SHADOWS IN GRAVEWOOD

Stephanie Tyo

Stephanie Tyo

Stephanie Tyo

To my beloved daughter, Jasmine,

In the intricate dance of life, you are the most vibrant and cherished presence. This book is a sincere testament to the boundless love and inspiration you've infused into my world. Every word penned is a brushstroke, illustrating the depth of our connection.

Jasmine, you are my joy, my compass, and the guiding star that lights my path. May these written reflections stand as a timeless tribute to the extraordinary person you are evolving into. As you embark on your unique journey, let this book be a constant reminder of the enduring love and limitless possibilities that accompany you, my dear daughter.

With all my love,

Mom

CHAPTER 1

Gravewoods, a town shrouded in mystery and nestled deep within a dense forest, exuded an aura of intrigue and secrecy. The ancient buildings stood tall and proud among the trees; their dark brick facades blanketed with ivy, crawled up their sides over many decades. Each structure had its own story—whispers of past lives echoing through the narrow cobblestone streets.

In this town, there was a curious and daring 13-year-old boy named Cameron Hawthorne. He had short, messy brown hair and eyes that sparkled with mischief, and his grin hinted at a mind that was always plotting his next adventure. His wiry frame, clad in jeans and a faded t-shirt, stood out against the backdrop of Gravewood's antiquity.

"Mom, I'm going out to explore!" Cameron called out, excited as he glanced around their new home. His mother, Mrs. Eleanor Hawthorne, appeared at the door, her warm smile framed by medium-length brown hair.

"Alright, Cam," she sighed, knowing there was no point in trying to contain her son's restless energy. "Be cautious and stay within limits. We don't know this town yet."

"Of course, Mom," Cameron replied, rolling his eyes playfully. "I'll be back before dinner." He darted out the door, eager to uncover the secrets hidden within the corners of Gravewood.

As Cameron wandered the seemingly endless streets, he reveled in the cacophony of sounds around him: the distant cawing of crows, the rustling of leaves underfoot, and the faint whisper of wind through the trees. The air was heavy, with the smell of damp earth and decaying leaves—a rich, musky aroma clung to his clothes like a second skin.

"Gravewood is so different from the city," he mused, his thoughts racing with endless possibilities. "There's so much to discover here."

He couldn't shake there was something extraordinary waiting for him in this strange town—a mystery only he could solve. As he ventured deeper into Gravewood, Cameron's curiosity grew stronger, and he wouldn't rest until he uncovered every secret hidden within its ancient walls.

———

Cameron's heart pounded in his chest as he approached the entrance of Gravewood Middle School. The building loomed before him, a relic of days long past. Its gothic architecture cast eerie shadows on the overgrown courtyard. He glanced down at his new sneakers, scuffing them against the rough pavement as he contemplated the day ahead.

"Deep breaths," he reminded himself, inhaling the odor of wet stone and musty air. "You've got this."

Pushing open the heavy wooden doors, Cameron stepped into a dimly lit hallway, the atmosphere thick with anticipation. His footsteps echoed off the walls, the creaking floorboards beneath him adding an unsettling soundtrack to his first moments in this new environment. As he continued down the shadowy corridor, flickering lights overhead cast a ghostly pallor over his surroundings.

"Hello?" He called out hesitantly, his voice a whisper in the oppressive silence. "Is anyone here?"

"Hey!" a voice replied from somewhere nearby, shattering the stillness. A boy around Cameron's age appeared from around a corner, his eyes wide with excitement. "You must be new here! I'm Jake. What's your name?"

"Uh, Cameron," he stammered, extending a hand in greeting. "Cameron Hawthorne."

"Nice to meet you, Cameron!" Jake exclaimed, shaking his hand vigorously. "I'll show you around. This place can be pretty creepy, but you'll get used to it."

"Thanks," Cameron said, forcing a smile as they walked side by side. Inwardly, he marveled at how quickly he made a connection in this unfamiliar setting.

As they traversed the labyrinthine hallways, Cameron couldn't help but notice the peculiar details permeating every corner of the school: doorways led to seemingly endless staircases; strange symbols adorned the walls and floors; whispers echoed from the very air itself.

"Jake," he asked cautiously, "is it just me, or is there something... off about this place?"

"Off?" Jake replied, his brow furrowing in thought. "I guess you could say that. Gravewood has a lot of history, and some of it's pretty spooky. But don't worry—we've all got each other's backs here."

Cameron nodded, reassured by Jake's words. Despite the eerie atmosphere, he couldn't deny the thrill coursing through his veins at the prospect of exploring these mysterious halls with new friends by his side.

"Besides," Jake continued with a grin, "life would be pretty boring without a little mystery, right?"

"Right," Cameron agreed, his own mischievous smile returning to his face. With newfound resolve, he followed Jake deeper into the shadows of Gravewood Middle School, eager to uncover the secrets that awaited them within its haunted walls.

As Cameron rounded a shadowy corner, Jake left to head to his class, Cameron's schedule clutched in one hand and a worn map in the other, he stumbled upon a group of students huddled together in a small alcove. Their animated voices bounced off the stone walls, creating an inviting contrast to the eerie silence that dominated the rest of the school. Intrigued, Cameron took a step closer, hoping to make some new friends on this nerve-wracking first day.

"Guys, check this out," said a blonde-haired girl with piercing blue eyes, her finger tracing a peculiar pattern on the wall. "Do you think it's some kind of code?"

"Could be," mused a boy with short black hair and glasses, adjusting them as he squinted at the design. "Or maybe a prank by some bored students."

"Personally, I think it's a secret message from the ghosts haunting Gravewood," declared a petite girl with curly red hair, her voice dripping with sarcasm.

"Ellie, not everything is about ghosts," sighed a dark-haired girl, her brown eyes rolling in exasperation as she fiddled with her camera.

"Hey, um, sorry to interrupt," Cameron said hesitantly, drawing their attention. "But do any of you know where room 207 is? I'm kind of lost."

The bespectacled boy, Oliver "Ollie" Thompson, stepped forward with a friendly smile. "Sure thing. It's down the hall and up the stairs. We're actually headed there too. I'm Ollie, by the way."

"Nice to meet you, Ollie. I'm Cameron Hawthorne." Cameron's nervousness began to dissipate as he smiled back. "This place is like a maze."

"Tell me about it," agreed Ellie Sinclair, the blonde girl who had been studying the wall earlier. "I've been here for a year, and I still get lost sometimes. It's like the school is alive, always changing."

"Or maybe it's just old and creepy," Natalie Martinez chimed in, snapping a photo of the peculiar pattern on the wall.

"Anyway," interjected Eleanor "Ellie" Grayson, her green eyes twinkling with impish delight. "Since we're all going to the same class, why don't you stick with us? Plus, they say there's strength in numbers, after all."

"Sounds good to me," agreed Cameron, his mischievous grin returning as he fell into step beside them. He sensed this group shared his sense of adventure and curiosity, and he was eager to see what mysteries they might uncover together.

"By the way," Ellie said, casting a sidelong glance at Cameron, "did you notice anything strange about Gravewood since you got here?"

Cameron hesitated, recalling the eerie atmosphere and whispers he experienced earlier. "Yeah, I did. But then again, Jake told me every school has its secrets."

"True," Ollie mused, "but Gravewood has had more than its fair share."

"Great," Ellie grinned, rubbing her hands together with anticipation. "I can't wait to find out what other surprises this place has in store for us."

As they walked together toward room 207, their laughter and excited chatter filled the dimly lit hallway, momentarily banishing the ghosts and shadows lurking in the corners of Gravewood Middle School.

Cameron couldn't help but notice the hushed whispers trailing them as they ventured down the hallway, their newly formed pack drawing curious glances from other students. He tasted the gossip in the air—thick and tinged with a hint of jealousy.

"Hey, Ellie!" called a tall girl with red-streaked hair, leaning against a row of lockers. "I heard you guys were poking around in the old basement yesterday. Find anything interesting?"

"Maybe," Ellie replied with a coy smile, her eyes darting to her new friends for a fleeting moment. "Nothing we can't handle."

"Nice!" the redhead smirked, giving the group an approving nod before sauntering away.

"It seems like words travel fast around here," Cameron muttered under his breath, feeling the weight of expectation settle on his shoulders. He had never been one to shy away from a challenge, but something about Gravewood made him feel like he was being watched—scrutinized by unseen eyes.

"Didn't you know?" Ollie joked, elbowing Cameron playfully in the ribs. "This place is like one big game of telephone. You whisper something at one end, and by the time it reaches the other side, it's turned into a full-blown urban legend."

"Speaking of legends," Natalie chimed in, her camera swinging from its strap around her neck. "I've been doing some research on the history of Gravewood, and I found some pretty interesting stuff."

"Like what?" Ellie asked, her green eyes alight with curiosity.

"Did you know this entire area used to be a burial ground?" Natalie whispered dramatically, casting a glance over her shoulder as if she expected a ghost to materialize out of thin air. "They say there are still artifacts hidden all over the school, relics from a time long past."

"Really?" Cameron's pulse quickened at the thought, his imagination running wild with images of ancient treasures and forgotten secrets. "Do you think we could find some?"

"Sure," Natalie shrugged, her enthusiasm infectious. "I mean, if we're willing to go poking around in some dark, creepy corners."

"Sounds like a plan," Cameron grinned, his mischievous streak rearing its head once more. "Who knows what we might uncover?"

"Count me in," Ollie agreed, his eyes twinkling with excitement.

"Me too," Ellie added, always eager for a new adventure.

"Great," Natalie said, clapping her hands together with determination. "Then it's settled. We'll meet up after school and see what we can find."

As they filed into their next class, a surge of anticipation coursed through Cameron's veins. He was no stranger to mysteries, but Gravewood seemed different—as if the walls held secrets waiting to be discovered. And with his newfound friends by his side, they would unravel the enigma of Gravewood Middle School.

As the day progressed, Cameron eagerly counted down the moments until he could meet his newfound friends and delve into the business that awaited them.

As the final bell rang, Cameron and his new friends gathered in the school library. The hushed whispers of students studying and the faint scent of old books filled the air, setting the perfect atmosphere for their investigation into Gravewood's past.

"Okay, guys," Cameron said, eyes scanning the shelves. "Let's split up and see what we can find about this place." The group nodded in agreement, each heading toward a different section of the library.

Cameron found himself drawn to a dusty, forgotten corner where ancient volumes lined the walls. He pulled one from the shelf, its leather cover worn with age. As he flipped through the yellowed pages, something fell out onto the floor. Curiosity piqued, Cameron picked it up, revealing an old photograph from the 1860s.

The image depicted a group of stern-faced individuals standing in front of Gravewood Middle School. Despite their serious expressions, there was something unsettling about their eyes, as if they held secrets never meant to be discovered.

"Guys, check this out!" Cameron called, unable to contain his excitement. His friends quickly gathered around, their faces mirroring his astonishment.

"Wow," whispered Ellie, her blue eyes fixated on the photograph. "This must be one of the first classes to attend Gravewood."

"Look at their eyes," Natalie murmured, shuddering involuntarily. "There's something... off about them."

"Maybe they knew something we don't," Ollie suggested thoughtfully, adjusting his glasses.

"Only one way to find out," Ellie chimed in, her determination shining through. "We need to learn everything we can about these people and the school's history."

"Agreed," Cameron nodded, his heart racing with excitement as he clutched the photograph tightly. "We'll dig deeper, uncover every secret Gravewood has been hiding all these years."

"Where should we start?" Ellie asked, her eyes scanning the library for clues.

"Old newspaper archives," suggested Cameron. "We can look for any articles that mention the people in this photo."

"Good idea," Natalie said, already snapping a picture of the photograph to aid their research. "And I'll see if there are any photographers' records from that time. There might be some information about the subjects."

"Let's not forget the school itself," Ollie pointed out. "There could be hidden rooms or passages that hold more answers."

"Right," Ellie agreed. "We'll tackle this mystery from every angle and leave no stone unturned."

The group dispersed; each member eager to uncover the truth behind the eerie photograph. As Cameron delved into the archives, he couldn't shake the feeling that they were on the cusp of something extraordinary—something that would change their lives forever. And with his newfound friends by his side, Cameron knew no secret, no matter how dark or supernatural, would remain hidden for long.

Cameron's pulse quickened at the thought as he and his friends huddled together around the ancient photograph, their reflections flickering in the dim library light. The air felt thick with anticipation as they whispered theories about the people captured within the faded image.

"Could it be... a secret society?" Natalie ventured, her brown eyes widening at the thought. "Maybe they were involved in some kind of ritual or dark magic?"

"Or perhaps they're trapped," Ollie suggested, pushing his glasses up on his nose. "Their spirits might be bound to the school, waiting for someone to set them free."

"Whatever it is," Ellie chimed in, blue eyes flashing with excitement. "I have a feeling it's going to lead us on an incredible adventure."

Cameron grinned, his heart swelling with camaraderie as they all eagerly shared their thoughts. There was something invigorating about this newfound friendship—a kinship forged in curiosity and a hunger for the unknown. He couldn't help but imagine the thrill that awaited them as they delved deeper into Gravewood's history.

"Alright, team," Cameron declared, clapping his hands together. "We've got our mission: uncover the secrets of this photograph and explore every inch of Gravewood Middle School. "Are you with me?"

"Absolutely!" Ellie replied with determination, her curly red hair bouncing as she nodded her head.

"Count me in," agreed Natalie, a fire ignited in her artistic soul.

"Let's do this," Ollie said firmly, loyalty shining in his eyes.

"Nothing can stop us," added Ellie, her voice filled with the confidence of a seasoned detective.

As the group dispersed to begin their research, Cameron couldn't shake the sense of foreboding settling over him like a heavy fog. The floorboards groaned and whispered from afar, their eerie creaks seeming to mock them, alluding to the sinister secrets lurking just beyond their reach. But with his newfound friends by his side, they would face any supernatural challenge that awaited them.

"Ready for whatever comes our way," he whispered to himself, feeling the weight of the photograph in his pocket. And as the wind outside picked up and rattled the library windows, Cameron couldn't help but feel Gravewood itself watching, waiting to see what mysteries they would uncover within its haunted halls.

CHAPTER 2

Under the cloak of shadows, Cameron and his newfound friends stealthily approached the imposing gates of Gravewood Middle School. The moon cast distorted shadows as they navigated through the courtyard, its eerie silence broken only by the faint rustling of leaves. Taking advantage of a partially ajar window, Cameron skillfully slid it open, the aged hinges letting out an ominous squeak. The group, now inside, tiptoed through dim hallways, the flickering overhead lights casting ominous shadows on the peeling walls. The air seemed to thicken with every step, carrying a palpable sense of foreboding as they ventured deeper into the heart of the school. The creaking floorboards and distant echoes of whispers taunted them, hinting at the dark secrets lying beyond their grasp.

As they ventured into the basement, the air heavy with a musky dampness, a chill crept through the very foundations of Gravewood Middle School's basement. Shadows clung to every corner and crevice as if trying to hide from the dim glow of the solitary lightbulb struggling against the darkness. The walls, lined with a patchwork of cobwebs, seemed to have absorbed the whispers and secrets of countless generations; one could almost hear the echoes of time gone by.

Cameron stood at the top of the creaky wooden stairs, his heart pounding in anticipation. The mischievous grin plastered across his face belied the fear gnawing at him—the fear of being alone, left behind by friends who would never understand his thirst for adventure. He swallowed hard, pushing the thought away. "Are you guys ready?" he asked, turning to his new friends.

Ellie, a tall girl with curly red hair and freckles dancing across her cheeks, nodded hesitantly, her eyes wide with excitement and uncertainty. Beside her, the quiet and studious Ollie clutched a flashlight in one hand and an old map of the school in the other. They all heard stories about the basement—whispers of long-lost treasures and forgotten secrets—but none of them ever dared to venture into its depths until now.

"Let's do this," Cameron declared, taking the first step down into the bowels of Gravewood Middle School. Ellie and Ollie followed closely behind, their hearts racing in unison as they descended into the unknown.

"Does... does anyone else feel that?" Ellie whispered, rubbing her arms as goosebumps rose on her skin. "It feels like someone's watching us."

"It's probably just our nerves," Cameron replied, forcing a confident smile. In truth, he felt it too—an unsettling sensation they were not alone in the darkness. He shook it off, refusing to let fear hold him back.

As they continued to venture deeper into the basement, the air grew colder and heavier, thick with a palpable sense of mystery. Each step revealed more secrets hidden within the shadows, drawing them further into the heart of the unknown.

The creaking floorboards beneath their feet echoed through the dimly lit hallways, each step sending shivers down their spines. Shadows danced along the walls, distorted by the flickering light from Cameron's flashlight. It was as if the air was alive with anticipation.

"Wow," Ellie breathed, her voice barely audible. She reached out a trembling hand to touch a dusty bookshelf, its shelves sagging under the weight of ancient leather-bound volumes. "This place is like a museum."

"Or a graveyard," Ollie muttered, hugging himself for comfort.

As they continued deeper into the basement, they discovered more and more relics from the past. A tarnished silver chalice lay on an old wooden table, its rim adorned with intricately carved patterns that only hinted at its former beauty. Natalie couldn't resist capturing the scene with her camera, the click of the shutter echoing through the silence.

"Guys, look at this," Ellie called out, kneeling beside a dusty trunk. Her fingers traced the outline of a faded crest on the lid, her eyes wide with awe. "Do you think it belonged to someone important?"

"Only one way to find out," Cameron said, his usual impulsive self taking over. He flipped open the latch and lifted the lid, revealing a treasure trove of forgotten artifacts—a rusted pocket watch, a yellowed envelope sealed with wax, and a delicate lace handkerchief.

"Imagine the stories these things could tell," Ellie murmured, carefully picking up the envelope. The paper crinkled in her grasp, and she hesitated for a moment before breaking the seal. Inside a single sheet of parchment, covered in elegant script long since faded. "I can't make out anything," she admitted, disappointment clouding her features.

"Maybe Millie can help us figure out what it says," Cameron suggested, his curiosity piqued. "We should take it to her."

"Are you sure?" Ollie asked, his voice wavering. "I mean, what if we're not supposed to be touching any of this stuff?"

"Ollie's right," Natalie chimed in, capturing another eerie photograph. "This place feels... off. Maybe we shouldn't be messing with things that don't belong to us."

Cameron hesitated, torn between his thirst for adventure and the unease that grew stronger with each passing moment. The air grew colder still, and a chill seeped into their very bones. It was as if the basement itself was urging them to turn back and leave its secrets undisturbed.

"Let's just take the letter," Cameron finally decided, shoving the envelope into his backpack. "We'll ask Millie about it tomorrow. For now, let's get out of here."

"Good idea," Ellie agreed, her eyes darting nervously around the room. "Something tells me we've overstayed our welcome."

Cameron led the way, his flashlight beamed, dancing along the floor as they ventured deeper into the basement. The flickering lightbulbs overhead cast eerie shadows on the walls, their dim glow barely penetrating the gloom. He couldn't shake something lurking beyond the edge of their vision, watching them with unseen eyes.

"Guys, check this out!" Ellie called out excitedly, her voice muffled by the oppressive atmosphere. She held up an old book, its leather cover cracked and worn. "It's like we've stepped back in time."

"Wow," Natalie whispered, snapping a photo of the dusty tome. "Everything down here is so ancient."

"Creepy is more like it," Ollie muttered, hugging himself as if to ward off the chill settling over him. "I don't like this place. It feels like we're being watched."

"Come on, don't be such a scaredy-cat," Cameron teased, though he couldn't deny the growing sense of unease gripping him as well. As much as he wanted to explore the basement's secrets, a part of him longed to escape back to the safety of the school above.

"Can you imagine all the things that have happened down here?" Ellie mused, running her fingers over a tarnished silver chalice that lay forgotten on a dusty shelf. "There must be so many stories hidden within these relics."

"Stories that should probably stay hidden," Ollie insisted, his eyes darting nervously around the room. "We shouldn't be messing with things we don't understand."

"Relax, Ollie," Cameron said, trying to sound more confident than he felt. His heart raced as they continued to explore the basement, the air thick with anticipation and unspoken fears. "We're just looking. What's the worst that can happen?"

"Maybe we should head back," Natalie suggested, her voice quivering slightly. "We've seen enough, haven't we?"

"Let's just look a little further," Cameron urged as he swallowed hard, forcing himself to push forward in spite of the mounting dread threatening to overwhelm him. The shadows grew darker and more menacing as if drawing strength from their unease.

Cameron led the way as they ventured deeper into the basement, his flashlight beam slicing through the darkness like a blade. The air grew colder, and a faint, musty odor crept into their nostrils. Their footsteps echoed eerily, mingling with the sound of water dripping from unseen pipes overhead.

"Look at this," Ellie whispered, her voice shaking slightly. She shone her flashlight on a dusty wooden box, revealing ornate carvings of strange symbols dancing in the shadows. "What do you think it is?"

"Maybe it's some kind of puzzle box," Ellie suggested, her curiosity piqued despite the unsettling atmosphere. "We can try to open it."

"Are you kidding?" Ollie protested, adjusting his glasses nervously. "Who knows what's inside? It might be cursed or something!"

"I don't believe in curses," Cameron scoffed, but there was a hint of doubt in his voice. "Besides, we're not going to touch it. We're just looking, remember?"

"Guys, look at this!" Natalie called out; her artistic instincts drawn to an ancient-looking tapestry hanging on the wall. It depicted a menacing figure standing atop a hill, surrounded by a stormy sky. "This must have been made centuries ago. I wonder who that person is?"

"It can be anyone," Cameron replied dismissively, trying to tamp down the growing unease within him. His mind raced with thoughts about what lurked in the depths of the basement. "Let's keep moving."

As they continued to explore the shadowy corners of the basement, they encountered more relics of the past: rusted daggers with intricately engraved hilts, shelves lined with leather-bound books whose titles had long since faded, and a cracked mirror whose reflection distorted their faces in unsettling ways.

"Ugh, this place gives me the creeps," Ellie muttered, hugging herself tightly as if to ward off a chill. "I don't like it here."

"None of us do," Ellie admitted, her eyes scanning the room warily. "But there's something strangely fascinating about it, too. It's like we're unearthing secrets that were never meant to see the light of day."

"Maybe they shouldn't," Ollie insisted, his voice more than a whisper. "We don't know what kind of forces we could be dealing with."

"Come on, Ollie," Cameron teased, trying to lighten the mood. "You're starting to sound like one of those paranoid characters in a horror movie. Next, you'll be telling us not to split up."

"Actually, that's not a bad idea," Natalie chimed in. "We should stick together. Who knows what can happen down here?"

"Fine," Cameron agreed begrudgingly, though his thoughts betrayed him: *Maybe they're right. Maybe this place is dangerous. But I can't let them see how scared I am. I have to be brave for all of us.*

"Let's just keep going," he said firmly, forcing himself to move forward despite the dread gnawing at his insides. As they delved further into the darkness, each mysterious artifact and relic held an ominous secret, beckoning them closer to an unseen danger.

The dim, flickering light of their flashlights glinted off a dusty glass frame as Cameron's foot nudged it out from under a pile of yellowed newspapers. The group gathered around, the tension in the air ratcheting up another notch.

"Look at this," Natalie whispered, carefully picking up the old photograph with trembling hands. A chill ran down Cameron's spine as his eyes fell upon the dark figure dominating the center of the frame: Gideon Blackwell. Tall, gaunt, and with hollow cheeks, his piercing eyes bore into Cameron's very soul.

"Who is that?" Ollie asked, a hint of fear creeping into his voice.

"His name's Gideon Blackwell," Ellie said, her own voice unsteady. "He's got quite a reputation around Gravewood. They say he's been here since the 1860s."

Cameron couldn't tear his gaze away from the unsettling image. Despite the fear gripping him, his curiosity piqued.

"What do you mean he's been here since the 1860s? That's over a hundred years ago."

"Nobody knows for sure," Ellie replied, swallowing hard. "Some people think he's a ghost or some other supernatural being. Others think he's just an urban legend."

"Urban legend or not, he looks creepy," Ollie shuddered. "It's like he's staring right at us."

"Maybe we should put it back," Natalie suggested, her eyes darting nervously around the shadowy basement. "This whole place is giving me the creeps."

But Cameron's mind raced, thoughts whirling faster than he could process them. There was something about Gideon Blackwell that called to him—a mystery begging to be unraveled. He needed to know more. "Wait," he said, gripping Natalie's wrist before she could discard the photograph. "Maybe we should keep it. There might be a reason we found it—something important."

"Are you sure?" Ellie asked, her brow furrowed with concern. "It doesn't feel right to take things from here."

"Right or not, I can't shake the feeling this photo is significant," Cameron insisted, his voice firm despite the pounding of his heart. "I need to know more about Gideon Blackwell and why he's still a part of Gravewood. Maybe if we can figure out who—or what—he is, we can put an end to whatever's is going on in our town."

A heavy silence enveloped the group as they weighed Cameron's words, unease and curiosity warring inside them. The basement pressed in closer as if urging them to decide.

Finally, Ollie sighed. "Okay, let's do it. But we have to be careful—there's no telling what kind of trouble we could be getting ourselves into."

Cameron nodded solemnly, determination flooding through him. He knew they were on the brink of something much larger than themselves, something that threatened not only their own safety but of everyone in Gravewood. And as the darkness closed in around them, he couldn't help but wonder: What would happen next?

"Are you sure about this?" Ellie asked, her voice wavering slightly. She glanced around the dim basement, unease settling into her bones. "We don't know what we're dealing with here."

"Exactly," Cameron responded, his grin unwavering. "That's why we need to find out." He held the photograph up to the flickering light, studying Gideon Blackwell's ominous figure intently. The shadows danced across his face, heightening the sense of danger lingering in the air.

"Okay, but we have to be cautious," Ollie chimed in, eyeing the photograph warily. "No telling what kind of trouble we could get into."

"Agreed," Cameron said, tucking the photograph into his backpack. "But if we're going to solve this mystery, we can't let fear hold us back."

As the group moved deeper into the basement, their footsteps echoed off the damp walls, creating an eerie soundtrack for their descent.

"We're getting closer," Cameron whispered, more to himself than his friends. "I can feel it."

"Wait," Ollie suddenly said, stopping in his tracks. "Did you hear that?"

Cameron strained his ears, searching for any sound beyond their own breathing and the creaking of the old floorboards. For a moment, there was nothing but silence. Then, without warning, a bone-chilling scream pierced the darkness, echoing through the basement like a banshee's wail.

"Wh-what was that?" Ellie stammered, her eyes wide with terror.

Cameron gripped the straps of his backpack tightly, his heart pounding in his chest as adrenaline coursed through his veins. "I don't know," he admitted, fear sharpening his voice. "But I think we're about to find out."

The three friends exchanged anxious glances before cautiously moving towards the source of the scream, each step weighed down with trepidation. As they inched closer to the unknown, Cameron couldn't help but wonder if they finally uncovered a key piece of the puzzle—or if they sealed their own fate.

CHAPTER 3

As they walked through the town, the eerie sensation of being watched intensified. The whispers of the past grew louder, and the shadows cast by the ancient oaks danced menacingly on the cobblestones beneath their feet. Cameron thought that the mysterious photograph possibly awakened a part of Gravewood that had laid dormant for centuries, and the town would never be the same again.

The moment Cameron's fingers brushed against the old photograph; it was as if Gravewood itself shuddered. Their innocent curiosity would bring forth such consequences, and they certainly didn't realize the danger lurking beneath the town's picturesque façade.

Cameron's heart raced as he recalled the strange events that transpired earlier in the day. He and his friends, Ellie, Ollie, and Natalie discovered an eerie old photograph of Gideon Blackwell, a man whose chilling presence haunted Gravewood since the 1860s. They couldn't shake the photograph held a dark secret, one they determined to uncover.

The picturesque town of Gravewood had always been a place where time stood still. Ancient oak trees lined the cobblestone streets, their gnarled branches casting eerie shadows on the ground below. The air was heavy with the scent of autumn leaves, and a faint mist clung to the ground like a silent specter. Though the town appeared quaint and charming on the surface, a sense of foreboding hung in the air as if the spirits of the past were still very much alive.

"Guys, I can't stop thinking about that photograph," Cameron confessed, his messy brown hair blowing in the gentle breeze. "There's got to be more to it than meets the eye."

"Me neither," Ellie agreed. Her piercing blue eyes scanned their surroundings as if searching for clues. "I have this nagging feeling that we've stumbled upon something big—something that can change Gravewood forever."

Ollie shivered, adjusting his glasses nervously. "I don't know if I want to find out what it is, though. What if it's something dangerous?"

"Ollie's right," Natalie chimed in, her artistic gaze fixed on the horizon. "What if our curiosity puts us all in danger? I don't want to risk our lives just to solve a mystery."

As the group contemplated their next move, Ellie clenched her fists, her fiery red curls bouncing with determination. "We can't just ignore this, you guys. If there's something wrong in Gravewood, we have to find out what it is and fix it!"

Cameron looked at his friends, concern etched on his face. His fear of isolation battled with his daring nature. "What if, by digging deeper into this mystery, I end up losing my friends?" he thought.

"Alright," Cameron said hesitantly. "Let's try to figure out what's going on. But we have to be careful. We don't know what we're dealing with."

"Did you guys feel that?" Ellie asked, her intuition sending a chill down her spine.

"Feel what?" Cameron replied, trying to sound nonchalant despite the unease gnawing at him. The others exchanged glances but didn't answer, each harboring their own fears as they continued through the town.

As night fell upon Gravewood, strange occurrences began to manifest. Streetlights flickered erratically, casting eerie shadows as if reaching out for the group. A cacophony of unexplained noises echoed through the streets—faint whispers, distant footsteps, and the creaking of unseen doors. Objects in storefront windows trembled inexplicably, their movements almost imperceptible but undeniably unnatural.

"Guys, something isn't right," Ollie whispered, his voice trembling as he clutched the straps of his backpack. His glasses fogged up with every breath, making it almost impossible to see the unsettling events unfolding around them.

"Agreed," Natalie muttered, her fingers gripping her camera tightly. She tried to capture the odd phenomena on film, but the images couldn't convey the chilling atmosphere that now enveloped Gravewood.

Cameron's thoughts were a whirlwind of fear and determination. His heart raced, each beat pounding harder against his chest. "We've unleashed something terrible," he realized, "and we have to set things right before it's too late." He glanced around at his friends, their faces lit by the stuttering streetlights, and saw the same resolve mirrored in each pair of eyes.

"Alright," Cameron said, forcing conviction into his voice. "We need to get to the bottom of this. Whatever's happening, we've got to find a way to stop it."

"Agreed," Ellie chimed in, her small frame trembling with both fear and courage. "We can't let Gravewood be consumed by this... curse."

"Curse?" Ellie questioned, her blue eyes wide with trepidation. "Is that what you think this is? Some sort of supernatural punishment?"

"Maybe," Cameron admitted, his mind racing with the implications. "But whatever it is, we'll face it together."

As the group pressed on, they knew their lives would never be the same again. The shadows whispered warnings, but they couldn't turn back now. With each step, the supernatural forces swirling around them grew stronger, and the once-peaceful town of Gravewood became a battleground for the souls of its inhabitants.

"Stay close," Cameron whispered as he led his friends deeper into the darkness. "Whatever happens, we've got to stick together."

And so, the group of friends braced themselves for the unknown, unaware of the full extent of the danger that awaited them in the shadows of Gravewood.

Cameron's heart pounded in his chest as he stared at the flickering streetlights, unable to shake the nagging fear they unleashed something terrible upon Gravewood. The air was thick with a sinister energy, and every shadow concealed unspeakable horrors. Beside him, Ellie shivered, pulling her jacket tighter around her petite frame.

"Guys," she stammered, her voice barely audible above the eerie silence. "Do you think we're really dealing with a curse here?"

Ellie bit her lip, her blue eyes wide with trepidation. "I don't know, but we've got to find out what's going on. People are going to get hurt if we don't do something."

"Exactly," Cameron agreed, his mind racing with the implications of their actions. The weight of responsibility bearing down on him and his fear of isolation only intensified his determination to protect his friends from the unknown danger lurking in Gravewood.

"Okay, we need a plan," he said, forcing conviction into his voice. "We should go back to the basement where we found the photo. Maybe there's something else down there that can help us figure out how to stop this."

The others exchanged uneasy glances, each one struggling to quell the rising panic within them. Returning to the basement meant confronting the source of the supernatural events plaguing their town, but they also understood there was no other choice.

"Right," Ellie said, her voice trembling slightly. "Let's do it. But we need to be careful."

"Agreed," Ellie chimed in, steeling herself against her own fear. "We'll stick together, no matter what happens."

As the group retraced their steps through the haunted streets of Gravewood, they couldn't help but notice the strange occurrences escalating all around them. Windows rattled in their frames, and eerie whispers floated on the wind, sending shivers down their spines. But despite the mounting dread, they pressed on, their resolve only growing stronger with each step.

"Whatever we find down there," Cameron thought, his heart pounding in his ears, "we'll face it together. We won't let this curse tear us apart."

With every passing moment, the friends drew closer to the terrifying truth hidden in the basement, unaware of the full extent of the danger that awaited them in the shadows of Gravewood.

The air in the basement was damp and cold, chilling the group to the bone as they descended the creaky stairs. Shadows danced on the walls, taking on grotesque forms and mocking their fear. Natalie clutched her camera tightly, her artistic eye drawn to the eerie beauty of the scene despite her terror.

"Alright, everyone, spread out and search for any information or possible clues," Ellie instructed, trying to maintain an air of authority despite her pounding heart.

As they began to comb through the dusty shelves and cobweb-covered corners, Natalie's flashlight flickered over an ancient wooden chest tucked away beneath a rotting tarp. With cautious steps, she approached the chest, feeling its rough, splintered surface beneath her fingertips.

"Guys, come take a look at this," Natalie called out, her voice above a whisper.

Cameron, Ellie, and Ollie gathered around the chest; their breaths held tight. With trembling hands, Natalie carefully lifted the lid, revealing a hidden compartment within. "Whoa," Cameron breathed, peering into the dark recesses of the chest. "What is that?"

Natalie reached in and pulled out a worn leather-bound journal, the pages yellowed with age. The date "1800" was etched on the cover, along with the name Gideon Blackwell.

"Guys," Natalie said, her voice filled with a mix of excitement and dread. "I think I found something important."

"Read it," Ellie urged, her curiosity overcoming her fear. "Maybe it can tell us how to stop the curse."

Natalie hesitated for a moment, her fingers tracing the embossed letters on the journal's cover. She knew opening its pages might lead them deeper into the darkness, but she also understood their only hope of saving Gravewood lay within its secrets.

"Okay," Natalie whispered, her heart pounding like a drum. "Here goes."

As the group huddled together, flashlights illuminating the fragile pages, they held their breath and began to read Gideon Blackwell's chilling words.

Natalie's eyes scanned the faded ink, her voice steady as she read aloud. "I, Gideon Blackwell, do hereby document the events that transpired on the cursed night of October 31st, 1862..." The others leaned in closer, each word drawing them deeper into the haunting tale.

Cameron felt a sudden chill, colder than before, and shivered involuntarily. He glanced around, searching for an open window or door which would explain the drop in temperature. But there none to be found.

"Guys," Ollie murmured, his breath visible as he spoke, "is it just me, or is it getting really cold in here?"

Ellie wrapped her arms around herself, nodding in agreement. "It's like someone left a freezer door open."

Just then, an unexpected gust of wind tore through the room, causing the old pages of the journal to flutter wildly. Natalie struggled to hold onto it, her knuckles turning white from the effort. And in an instant, the flashlights flickered and went out, leaving the group engulfed in darkness. All of them dropped their flashlight.

"Ah!" Ellie cried out, latching onto Ollie's arm. "What just happened?"

"Everyone, stay calm," Cameron urged as his pulse raced. "We need to find our flashlights. They must've just...shut off or something."

As they fumbled in the dark, their hands brushing against the cold stone walls and dusty shelves, an eerie silence settled over the basement. Then, faint whispers emerged from the shadows, drifting in and out of earshot like ghostly echoes. Footsteps followed suit, tapping softly on the wooded floor.

"Can you guys hear that?" Ellie asked, her voice wavering with fear.

"Y-yeah," Ollie stammered, clutching Ellie tighter. "It sounds like...whispers and footsteps."

"Maybe it's the wind?" Ellie suggested, trying to rationalize the unnerving sounds.

The air stilled, and every instinct in her body screamed they were not alone. She swallowed hard, summoning the courage to voice her thoughts. "I think...I think we might have unleashed something when we found this journal. Something that doesn't want us here."

The group exchanged wordless glances, their hearts pounding in unison as they faced the terrifying reality of their situation. They ventured too far into the darkness, and now, they would have to face the consequences.

The basement air was thick and oppressive, its weight pressing down on their chests, making it difficult to breathe. The darkness swallowed them whole, leaving no trace of their existence. As they huddled together, a sense of foreboding crept up on them, like tendrils of icy fingers wrapping around their spines.

"Guys," Cameron whispered. "Do you feel that?"

"Feel what?" Ellie asked, her breath coming in short, panicked gasps.

"Like...like something's watching us," he replied, trying to keep his own fear at bay. "An invisible force or something."

"What do we do?" Ollie's shaky voice cut through the silence, betraying his fear of abandonment.

"Stay close," Natalie implored, her grip tightening on the journal as if it were a lifeline. "We need to stick together."

As they pressed closer, their breath shallow and ragged, the whispers grew louder, evolving into an ominous hum resonating within their bones. The footsteps echoed throughout the basement, growing nearer with each passing second.

"Maybe we should leave," Ellie proposed, her small frame trembling against the cold stone wall.

"Wait," Ellie interrupted, her piercing blue eyes narrowing as she tried to focus on the sounds around them. "Listen."

Suddenly, a chilling voice filled the air, speaking in a language they couldn't understand. It was as if the very atmosphere itself came alive, whispering ancient secrets and forbidden knowledge. The eerie cadence sent shivers down their spines, freezing them in place.

"Wh-what is that?" Ollie stammered, gripping Ellie's hand tightly.

"I don't know," Cameron admitted, his fear of isolation creeping up on him as the alien words swirled around them. "But it can't be good."

"Maybe it's a warning," Natalie speculated, her own fear of the unknown gnawing at her. "Or...or a curse?"

"Whatever it is," Ellie declared, her voice firm despite the terror threatened to consume her, "we can't let it control us. We need to find a way to break this curse or whatever we've unleashed."

"Right," Cameron agreed, his determination returning as he squeezed his friends' hands. "We're not going to let some creepy voice scare us away. We'll figure this out together."

As one, they nodded, their resolve hardening like steel in the face of adversity. They ventured into the darkness, and now they would do everything in their power to protect each other, their town, and themselves from the supernatural forces they'd unleashed.

"Let's get out of here," Ellie whispered, leading the group through the oppressive shadows towards the faint promise of light at the top of the stairs. And as they ascended, the chilling voice followed them, an unrelenting reminder of the danger they now faced.

The voice suddenly changed, morphing into a language they could understand. "Leave Gravewood and never return," it warned, its tone icy and menacing. "Or face the wrath of Gideon Blackwell's spirit."

Ellie's heart hammered in her chest as she exchanged frightened glances with her friends.

"Who are you?" Cameron demanded, his voice shaky but defiant. "Why are you doing this?"

"Could it be Gideon Blackwell?" whispered Natalie, her eyes wide with terror.

"Enough!" Ollie shouted, trying to muster courage. "We're not leaving! We'll find a way to break this curse!"

As if responding to their collective defiance, the room grew colder still, an unearthly chill seeping into their bones. The presence tested them, sizing up their resolve.

"Go ahead," Ellie challenged the unseen force, her fear of losing her friends driving her to stand her ground. "Do your worst. But we won't back down. We will save Gravewood."

"Yeah!" Ellie agreed, gripping Ollie's hand tightly for support. "You can't scare us away!"

For a moment, the chilling silence hung heavy in the air, as if the specter was considering their words. Then, the voice spoke again, its tone low and dripping with malice. "Very well," it hissed, the words echoing through the dark basement. "But remember...you have been warned."

The temperature returned to normal, and the oppressive atmosphere dissipated like fog in the sunlight. The group stood there, trembling but resolute, knowing they'd faced the first test of their newfound mission.

"Let's get out of here," Ellie whispered, her voice still shaking. "We need a plan."

"Agreed," Cameron said, his determination overriding his fear of isolation. "But first, let's make sure we have everything we need from this basement."

"Whatever we face," Natalie added, clutching the journal tightly to her chest, "we'll do it together. We're stronger as a group."

With a deep breath, they began to gather their flashlights and any other items that might prove helpful in their quest. The road ahead would be fraught with danger, but together, they were determined to save Gravewood and break the curse that threatened to consume them all.

Cameron's heart pounded in his chest, the blood rushing in his ears as if it were trying to drown out the lingering threat of Gideon Blackwell's spirit. The others stood around him, their faces pale and their eyes wide with fear.

"Did that just happen?" Ollie asked, his voice small and lost amid the cold darkness surrounding them.

"Unfortunately, yes," Ellie replied, her blue eyes shimmering with fierce determination. "But we're not backing down. We need to find a way to break this curse."

"Right," Natalie said, her grip on the journal tightening. "We can't let Gravewood be destroyed by some vengeful spirit. We live here, and we love our home."

"Exactly." Cameron squared his shoulders, trying to ignore his fear of isolation. He needed to be strong for his friends. "Let's get our stuff together and come up with a plan."

As they gathered their belongings, the air around them chilled even further. Shadows danced along the walls, taunting them with unseen horrors. The scent of damp earth and decay filled their nostrils while a distant creaking echoed through the basement like the footsteps of a long-lost soul.

"Guys," Ellie whispered, her breath visible in the freezing air. "Do you feel that? Like...like something is watching us?"

"Maybe it's just our nerves," Ollie offered, though his glasses fogged up from the sudden drop in temperature.

"Or maybe it's Gideon Blackwell's spirit," Ellie suggested, a shiver running down her spine. "He did warn us, after all."

"Either way," Cameron said, swallowing hard against his rising panic, "we need to stick together. No one should ever be alone in this place again."

"Agreed," they all murmured, their voices barely audible above the sound of their beating hearts.

"Alright," Natalie said, her eyes darting nervously around the room. "Let's go."

As they turned to leave, a loud crash resounded from upstairs, shaking the foundations of the school. The sound was followed by a cacophony of screams and whispers, as if the entire building had been thrown into chaos.

"Wh-what was that?" Ollie stammered, his eyes wide behind his fogged-up glasses.

"Something bad," Cameron replied, his voice trembling as he gripped his flashlight tightly. "And it's happening right now—in our school."

"Come on," Ellie urged, her fear momentarily overshadowed by her need to protect her fellow students. "We have to find out what's going on."

"Stay together," Ellie reminded them, her small frame shaking with terror. "Whatever is happening, we'll face it as a group."

"Right," they all said in unison, their voices shaky but determined.

With trepidation heavy in their hearts, they moved cautiously toward the basement stairs, unaware of what awaited them above. The eerie silence had been replaced with the unsettling sounds of supernatural chaos.

As they climbed the stairs, Cameron couldn't help but wonder if they were already too late. They were about to discover the full extent of Gideon Blackwell's wrath. Did they have the strength to break the curse and save their town?

CHAPTER 4

Cameron's heart pounded in his chest as he and his friends approached the local library, their steps sounding like muted thunder against the cobblestone path. In his mind, he replayed the chilling image of Gideon Blackwell from the old photograph they discovered. The gaunt man with hollow cheeks and dark eyes pierced through him and haunted Cameron's thoughts. They needed answers about the curse and Gideon's spirit, and Millie Finch was the only person who could help them.

The heavy wooden doors creaked open, revealing the dimly lit space that housed years of Gravewood's secrets. Rows upon rows of dusty books stretched out before them, like ancient guardians keeping watch over untold stories. The smell of old paper, leather bindings, and ink permeated the air, wrapping around them like a musty embrace.

"Hello?" Cameron whispered hesitantly, as if speaking too loudly would disturb the ghosts of the past who lingered among the bookshelves. His friends exchanged nervous glances, their own fear and uncertainty mirroring his own. Despite their shared apprehension, they were determined to uncover the truth about Gideon Blackwell's spirit and the curse that plagued their town.

"Let's find Millie," Cameron said softly, his breath clouding the cold air. His friends nodded in agreement, and they ventured deeper into the library, their footfalls muffled by the thick layer of the dust covering the floor.

As they moved through the dimly lit space, a growing sense of unease washed over Cameron. The shadows cast by flickering candles danced on the walls, morphing into sinister shapes, making his skin crawl. He rubbed his arms to dispel the goosebumps formed, his thoughts occupied by the unknown dangers they might face in confronting Gideon's spirit.

"Remember, we're doing this for Gravewood," he told himself, trying to quell the fear threatened to overtake him. His friends were anxious, too, their eyes darting around the library's dark corners and seeking any hint of Millie Finch or the answers they so desperately needed.

"Guys, we have to stick together," Cameron urged, his voice wavering slightly. "We're stronger as a team, and we can break this curse if we work together."

His friends exchanged determined looks, nodding in agreement. With renewed resolve, they continued their search for Millie Finch, eager to learn everything about Gideon Blackwell's spirit and the ancient ritual that brought such darkness upon their town.

Cameron's heart pounded in his chest, the chilling silence of the library amplifying his every breath. His friends huddled close, their eyes darting from one dark corner to another. The creaking of old floorboards beneath their feet and the distant rustling of turning pages sent shivers down their spines.

"Ah, there you are," said a gentle voice, breaking the eerie silence. Cameron looked up to see Millie Finch standing before them, her warm smile cutting through the darkness like a ray of sunshine. Her short gray hair framed her kind, wrinkled face, and the spectacles perched on her nose gave her an air of wisdom.

"Millie, we need your help. We want to know about Gideon Blackwell," Cameron said, his voice strained with urgency. He glanced at his friends, who nodded in agreement, their faces etched with worry.

"Of course, dear," Millie replied, her eyes twinkling with compassion. "Follow me."

She led them through the library, her passion for history evident in every step. She pointed out various sections dedicated to Gravewood's past, her excitement palpable as she recounted tales of the town's founding and the early settlers who carved out their lives in this once-untamed wilderness.

"Many secrets lie hidden within these books," she told them, her voice soft yet warm, like a crackling fire on a winter's night. "The history of Gravewood is vast and complex, filled with triumphs and tragedies, heroes and villains, and a dark and twisted past. And it's our responsibility to preserve these stories so future generations can learn from our past."

Cameron listened, captivated by Millie's words, as she guided them deeper into the labyrinth of shelves. The musty scent of old paper filled his nostrils, and he could almost feel the weight of the countless stories surrounding them.

"I've noticed peculiar occurrences since yesterday," Miller remarked, her voice carrying a hint of unease. Continuing, she added, "The atmosphere in Gravewood has shifted, as if the specter of Gideon Blackwell looms over us."

"Here," Millie said, stopping in front of a dusty display case filled with ancient artifacts. "This is where we can begin to unravel the mystery of Gideon Blackwell's curse."

Cameron's heart raced as he stared at the objects before him, each one a piece of Gravewood's dark and twisted past. He sensed the growing tension among his friends, but their resolve held strong, fueled by a determination to save their town from the clutches of an evil long thought dead.

"Millie, please tell us everything you know about Gideon Blackwell and the ritual that cursed our town," Cameron pleaded, desperation evident in his trembling voice.

"Remember," Millie warned, her voice heavy with concern, "knowledge is power, but it can also be dangerous. Proceed with caution, and never underestimate the forces that have been unleashed upon our town."

With her words echoing in their minds, Cameron and his friends steeled themselves for the challenges ahead, knowing their journey into the darkness had only begun.

Cameron's pulse quickened as Millie ushered the group into a dim alcove, away from the prying eyes of other patrons. The creaking of the library floorboards beneath their feet's echoed through the hushed space like whispers in the dark. A single flickering light bulb that dangled above a table groaned under the weight of dusty tomes and yellowed documents, casting eerie shadows on the walls. The air was thick with the musky scent of decaying paper and the faint tang of old ink.

"Here," Millie said, gesturing towards the table with a wrinkled hand. "I've gathered everything I can find about the ancient ritual and Gideon Blackwell." Her eyes gleamed with equal parts excitement and trepidation, betraying her deep-rooted connection to Gravewood's history.

"Thank you, Millie," Cameron murmured, his voice barely audible in the silence enveloping them. His heart hammered in his chest as he reached out to touch one of the books, its leather cover cracked and brittle beneath his trembling fingers.

Millie cleared her throat and leaned farther over the table. "The ritual dates back to the early days of Gravewood, when the town was still struggling to survive," she began, her voice wavering with emotion. "A desperate act, born out of fear and suffering, its consequences have haunted us ever since."

"Like Gideon's spirit?" asked Ellie, her eyes wide and fearful. She clutched her backpack strap as if it were a lifeline.

"Exactly," Millie nodded solemnly. "Gideon Blackwell, already a troubled soul, was consumed by darkness long before the ritual took place. When the townspeople sought to harness his power for their own benefit, they unknowingly unleashed a curse far greater than any of them could have imagined."

Cameron's stomach churned at the thought, his palms slick with cold sweat. "So, what's the connection between Gideon's spirit and the curse?"

"Legend has it," Millie continued, her voice a whisper, "that Gideon's spirit was bound to the town by the ritual, forever trapped in an eternal struggle for power and control. As the generations passed, his malevolence only grew stronger, seeping into the very fabric of Gravewood itself."

"Is there anything we can do to break the curse?" asked Ellie, his voice strained as he tried to maintain his composure.

"Breaking a curse of this magnitude is no easy task," Millie cautioned, her eyes clouding over with worry. "But I believe that if you can confront Gideon's spirit and sever its connection to the town, you may just have a chance at setting things right."

"May" wasn't the most reassuring word, but Cameron clung to the hope it offered. With every fiber of his being, he knew they had to try. For the sake of Gravewood and its people, they would face the darkness lurkingwithin.

Cameron's eyes darted across the weathered pages as he listened to Millie's revelations, his mind racing to piece together the puzzle. The weight of each word settling in his chest—a growing pressure threatened to suffocate him. The more he learned, the more he understood the gravity of the situation they faced.

"Millie," Cameron whispered, forcing himself to speak through the tightness in his throat, "what has the curse done to Gravewood over the years?"

"Ah, dear child," Millie sighed, her voice heavy with sorrow. She paused, taking a deep breath, before continuing. "The curse brought about a great deal of darkness and misfortune. Unexplained accidents, unspeakable tragedy... even the air we breathe seems tainted by its presence."

"Like the fog?" Natalie asked, recalling the eerie mist that rolled into town the night before.

"Exactly," Millie confirmed, nodding gravely. "The fog is but one manifestation of Gideon's lingering malevolence. There have been countless other incidents throughout Gravewood's history that can be attributed to his curse."

Millie's eyes took on a distant, haunted look as she recounted an unsettling tale from decades past. "When I was just a girl, there was a terrible storm that struck the town without warning. The rain fell like daggers, and the wind howled like a banshee. Many lives were lost that fateful night, and those who survived spoke of seeing Gideon Blackwell's twisted visage within the storm clouds."

Cameron shuddered at the image, feeling as though icy fingers were tracing down his spine. He glanced around at his friends, noting their pale faces and wide, fearful eyes. They all recognized the danger that lurked within Gravewood, but acknowledging it only made it more real, more terrifying.

"Is there any way to protect ourselves from the curse while we try to confront Gideon's spirit?" asked Ellie, his voice shaky but determined.

Millie hesitated, her eyes searching the dusty bookshelves as if seeking a glimmer of hope. "There is no surefire way to guard against the curse," she admitted softly. "But I believe strength can be found in unity and unwavering resolve. The curse feeds on fear and despair, so you must stand tall in the face of darkness."

"Easy for you to say," muttered Ollie under his breath, though there was no bite to his words. The fear gripping them all was palpable, pressing down upon them like a smothering blanket.

"Nothing about this will be easy," Millie acknowledged, her gaze steady and sincere. "But you must not lose sight of what you're fighting for. Gravewood is more than a town—it's a home, a community. And you, my brave young friends, carry within you the power to save it from the shadows that have long held it captive."

As Cameron absorbed Millie's words, something stirred deep within him. It was small and fragile, yet fierce in its determination: hope. For the first time since learning of the curse, he believed they might stand a chance against the darkness.

And with belief, they would face whatever horrors awaited them together.

Cameron's heart pounded in his ears like the distant beat of a thousand drums, each thud echoing through him and stirring up questions that begged to be answered. His fingers curled into fists at his sides as he turned to face Millie, his eyes wide with a mix of fear and determination.

"Millie," he began, his voice raw with emotion, "how do we even begin to confront Gideon Blackwell's spirit? How can we make sense of all this?" He gestured around them, indicating the stacks of books, the ancient scrolls, and the layers of Gravewood's history surrounding them like ghosts of a forgotten past.

"Ah, dear boy," Millie replied, her eyes softening with sympathy. She pushed her spectacles up her nose and sighed heavily. "Tackling such dark forces will require both knowledge and courage. You must understand what you're up against before you can hope to face it."

"Then tell us," Ollie urged, his voice trembling slightly. "Tell us everything you know about Gideon Blackwell's spirit."

"Very well." Millie licked her lips nervously, then leaned forward, her voice dropping to a whisper as she began to speak. "Gideon's spirit is like a storm—unpredictable, relentless, and utterly devastating. It feeds on fear, drawing strength from the terror it instills in those it haunts. The curse has only served to amplify its power, allowing it to wreak havoc on our town for generations."

"Is there any way to stop it?" Cameron asked, clenching his jaw as the weight of their task settled around him like a cloak made of lead.

"Only by breaking the curse can you truly banish Gideon's spirit from Gravewood," Millie explained, her voice heavy with the burden of her knowledge. "But you must tread carefully, for his spirit is cunning and malicious, ever seeking to twist your actions against you."

Cameron's thoughts raced as he took in Millie's words. How could they hope to outsmart such a malevolent force? And yet, the thought of doing nothing—of allowing Gideon Blackwell's spirit to continue terrorizing Gravewood— was unthinkable.

"Where do we start?" he asked, his voice barely audible above the sound of his own heartbeat. "What's our first step?"

"Your first step," Millie began hesitantly, "is to learn all you can about the curse and its origins. You must delve into Gravewood's darkest corners and uncover the truth that has been hidden for so long."

"Can we trust the people of Gravewood to help us in this quest?" Ollie inquired, his brow furrowed with concern.

"Trust is a fragile thing, my dear boy," Millie warned, her eyes clouded with sorrow. "But remember that even the most fearful heart can be swayed by the power of hope. Reach out to those who are willing to listen and stand beside you but be wary of the shadows that lurk beyond sight."

"Thank you, Millie," Cameron murmured, his gratitude shining brightly amidst the darkness of the library. With renewed purpose, he faced the uncertain path ahead, knowing he and his friends would need every ounce of courage and determination they possessed to confront Gideon Blackwell's spirit and break the curse that long plagued their town.

A heavy silence settled over the dim library, the weight of Millie's words pressing down on Cameron and his friends.

"Remember," Millie said gently, her voice soft yet resolute, "you are not alone in this journey. There are others who have faced similar darkness, and their knowledge can guide you." Her eyes met each of theirs in turn, instilling a sense of camaraderie and determination that chased away a fraction of the fear gnawing at their hearts.

"Thank you, Millie," Cameron managed to say, his throat tight with emotion. His fingers trembled as he reached out to clasp her frail hand, drawing strength from the warmth of her touch.

"Be brave, young ones," Millie urged, giving his hand an encouraging squeeze before releasing it. "And trust that the light will always find a way to break through the shadows."

The group nodded, their expressions resolute, as they prepared to leave the sanctuary of the library. Each one felt the gravity of their mission settling upon their shoulders like a cloak, both daunting and empowering in its enormity. As they stepped toward the exit, the oppressive presence of

Gideon Blackwell's spirit lingering beyond the threshold, a sinister force threatened to extinguish the hope Millie kindled within them.

"Wait," Millie called out suddenly, causing the group to halt in their tracks. She hurried to a nearby shelf and removed a tattered, leather-bound book with trembling hands. "Take this with you," she instructed, handing it to Cameron. "It contains the stories of those who have faced the supernatural before. May it help you navigate the unseen world that now lies before you."

Cameron clutched the book to his chest, the leather cool and worn beneath his fingertips. The echoes of those who came before him, their experiences bound within the pages, waiting to offer guidance and wisdom.

"Thank you," he whispered, his eyes filled with gratitude as he looked at Millie one last time. Then, with a deep breath that did little to steady his racing heart, Cameron turned and led his friends out of the library, each step taking them further into the shadows obscured their path.

CHAPTER 5

The basement door creaked open, revealing the dim space below. Cameron led the way down the stairs, followed closely by Ellie, Ollie, and Natalie. As they descended, each step was accompanied by a groan from the old wooden floorboards beneath their feet. The musty smell of damp earth and long-forgotten memories wrapped around them like a suffocating blanket.

"Guys, I can't believe we're actually doing this," whispered Natalie, nervously fiddling with the strap of her camera.

"Come on, Nat, where's your sense of adventure?" Cameron replied with a mischievous grin, his eyes scanning the room for anything unusual.

"Easy for you to say," Ellie muttered, her small hands gripping the railing tightly as she took in the eerie atmosphere.

"Look at all this stuff," Ollie said in awe, adjusting his glasses as he peered at a dusty display case. "It's like stepping back in time."

"Exactly," agreed Ellie, her blue eyes alight with curiosity as she surveyed the room. "There must be so much history here just waiting to be discovered." She couldn't help but feel a thrill at the prospect of piecing together the puzzle before them despite the unsettling ambiance.

"Let's not forget why we're here," Cameron reminded them, his voice betraying a hint of unease. "We need to figure out what's going on with these supernatural occurrences, and we won't do that by standing around."

"Right," said Ellie, drawing herself up to her full, albeit petite, height. "We'll find the answers we need, no matter how scary it gets."

As the friends began to explore the basement, their footsteps echoed in the silence, punctuated by the creaks and groans of the aging building. The weight of history pressing down on them as if the very walls were whispering secrets from long ago.

"Guys," Ellie called out softly, her voice audible above the sounds of the basement. "Over here! I think I've found something."

The group gathered around a dusty table strewn with ancient-looking documents and artifacts, all seemingly connected to the town's past. As they examined the items, the chilling atmosphere intensified, as though the spirits of those who come before them were watching from the shadows, waiting for their story to be told.

The friends continued their exploration, each step echoing softly through the cavernous basement. Ollie hesitated, reaching out to touch a tarnished silver locket that lay half-hidden beneath a yellowed newspaper. He looked up at Natalie, who was rifling through a stack of old photos. "Hey Nat, check this out," he whispered, holding the locket up for her to see.

"Wow," she replied, taking it from him. "It's beautiful but also kind of creepy, don't you think?"

"Definitely," Ollie agreed, shivering involuntarily as the temperature in the room dropped several degrees.

"Guys?" Cameron's voice was tense, his eyes glued to something in the distance. "I think we've got company."

Ellie followed his gaze and gasped. "Gideon Blackwell..."

The air crackled with energy as the spirit made its first appearance before them. The dim lights flickered ominously, casting unsettling shadows on the walls. The presence of

Gideon Blackwell was palpable, like a force pressed down upon them, making it difficult to breathe.

"Is it...is it really him?" Ellie stammered, her voice barely above a whisper.

"Seems like it," Ollie muttered, trying to sound braver than he felt.

"Stay calm, guys," Cameron urged, his face pale but determined. "We need to figure out why he's here. Maybe he can help us understand what's been happening."

"Yes, we have to try and communicate with him," Ellie said resolutely, her passion for history momentarily overpowering her fear. "This could be our only chance to get answers."

"Okay, let's do this," Cameron said, nodding his agreement. "Gideon Blackwell, if you can hear us, we need your help."

For a moment, the only sound in the room was their own ragged breathing as they waited for a response from the spirit.

"Please," Ellie added, her voice quivering.

Wide-eyed expressions filled the faces of Cameron, Ellie, Ollie, and Natalie, as they stared at Gideon Blackwell's spirit. Their bodies trembled, an involuntary reaction to their growing fear and awe. The air crackled with energy, with each breath feeling heavier than the last.

"Is this really happening?" Ollie stammered, his voice cracking. "I mean, we're actually seeing a ghost!"

"Keep it together, Ollie," Cameron whispered, trying to sound braver than he felt. His knuckles turned white as he clenched his fists, desperate for some semblance of control.

Ellie's heart raced in her chest, but she couldn't tear her eyes away from the vengeful spirit. Her love for history and insatiable curiosity pushed her forward, even as terror gnawed at the edges of her thoughts. She blinked back tears as her mind raced, searching for any connection between the artifacts they'd discovered and the curse that plagued their town for generations.

"Guys, look at these old newspaper clippings," Ellie said as she pointed to a dusty scrapbook on a nearby shelf. Trembling fingers traced the yellowed pages, piecing together fragments of stories long forgotten. "It says here Gideon Blackwell was accused of witchcraft, but he claimed innocence until the very end."

Gildon Blackwood pointed at the scrapbook. "Maybe he's trying to tell us something," Ellie suggested, her eyes darting between the scrapbook and the spirit hovering before them. "We need to listen to him."

"Right," Ellie agreed, determination pushing her past her fear. "We can't be afraid, not now. We need to find the truth hidden within these relics, no matter how terrifying it may be."

As she continued to analyze the artifacts, the other friends could see Ellie's intuition at work, connecting the dots between the town's history and the curse that haunted it for centuries. Their fear began to give way to curiosity, the desire to uncover the truth propelling them forward.

"Look at this symbol," Ellie said, pointing to an old book with a strange marking on the cover. "It matches the one we found on that locket."

"Then let's figure this out together," Cameron declared, his gaze locked on Gideon Blackwell's spirit. "We have to put an end to this nightmare once and for all."

As the friends huddled together, their hearts pounding in unison, they were more determined than ever to face the supernatural forces that threatened their town. The chilling atmosphere of the basement closed in around them, as if urging them to uncover the dark secrets hidden within its walls.

"Does anyone have any idea what Gideon Blackwell wants?" Ollie asked, his voice quivering as he stared at the spirit hovering before them.

"Maybe he's trying to tell us something," Ellie suggested, her eyes darting around the dim basement, searching for any clues that might help them decipher his message.

"Or maybe we've disturbed him," Natalie whispered, clutching her arms tightly around herself as a shiver ran down her spine. "Maybe we should leave."

"Wait!" Ellie said suddenly, her fingers delicately tracing the intricate outline of the symbol on the book's cover. The symbol, an enigmatic convergence of intertwining lines and cryptic shapes, seemed to pulse with an otherworldly energy. Its presence on the aged pages hinted at a connection to Gravewood's rich and mysterious history as if each curve and intersection told a tale that transcended time.

"Look at these symbols and the way they connect to Gravewood's history," Ellie continued, her gaze fixed on the ancient emblem. The lines seemed to weave together like threads in a tapestry, binding the town to a narrative woven with secrets and echoes of the past. "I think Gideon Blackwell holds the key to breaking the curse, and this symbol might be the map to unraveling the hauntings in Gravewood."

"Are you saying that he could be... helping us?" Cameron asked, his brow furrowing in confusion.

"Helping or not, we need to figure out what he wants from us," Ellie replied, determination evident in her voice.

As the group continued to discuss their theories, the chilling atmosphere of the basement intensified with each passing moment. The flickering lights cast eerie shadows on the walls, and hair-raising whispers echoed through the air as if someone was watching and listening to their every word.

"Can you guys hear that?" Ollie asked.

"Stay focused," Ellie urged, her eyes scanning the artifacts surrounding them. "We can't let fear get the best of us. We have to find out what Gideon Blackwell is trying to tell us."

"Right," Natalie agreed, her breath coming in shallow gasps as she listened to the whispers closing in around them. "We have to put an end to this curse once and for all."

"Before it's too late," Ellie added, her voice barely audible above the unsettling sounds filling the basement.

As the friends huddled together, their hearts pounding in unison, they couldn't shake they were being watched from the shadows. With each passing second, the encounter with Gideon Blackwell's spirit grew more intense, urging them to unravel the mystery haunting their town for centuries.

Cameron took a deep breath, his heart pounding in his chest as he tried to summon the courage to speak. His voice shook as he addressed the spirit, "Gideon Blackwell, we want to understand why you're here. What do you want from us?"

The others stared at him, their eyes wide with fear and anticipation. The eerie whispers which had filled the room moments ago vanished, leaving an unnerving silence hanging in the air.

"Are you responsible for the curse plagues our town?" Ellie ventured, her blue eyes narrowed in determination. She reached out a trembling hand, almost as if to touch the invisible force surrounding them.

"Please," Ollie whispered, his voice cracking under the weight of his growing fear. "We only want to help."

The friends exchanged nervous glances, waiting for a response from the vengeful spirit. But the silence that followed their inquiries was even more oppressive than the chilling atmosphere that had enveloped them before. The air grew colder, and an unspoken understanding passed between them: Gideon Blackwell's motives remained shrouded in darkness.

As they stood there, their bodies rigid with tension, the silence was suddenly shattered by a loud crash from another part of the basement. They jumped, their hearts racing as the sound echoed through the dim space, causing dust to rise from the creaking floorboards.

"Wh-what was that?" Ellie stammered, her green eyes darting around the room as she clutched her arms tightly around herself.

"Maybe it's something falling over," Natalie suggested, her voice strained as she gripped her camera tight in her hands. She snapped a picture, hoping to capture anything that might give them a clue about what they're dealing with.

"Or maybe it's a warning," Cameron thought aloud, his eyes scanning the shadows for any sign of movement. The weight of his fear pressed down on him, but he refused to let it consume him.

"Whatever it is," Ellie said, her voice steady despite the chill crawling up her spine, "we need to figure out how to break this curse before it's too late."

As the friends exchanged worried glances, they knew their quest for answers had only begun. With each passing moment, the horrors lurking in Gravewood's shadows grew stronger, and they couldn't help but wonder if they would be able to withstand the darkness that threatened to consume them all.

Ellie's piercing blue eyes scanned the artifacts with determination, her hands trembling slightly as she brushed away layers of dust from a peculiar-looking relic. It was an old book, its leather cover worn and slightly tattered at the edges. The pages whispered secrets as she carefully flipped through them, her heart pounding in anticipation.

"Guys, I think I've found something!" Ellie exclaimed, her excitement palpable as the others gathered around her. Ollie peered over her shoulder, curiosity gleaming in his eyes.

"What is it, Ellie?" he asked, his voice barely audible in the tense silence.

"Look," she replied, pointing at a faint symbol etched into the corner of one of the pages. "This symbol... It matches the one on the pendant we found earlier, remember?"

Cameron nodded, his brow furrowing in concentration. "Yeah, you're right. But what does it mean?"

"Wait," Natalie interjected, her camera momentarily forgotten as she focused on the mysterious symbol. "I think I remember reading about this in the town's archives. It's an ancient sigil, used by the founders of Gravewood to protect the town from dark forces."

"Then why is it here, hidden in this book?" Ellie asked, her green eyes wide with fear. "And how is it connected to Gideon Blackwell's spirit?"

"Maybe it has something to do with the curse," Ellie mused, her thoughts racing as she tried to piece together the cryptic clues. "If we can figure out how to use this sigil, maybe we can break the curse and set things right."

"Let's hope so," Cameron said grimly. "Because the darkness in this town is growing stronger, and I'm not sure how much longer we can hold out against it."

The friends exchanged somber glances, each one silently acknowledging the weight of the responsibility now rested on their shoulders. As they climbed the creaking stairs and left the basement behind, their hearts pounded with a mix of fear and determination. Each step, bringing them closer to the heart of the darkness, threatened to consume Gravewood.

CHAPTER 6

The sun sank low in the sky, casting long shadows that crept like tendrils over the unkempt lawn of Jazz Whittaker's abandoned house. The once grand Victorian mansion now stood as a crumbling testament to Gravewood's haunted history. Its peeling paint and cracked windows reflect the neglect that consumed the once-vibrant estate. A tangled mess of vines and thorny brambles wrapped around its foundation, climbing up the sides to claim the house as their own.

A chilling breeze whispered through the twisted branches of the gnarled oak tree in the front yard, and an eerie silence enveloped the scene as the group of friends hesitantly approached.

"Are you sure this is the place?" asked Cameron, his voice barely audible as he stared at the looming structure with wide eyes.

"According to Jazz's journals," said Ellie, clutching the leather-bound book tightly to her chest, "this is where he lived before... well, you know." She swallowed hard, trying to keep her fear from seeping into her words.

Ollie shivered, pulling his jacket tighter around him. "I don't like it," he mumbled, glancing nervously over his shoulder as if expecting some unspeakable horror to leap out from the shadows. "This place gives me the creeps."

"Come on, guys," urged Natalie, taking a deep breath and stepping onto the creaking porch. "We have to find out what happened here. It could be our only chance to break the curse."

As they reluctantly followed her lead, the friends couldn't shake the unseen eyes watching them from the darkened windows. Their hearts raced with a mixture of curiosity and trepidation as they neared the warped wooden door, the weight of their task pressing down upon them like a suffocating fog.

"Here goes nothing," muttered Cameron, reaching out a trembling hand to grasp the rusted doorknob. The door creaked open with a haunting moan, revealing the dusty, cob-web-filled interior of Jazz Whittaker's forgotten home.

The air inside the house was heavy with dust and decay, making it difficult to breathe as they stepped across the threshold. The dim light filtered through the grimy windows cast eerie shadows on the peeling wallpaper and warped floor-boards, giving the impression of a place forgotten by time.

"Wow," whispered Natalie as she raised her vintage Polaroid camera, its worn leather casing telling tales of countless captures to immortalize the haunting scene before them. The camera whirred softly as it spat out an instant photograph, the image developing in the ethereal glow of Gravewood's mysterious ambiance. Each photo held a piece of the supernatural puzzle, a visual record of the spectral anomalies that danced in the shadows.

"This is like stepping into another world," Natalie marveled, carefully organizing the Polaroids in a worn leather album, each snapshot a portal into the paranormal. Her collection of eerie photographs, a tangible documentation of the inexplicable, served as both a testament to the haunting occurrences in Gravewood and a visual journal of their quest for answers.

"Another creepy world," Ollie added, adjusting his glasses and squinting into the gloom. "It's so dark in here."

"Let's split up and see what we can find," suggested Cameron, trying to sound braver than he felt. "Maybe we'll uncover some clues about Gideon Blackwell and the curse."

"Good idea," nodded Ellie, her eyes already scanning the cluttered rooms for anything that might reveal more about Jazz Whittaker's research. "We should cover as much ground as possible."

As they ventured deeper into the house, their footsteps echoed through the silent hallways, accompanied only by the distant creaks and groans of the decaying structure. The group was comprised of Cameron, the curious 13-year-old with short, messy brown hair; Ellie, with her keen intuition and eyes that seemed to pierce the supernatural veil; Miller, whose analytical mind sought patterns in the paranormal; Ellie, with her knack for deciphering symbols; and Natalie, the photographer capturing the eerie essence of Gravewood with her vintage Polaroid camera.

Each room they entered was locked in a state of disarray, filled with piles of yellowed newspapers, musty books, and strange artifacts that hinted at the eccentric historian's obsession with Gravewood's past. The group split up, exploring different corners of the house. Cameron and Ellie headed up-stairs, drawn by a faint whisper that seemed to beckon from the shadows. Meanwhile, Miller and Ellie delved into the his-torian's study, hoping to uncover clues within the labyrinth of books and manuscripts. Natalie, with her camera in hand, documented every step, capturing the silent tales embedded in the dilapidated rooms of Gravewood's enigmatic mansion.

"Guys?" called Ellie from a small study off the main hallway. "I think you need to see this."

Her friends gathered around her, staring down at the faded map spread out on the desk. It was covered in cryptic symbols and annotations, several of which appeared to be written in a language none of them recognized.

"Jazz must have been trying to piece together the history of the ritual," mused Ellie, tracing one of the mysterious symbols with her finger. "But why? What did he hope to gain?"

"Maybe he wanted to break the curse himself," suggested Ollie, a shiver running down his spine at the thought. "But something went wrong, and now we're stuck with it."

"Let's keep looking," said Cameron, feeling a renewed sense of urgency. "There has to be something here that can help us."

They split up once more, each drawn to a different room or section of the house by an inexplicable pull. As they sifted through Jazz's belongings, their fingers brushed against the dusty relics of Gravewood's dark history, sending shivers of unease rippling through them.

Cameron's footsteps echoed through the abandoned house as he ventured deeper into its shadowy depths. The air grew colder, and he shivered involuntarily, his breath visible in the dim light. The weight of the past pressed down upon him, the secrets of the house lurking out of reach.

"Curiosity killed the cat," Cameron muttered to himself, trying to lighten the mood as he entered a room filled with shelves upon shelves of old journals, letters, and photographs. The musty scent of decaying paper filled his nostrils, and he hesitated, feeling both drawn to the room and repelled by its eerie atmosphere.

"Okay, Gideon, let's see what you've been hiding," he whispered, running his fingers over the cracked leather bindings of the journals, tracing the faded ink of the letters. His heart quickened with anticipation, knowing within these pages lay the answers they sought.

As he delved deeper into the room, Cameron noticed an oddity in one of the walls—a section of wooden paneling out of place amidst the dust-covered books. He reached out tentatively, feeling the rough texture beneath his fingertips, and pushed gently. To his astonishment, the panel gave way, revealing a hidden compartment.

"Guys, I found something!" Cameron called excitedly, but no one answered. He hesitated for a moment, then decided to investigate further on his own.

Within the concealed space, Cameron discovered a rickety ladder leading upwards, beckoning him toward the unknown. Unable to resist the pull of curiosity, he began to climb, each rung creaking ominously under his weight. As he ascended, the air grew colder still, and a sense of foreboding settled over him like a shroud.

"Please don't let this be a mistake," he thought, regretting his earlier quip about curiosity. But it was too late to turn back now.

Cameron emerged into a cramped attic, dimly illuminated by a single shaft of moonlight filtering through a small window. The space was filled with cobwebs and shadows, but what truly caught his attention were the stacks of journals and letters piled haphazardly on an old wooden desk, the words "Gideon Blackwell" scrawled across many of the covers.

"Whoa," Cameron breathed, his heart pounding in his chest as he realized the magnitude of his discovery. He reached for the nearest journal, feeling the cold, leathery cover beneath his fingers.

"Okay, Gideon," he whispered, opening the book to the first page, his eyes scanning the faded handwriting. "Time to find out what you've been up to all these years."

With every word he read, a chill ran down his spine as the truth about Gideon Blackwell's involvement in Gravewood's dark past came to light. And as he continued to sift through the hidden trove of knowledge, he knew the key to breaking the curse lay within his grasp.

Cameron's hands trembled as he turned the brittle pages of the ancient journal, his eyes scanning the faded ink documenting Gideon Blackwell's descent into darkness. The words came alive in his mind, painting a terrifying picture of the ritual Gideon orchestrated over a century ago.

"'Under the blood moon, we gathered in secret,'" Cameron read aloud, his voice no more than a whisper. "The circle drawn, the incantations chanted, and the sacrifices made. But something went wrong—the forces unleashed were beyond our control."

His breath caught in his throat as he continued, uncovering the terrible truth about what transpired fateful night. As the shadows cast by the moonlight danced upon the walls, Cameron couldn't shake Gideon's spirit lurking nearby, watching him uncover the past.

"By the gods, Gideon..." he muttered, his voice trembling with a mix of disbelief and terror. His heart pounded like a frantic drumbeat as he pieced together the horrifying consequences of the ritual. The air thickened with a palpable sense of dread as the weight of realization pressed down on him.

In that haunting moment, he could almost hear the whispered echoes of an ancient incantation, the very words that Gideon Blackwell had dared to speak. The shadows in the room seemed to lengthen, casting an ominous shroud over the truth he uncovered. His hands trembled as he connected the dots, tracing the intricate lines that wove a tapestry of doom.

"You doomed us all," he finally whispered, the words hanging in the air like a sinister curse. The room, once filled with a quiet stillness, now pulsated with an unsettling energy, as if the very walls mourned the irreversible fate that had befallen Gravewood.

He flipped through the pages, trying to find anything that might help break the curse that plagued Gravewood for generations. But with each new revelation, he realized the magnitude of the task before him.

STEPHANIE TYO

"Why did you do it, Gideon?" Cameron asked in the empty room, frustration and fear knotting in his stomach. "Why would you risk everything for power?"

"Because I thought I could control it," came a voice from within the darkest recesses of his own thoughts, sending shivers down Cameron's spine. He shook his head, dismissing the eerie response as a product of his overactive imagination.

"Focus, Cameron," he told himself, flipping through another dusty journal. "There has to be a way to fix this."

As he delved deeper into Gideon's writings, he began to see how much the man lost in his pursuit of power. Friends turned against him, the family disowned him, and the town of Gravewood suffered as a result.

"Everything I've ever loved, destroyed by my own hand," Gideon's words echoed in Cameron's mind. "The curse will remain until the day a willing heart can undo what has been done."

Cameron's pulse raced as he realized the implications of this passage. A glimmer of hope flickered within him, but it was overshadowed by the burden of responsibility now placed on his young shoulders. If he were to break the curse, he would need to face Gideon's spirit head-on and find a way to make amends for the atrocities committed so long ago.

"Alright, Gideon," Cameron whispered, determination flooding through him. "If a willing heart is what you need, then I'll be the one to end this nightmare once and for all."

Elsewhere in Jazz's house, Ellie's piercing blue eyes scanned the dim, cobweb-veiled room as she tiptoed through the creaking floorboards. The air heavy with the scent of mildew and age, a far cry from the musty library where Cameron disappeared moments before. She could hear her own heart pounding in her ears, the rhythmic thud a testament to her apprehension.

"Come on, Ellie," she whispered under her breath, trying to gather her courage. "There's got to be something here that can help us."

As she ventured further into the room, she noticed the piles of artifacts and relics, each seeming to hold in their grasp the secrets of generations passed. Her fingers grazed over an intricately carved wooden box, dust motes dancing in the air around her. A shiver ran down her spine as she considered the stories it might contain.

"Looking for answers, huh?" Ollie's voice broke the silence, his glasses fogging up slightly from the dampness in the air.

"Always," Ellie replied, a hint of a smile crossing her face. "Gideon's past is our best chance at understanding what we're up against."

"Good luck," Ollie said, patting Ellie's shoulder reassuringly before departing to explore another section of the house.

Ellie continued her search, her keen intuition driving her towards a dusty corner of the room. There, partially hidden beneath a moth-eaten tapestry, she discovered an ancient-looking chest adorned with symbols she couldn't quite decipher. An unexplainable pull urged her to open it, her curiosity overriding any lingering fears.

"Here goes nothing," she muttered, lifting the heavy lid with a groan.

Inside, nestled among tarnished trinkets and brittle parchment, lay an ornate dagger with a hilt twisted like living vines. Its blade had darkened, as though stained by a long-forgotten sin. Ellie felt the weight of its history in her hands and knew instinctively this relic connected to Gideon's past.

"Is this what you used, Gideon?" she whispered, her voice wavering with uncertainty. "Did you spill blood with this blade to seal your fate?"

Her breath caught in her throat as she imagined the ancient ritual taking place, the air thick with fear and desperation.

The realization of the artifact's purpose gripped her heart like a vice, amplifying her determination to uncover the truth.

"Whatever secrets you're hiding," she murmured, clutching the dagger tightly, "we will find them, and we will put an end to this nightmare."

A chill swept through the room as Cameron, Ellie, and Ollie reconvened in the dim parlor, their faces etched with equal parts fascination and trepidation. The flickering light from a solitary candle cast eerie shadows across the walls, amplifying the sense of unease that had settled over them since entering Jazz Whittaker's abandoned house.

In the dimly lit corner of the mansion, Ollie's fingers brushed against the dust-covered surface of an antique side table. As he explored the forgotten nooks and crannies, his eyes fell upon a small wooden box nestled amidst a collection of forgotten curiosities. Intrigued, he carefully opened the lid, revealing a trove of intricately carved figurines. Each miniature sculpture seemed to defy the boundaries of normalcy, with grotesque details etched into their forms. The eerie craftsmanship held an otherworldly allure, casting an uncanny spell on Ollie as he marveled at the macabre beauty concealed within the forgotten corners of Gravewood's mysterious mansion.

"Guys, you won't believe what I found," Cameron said breathlessly, clutching a stack of leather-bound journals and letters to his chest. "These are Gideon Blackwell's personal writings, and they reveal so much about the ritual he performed."

"Check this out," Ellie added, holding up the mysterious dagger she discovered. "I'm sure it was used in the ritual. It feels like there's an incredible power within it—but also something dark and sinister."

Ollie nodded gravely, presenting his findings: a small wooden box filled with intricately carved figurines, each more grotesque than the last. "I think these were part of the ceremony, too. They're so detailed, and each one gives off a strange energy."

As the friends shared their discoveries, their minds raced with the implications of Gideon's involvement and the curse's origins. The pieces of the puzzle were starting to come together, but the full picture remained elusive.

"From what I've read," Cameron explained, flipping open one of the ancient journals, "Gideon was obsessed with immortality and believed that performing this ritual would grant him eternal life. But something went wrong, and instead of becoming immortal, he cursed himself and the town of Gravewood."

"Is there any mention of how to reverse the ritual?" Ollie asked, his eyes darting between Cameron and the artifacts scattered on the floor before them.

"Not yet," Cameron admitted, furrowing his brow in frustration. "But we have enough information here to start piecing it together. We need to figure out how to break this curse, not only for Gideon's sake but for the entire town."

"Agreed," Ellie chimed in, her grip tightening around the hilt of the dagger. "We've come too far to give up now. We owe it to everyone who suffered because of Gideon's mistakes."

The resolve in her words was infectious, and a flame of determination ignited within each of them. They faced a daunting task, one fraught with danger and uncertainty, but there was no turning back now.

"Let's do this," Ollie declared, his voice firm and resolute. "Together, we'll find a way to reverse the ritual and break the curse."

"Gravewood is depending on us," Cameron added, closing the journal with a resounding thud. "And we won't let them down."

As they stood united in their mission, the atmosphere in the room shifted. The weight of the past and the unknown future loomed over them, but they're undeterred. With each clue uncovered and every secret revealed, they moved closer to unraveling the dark mystery that ensnared Gideon Blackwell and the town of Gravewood for generations. And they determined to succeed, no matter the cost.

The wind howled outside the dilapidated house, its eerie moan a chilling reminder of the supernatural forces at play. Shadows flickered across the floorboards as Cameron, Ellie, and Ollie exchanged determined glances.

"Alright," Cameron said, his voice steady despite the fear gnawing at the edges of his thoughts. "We've got what we came for. Let's get out of here and figure out our next move."

"Agreed," Ollie murmured, casting one last glance at the dusty shelves revealing so many secrets. "I don't think I can take much more of this place."

As they turned to leave, Ellie hesitated, her hand still wrapped around the ancient dagger. The cold metal pulsed with energy, a tangible connection to the past and Gideon's twisted legacy.

"Hey," she whispered, her eyes intent on the blade. "Do you hear that?"

Cameron and Ollie paused, straining their ears to catch any sound above the relentless wind. And then they heard it—a faint, insistent whisper, like voices carried on the breeze, beckoning them towards an unknown fate.

"Is that...Gideon?" Ollie asked, his heart pounding in his chest.

"Or maybe it's the spirits he wronged," Cameron mused, unease tightening his stomach. "Either way, we need to be ready for whatever comes next."

The friends shared a nod of understanding, steeling themselves for the challenges ahead. They knew confronting Gideon's spirit would be no easy task, but the weight of Gravewood's suffering rested on their shoulders, and they refused to let fear hold them back.

"Let's go," Ellie said firmly, leading the way through the darkened halls of the abandoned house. The creaks and groans of the decaying structure echoed around them, a haunting soundtrack to their departure.

As they stepped out into the overgrown garden, the wind carried a sense of anticipation, as though the air charged with the knowledge of what was to come. The friends exchanged one last glance, their eyes filled with determination and a quiet understanding their journey was far from over.

"Whatever it takes," Cameron whispered, his gaze fixed on the horizon. "We'll find a way to break this curse and set things right."

"Gravewood is counting on us," Ollie added, his voice unwavering. "We won't let them down."

They turned their backs on the eerie house, its secrets now a small part of the larger mystery they sought to unravel. As they walked away, the wind picked up once more, carrying with it the faintest hint of a promise—a promise of danger, of sacrifice, and ultimately, of redemption.

And so, the friends pressed on, driven by their shared resolve, determined to confront Gideon's spirit and bring an end to the darkness plaguing their town for centuries. The night stretched before them, an uncharted path leading into the unknown, but they moved forward without hesitation, guided by their unwavering commitment to righting the wrongs of the past.

CHAPTER 7

Gravewood Middle School loomed like a towering relic of a bygone era, its creaking floorboards and dim hallways echoing the whispers of past secrets. Despite the ongoing use of the school, shadows still danced along the walls as the flickering overhead lights struggled to illuminate every corner, casting an eerie atmosphere over the bustling corridors. The building, though occupied, retained an undeniable air of mystery, its history woven into the very fabric of its walls, waiting to be unraveled by those curious enough to venture into its still-enigmatic depths.

"Guys, do you really think this is a good idea?" asked Ollie, his glasses glinting in the low light as he nervously tugged at his shirt collar.

"Relax, Ollie. We have to find out what's going on," Cameron replied, his messy brown hair bouncing with excitement. His mischievous grin betrayed his thrill at the prospect of uncovering a mystery.

"Cam's right," agreed Ellie, her curly red hair cascading down her back like a fiery waterfall. "We need to get to the bottom of all these strange occurrences." She held her chin high, determination burning in her eyes.

"Besides," added Natalie, her dark brown hair shimmering under the weak lighting, "this place gives me the creeps. The sooner we figure this out, the better." Her fingers twitched, itching to capture the scene with her camera. They couldn't risk being seen. The unknown loomed around them, and her heart raced with anticipation.

As the group huddled closer together, Ellie scanned the hallway, her piercing blue eyes missing nothing. " "We need to be cautious," she warned, her voice steady despite the tendrils of fear creeping up her spine. "Whatever we're dealing with, it's powerful."

"Okay, Ellie, any ideas on what we should do then?" Cameron asked, turning to face her. He swallowed hard, attempting to conceal the fear of isolation gnawing at him.

"First, let's gather information," she replied, her gaze intense. "We need to understand what we're up against."

"Agreed," said Ollie, his voice trembling slightly. "Let's stick together and stay alert." The weight of his fear of abandonment anchored itself in the pit of his stomach.

"Right," Ellie chimed in, her courage unwavering even as she internally battled with the fear of losing control. "We can do this, guys. We have to work together."

Natalie nodded, her artistic eye taking in every detail of their surroundings. "Okay, let's go," she said, her fear of the unknown momentarily pushed aside by her desire to find answers.

As the group ventured deeper into the darkened halls of Gravewood Middle School, whatever awaited them would test the limits of their friendship and courage. And yet, despite their fears and uncertainties, they pressed on, united in their determination to face the supernatural forces lurking in the shadows.

The secluded corner of Gravewood Middle School was shrouded in shadows, the dim light from a flickering overhead bulb casting eerie patterns on the cracked walls. Here, away from prying eyes, Cameron led the group into their impromptu meeting spot. The air was heavy with dust and the faint scent of mildew, further amplifying the mystery surrounding them.

"Alright," Cameron began, rubbing his hands together anxiously as he glanced at each of his friends. "We need to pool our information and figure out what's going on with this curse and Gideon Blackwell's spirit." His voice wavered, betraying his fear of isolation as he realized how much they were all relying on one another.

Ellie stepped forward, her blue eyes narrowing in determination. "I did some research on Gideon Blackwell in the school library. It turns out he faced a notorious trial back in the 1860s, accused of being a powerful occultist and rumored to have dabbled in dark magic." She hesitated for a moment, acutely aware of the pressure she put on herself to succeed. "It's possible his spirit is behind these strange occurrences."

"We need to be cautious," she warned, her voice steady despite the tendrils of fear creeping up her spine. "Whatever we're dealing with, it's powerful."

"Okay, Ellie, any ideas on what we should do then?" Cameron asked, turning to face her. He swallowed hard, attempting to conceal the fear of isolation gnawing at him.

"First, let's gather information," she replied, her gaze intense. "We need to understand what we're up against."

Ollie, the quiet voice of reason among them, adjusted his glasses and nodded gravely. "That would explain the supernatural events we've been experiencing," he said, feeling his fear of abandonment creeping up on him as he clung to the hope of understanding the situation better.

Natalie spoke up next, her fingers fidgeting with the strap of her camera. "I've captured some strange things in my photos lately," she admitted, her artistic mind reeling with the possibilities. "Faint outlines of figures, unnatural shadows... Maybe they're connected to Gideon Blackwell." Her fear of the unknown gnawed at her, but she wouldn't let it consume her.

Ellie, tiny yet fierce, clenched her fists and looked around the circle. "We can't let this go on," she declared, her fear of losing control momentarily overshadowed by her determination. "If Gideon Blackwell's spirit is causing all this trouble, we need to find a way to stop him."

"Agreed," Cameron said, his heart pounding with anticipation. "Let's keep our eyes and ears open for more information. We'll meet back here tomorrow after school to share what we've learned."

Each member felt a mix of dread and determination. The stakes were high, and they couldn't afford to make any mistakes. But with their combined strengths and unwavering friendship, they're ready to face whatever supernatural forces Gideon Blackwell has in store for them.

Cameron stared at the flickering fluorescent light in the hallway, casting eerie shadows on the peeling paint of the school's walls. Facing Gideon Blackwell's spirit would require more than their small group; they needed as many allies as they could get. His thoughts raced with worry, but he had to be brave for his friends.

"Guys, we can't do this alone," Cameron said, his voice resolute. "We need to gather our classmates and join forces if we have any chance at breaking this curse."

Ellie nodded, her blue eyes filled with determination. "You're right, Cameron. We need to show them unity is the key to overcoming this supernatural threat."

Ollie adjusted his glasses nervously. "But what if they don't believe us? Or worse, what if they abandon us when things get tough?"

"Then we'll make them see the truth," Ellie replied fiercely, her red curls bouncing as she clenched her fists. "We have evidence, and we know what's at stake. We can't let our fears hold us back now."

As Ollie's insecurities gave way to resolve, Natalie held her camera close, ready to document their journey. "Let's go talk to our friends and classmates. We can start by showing them the photos I've taken and the information we've gathered so far."

They split up, each approaching different groups of students around the school. Cameron approached a group of boys huddled around a table in the cafeteria, his mischievous grin masking his inner worries. "Hey, guys, you won't believe what's happening in Gravewood. We need your help to stop it."

In the library, Ellie found a group of studious girls buried in their textbooks. She tapped her fingers on the table, trying to control her fear of failure. "We've uncovered something about the town's history that could change everything. We need your intelligence and problem-solving skills on our side."

Ollie approached a group of loners sitting under a tree outside, his kind-hearted nature shining through as he asked for their help. "We're facing something bigger than all of us, and we don't want anyone to be left behind. Will you join us?"

With her camera in hand, Natalie showed her mysterious photos to the school's art club, hoping to appeal to their creative minds. "There's something strange happening in this town, and we need your unique perspectives to help us understand it."

Ellie stormed into the gymnasium where the athletes practiced, her unwavering courage propelling her forward. "You guys are strong, fast, and fearless. We need you to stand with us against the supernatural forces threatening our town."

As the students listened with growing concern, each member of the group shared their discoveries and fears. They spoke passionately, urging their classmates to join them in confronting Gideon Blackwell's spirit and breaking the curse haunting Gravewood.

Their words resonated with the students, sparking a fire within them. As they agreed to help, Cameron felt a surge of hope. They were no longer alone; they had an army of friends and allies ready to stand with them against the darkness.

"Alright," Cameron said, taking a deep breath. "Let's do this. Together."

The sun was below the horizon as shadows stretched across Gravewood Middle School, its creaking floorboards and dimly lit hallways echoing with whispered secrets. Cameron stood amidst the motley crew of classmates they assembled, his heart pounding in anticipation.

"Alright, guys," he said, his voice steady despite the fear gnawing at him. "We need to come up with a plan to confront Gideon Blackwell's spirit. We've all got different strengths and abilities, so let's figure out how each of us can contribute."

Ellie cleared her throat, her keen intellect shining through her confidence. "From what we've gathered, this ancient ritual seems to be connected to the curse. If we can understand it and counteract it, we might have a chance against Gideon."

"Exactly," chimed in Ollie, his eyes alight with determination. "And we've got some pretty amazing people here. The art club has a talent for seeing things from different angles; maybe they can help us find clues we've missed."

Natalie's fingers twitched over her camera, her desire to capture the truth unwavering. "I'll keep taking pictures, documenting everything we find. Who knows? Maybe something will show up that leads us to the solution."

Ellie paced back and forth, her courage fueling her restless energy. "And don't forget about the athletes. We're fast and strong, and we won't back down from a fight. If there's any physical challenge we need to overcome, we'll be ready."

Cameron nodded, his mind racing with possibilities. He glanced around the room, taking in the faces of those who joined their cause: the bookworms, the artists, the athletes, and everyone in between. They're an unlikely alliance, bound together by the need to protect their town and break the curse that threatened to consume them all.

"Okay, so we've got brains, brawn, and creativity on our side," he mused, his thoughts tumbling out in a torrent. "But what about the ritual itself? What do we know?"

The assembled group grew quiet as they considered the fragments of information they gathered. Ellie finally broke the silence. "We know it's old—possibly even ancient—predating Gravewood itself. And there's definitely a connection to Gideon Blackwell."

"Right," Ollie agreed. "Maybe the town was built on some sort of sacred ground, and that's why his spirit is still here. We need to figure out how to break that connection."

As their classmates murmured in agreement, the weight of responsibility settled upon Cameron's shoulders. They come together as one, united by a common goal: to face the supernatural terror that haunted their town. Whatever the future held, they would face it together. And with any luck, they would emerge victorious.

Cameron stared at the motes of dust drifting through a sliver of sunlight filtered into their secluded corner of the school. The distant echo of creaking floorboards and the hum of fluorescent lights set an eerie atmosphere, as though Gideon Blackwell's spirit lurked in the shadows.

"Alright, so we know we need to confront Gideon Blackwell's spirit," Cameron began, his voice wavering slightly with the weight of the task ahead. "But how do we actually do that?"

"Maybe we can lure him out somehow?" Ellie suggested, her fingers nervously fidgeting with the hem of her sweater. "Use some sort of bait or trap?"

"Sounds risky," Natalie interjected, her brows furrowed in concern. "What if we end up making things worse?"

"Or what if one of us gets hurt?" Ellie added, his eyes darting between his friends, gauging their reactions.

Ollie rubbed his chin thoughtfully. "I wonder if there are any rituals or spells we can use to weaken him first. Give us a fighting chance."

Cameron chewed on the inside of his cheek as he considered each idea. He sensed the fear radiating from his friends but also their unwavering determination. They come this far; they couldn't back down now. "What if we combine both approaches? Find a way to lure him out, but also research any possible rituals or spells that could give us an edge."

The group exchanged apprehensive glances, silently weighing the potential outcomes. Finally, Natalie spoke up. "It's risky, but I think it's our best shot. And we can't just do nothing."

"Agreed," Ollie said, his voice firm. "We're stronger together. We'll find a way to make this work."

"Okay," Ellie nodded, taking a deep breath. "Let's do it."

"First, we'll need to gather as much information as possible about Gideon Blackwell and any potential weaknesses or vulnerabilities," Cameron outlined, his tone resolute. "Then, we'll look into rituals and spells that can help us in our confrontation. And finally, we'll devise a plan to lure him out, making sure everyone has a role to play and knows what to do."

As the group nodded in agreement, Cameron felt a surge of determination coursing through him. Their path was fraught with danger, but together, they would face the supernatural terror head-on. For Gravewood, for their friends and family, they would confront Gideon Blackwell's spirit and break the curse once and for all.

Cameron's eyes scanned the circle of his friends, each face determined and resolute. "Alright, let's assign roles based on our strengths," he said, his voice steady.

"Ellie, you'll be in charge of researching spells and rituals that can aid us in the confrontation. Your resourcefulness will be invaluable in finding what we need."

Ellie nodded solemnly, her curly red hair bouncing as she jotted down notes on a small notepad. "Got it. I'll have a list ready by tomorrow."

"Ollie, your loyalty and level-headedness make you the perfect person to help devise our plan for luring Gideon Blackwell out," Cameron continued. Ollie adjusted his glasses and gave a determined nod, accepting the responsibility without hesitation.

"Nat, your creativity and keen eye will be crucial in scouting the area, finding potential spots for the confrontation, and documenting everything with your camera." Natalie cradled her beloved camera in her hands, determination shining in her brown eyes.

"Ellie, you'll be our go-to historian. We need you to dig deep into Gravewood's past, find any information about Gideon Blackwell, and identify any weaknesses or vulnerabilities." Ellie's piercing blue eyes met Cameron's, acknowledging the gravity of her task.

"Lastly, I'll coordinate everything and make sure our plans come together seamlessly," Cameron finished, clenching his fists with resolve. The group exchanged glances, their stead-fast commitment to one another evident.

With their roles assigned, they moved on to gathering the necessary materials and resources for their plan.

Ellie scoured dusty tomes and ancient scrolls in the dimly lit corners of the Gravewood Library, her keen eyes sifting through the arcane knowledge hidden within the pages. The air was heavy with the scent of musty parchment as her fingers traced over faded ink, exploring the secrets of spells and rituals that might grant them an advantage in their supernatural quest.

Having recruited a group of intrepid allies, she led them through the labyrinthine shelves, each step echoing with the hushed anticipation of the unknown. The library, a reposito-ry of Gravewood's mystical history, held the key to unraveling the secrets of Gideon Blackwell and the dark forces at play.

"These tomes hold the answers we seek," Ellie declared, her voice carrying a whisper of excitement. "If we're to confront the spirit of Gideon Blackwell, we need every advantage we can find. Let's gather the knowledge and spells that will guide us through the shadows." The group, united in purpose, dis-persed among the aisles, each member scouring the ancient texts for the arcane wisdom that might tip the scales in their favor.

In the shadowed corners of the library, Ollie and Ellie pored over old maps and historical documents, the creaking floorboards beneath them a constant reminder of the eerie atmosphere they now inhabited. The scratch of their pencils on paper joined the chorus of whispers as they pieced together the puzzle of Gideon Blackwell's past.

Natalie ventured into the dimly lit halls of Gravewood, her camera capturing every nook and cranny that could potentially serve as a battleground against the supernatural foe. Her heart pounded in her chest, the chilling air around her prickling her skin like icy needles.

As the sun began to set, casting long shadows across the middle school, the group reconvened in their secluded corner, laden with tools, artifacts, and notes. They shared their findings, excitement, and trepidation intermingling as they realized the magnitude of the task before them.

"Remember," Cameron said, locking eyes with each of his friends, "we're all in this together. Every one of us has a part to play. And together, we'll break this curse and free Gravewood from Gideon Blackwell's grip."

A newfound sense of unity enveloped them, their hearts beating in unison as they prepared to face the unknown. With each passing moment, the anticipation grew, and they knew there was no turning back. The supernatural forces awaited them would soon be confronted by the unwavering courage of five determined friends.

Cameron couldn't help but notice the tightening grip his friends had on their newfound tools and artifacts as they gathered in their hidden corner. The dim light from a flickering bulb cast eerie shadows across the room, making it seem as if they were surrounded by unseen forces.

"Alright, then," he said, his voice steadier than he thought it would be. "We know our roles. Ellie, with her extensive research, will lead the incantations to weaken Gideon's spiritual presence. Ellie, armed with her knowledge of symbols, will set up protective wards to shield us. Natalie, your photographs will serve as a conduit, capturing the ephemeral moments as we confront the spirit. Cameron, you and I will be the anchors, keeping the group grounded in this realm while the ritual unfolds."

He took a deep breath, the weight of their collective purpose settling on his shoulders. "And we have each other. Whatever happens next, we'll face it together. Gravewood is counting on us. Let's execute this plan with precision and determination. Our actions tonight will shape the destiny of this town." The group exchanged determined glances, ready to confront the unknown and lift the veil on Gravewood's paranormal mysteries.

The flickering light gain strength as their resolve solidified, casting a warm glow on the determined faces of the five friends. They stood shoulder to shoulder, their hands clasped in a tight circle, drawing strength from each other's presence.

"Let's do this," Ellie whispered, her breath visible in the chilly air. "For Gravewood. For everyone who's been affected by this curse."

"Ready?" Cameron asked, his heart pounding with both fear and anticipation.

"Ready," they answered in unison, the word echoing through the dimly lit halls, a testament to their unwavering bond.

As the sun dipped below the horizon, enveloping Gravewood Middle School in darkness, the five friends stepped out of their sanctuary, ready to face the supernatural forces that awaited them. Together, they would confront the unknown, armed with the knowledge their friendship was stronger than any curse or vengeful spirit. And with each step they took, their determination grew, fueled by the unbreakable bond they shared.

CHAPTER 8

The curse of Gravewood haunted the small town for generations. The group of unlikely friends—Cameron, Ellie, Ollie, Natalie, and Ellie—banded together to unravel its mysteries. With help from Millie Finch, the elderly librarian, they unearthed old records and dug up buried secrets. Now, with their determination driving them forward, they found themselves standing before the entrance to a series of secret tunnels beneath the town.

"Guys, this is it!" Cameron whispered excitedly, his mischievous grin evident even in the dim light. "We're about to uncover the truth about this curse."

"Finally," Ellie replied, her blue eyes sparkling with anticipation. She adjusted her backpack, feeling the weight of the history books she carried, reminding her of the importance of their mission.

"Wait," Ollie cautioned, pushing up his glasses. "We need to be careful down there. We don't know what we might find."

"Ollie's right," agreed Natalie, clutching her camera close to her chest. "This could be dangerous."

"Come on," Ellie chimed in, her red curls bouncing as she stood on her tiptoes to peer into the darkness. "We've come this far. We can't turn back now."

As they stepped cautiously into the shadowy entrance, a wrought-iron gate loomed before them, adorned with ominous symbols and a prominent warning sign. The gate stated in bold letters: "Warning: Danger Beyond. Authorized Personnel Only."

A shiver ran down Cameron's spine as he read the foreboding message. "Looks like they don't want just anyone venturing down here," he remarked, his eyes flicking to the group. "This must be where the real secrets lie. We're in for a challenging journey." Determination glinted in their eyes as they collectively decided to breach the forbidden threshold, ready to unveil the mysteries concealed within the depths of Gravewood's clandestine tunnels.

"Wow," Ellie breathed as they ventured further into the tunnel, her voice echoing off the damp walls. "Can you believe we're actually doing this?"

"Believe it or not, we are," Ollie murmured, his gentle voice betraying a flicker of uncertainty. "Just remember, we need to stick together."

"Agreed," Natalie nodded, her eyes darting around the dimly lit passageway as she snapped photos. "We can't afford to get separated."

"Hey, I think I see something up ahead!" Ellie exclaimed, her voice hushed but full of excitement.

As they approached the spot where Ellie pointed, they found a series of strange markings etched into the walls. The symbols were ancient and otherworldly, reminiscent of the enigmatic carvings in the Gravewood Middle School and the mysterious books they had discovered.

"Look at these," Ellie whispered, running her fingers over the mysterious carvings. "They must be connected to the curse somehow." The group gathered around, their faces bathed in the dim light filtering through the tunnels. Ellie, with her extensive knowledge of occult symbols, squinted as she analyzed the intricate details.

Cameron, ever curious, pulled out the pages they had found in Gideon Blackwell's scrapbook, comparing the symbols etched on the walls to those in the book. "There's a similarity here," he observed, pointing at a particular motif. "These symbols are recurring, like a language. Maybe decoding them will unravel the mystery behind the curse." The group exchanged thoughtful glances, realizing that the symbols were the common thread tying together the paranormal occurrences in Gravewood. With newfound determination, they continued their journey, committed to deciphering the cryptic language that held the key to breaking the town's ancient curse.

"Let's keep moving," Cameron urged, his heart pounding in his chest. With each step, they're getting closer to unraveling the town's greatest secret and facing whatever supernatural forces lay hidden within the tunnels.

"Stay sharp, guys," Ollie warned, glancing anxiously at his friends. "We don't know what lies ahead."

"Whatever it is," Natalie said, determination shining in her eyes, "we'll face it together."

"Right," agreed Ellie, gripping Cameron's hand tightly. "We're in this until the end."

As they continued deeper into the tunnels, their flashlights flickering against the damp walls, the air heavy with anticipation, a sense of awe washed over Cameron at the power of friendship, and the depths of courage lay within each of them. Together, they would uncover the truth about Gravewood's curse and face the darkness haunted their town for far too long.

The dampness in the air clung to their skin as they ventured further into the ominous tunnels. The musty scent of decay, mixed with the earthy aroma of mold and mildew, filled their nostrils. Everything was shrouded in an eerie darkness, the only light coming from their flickering flashlights.

"Ugh!" Natalie shuddered, running her fingers along the cool, rough walls close in on them the deeper they went. "This place gives me the creeps."

"Me too," Ellie whispered, hugging herself tightly. The chill in the air seemed to intensify, and the group felt the weight of the unknown pressing upon them. "But we've got to keep going. We're so close to finding answers. The symbols on these walls, the ones from the school, and even the books—it's like they're all pieces of the same puzzle. If we don't push forward now, we might miss the chance to break the curse and save Gravewood."

The words hung in the air, a silent agreement settling among them. They steeled themselves against the encroaching darkness, their journey into the mysterious cave now infused with a palpable sense of urgency. Each step forward echoed with the anticipation of unraveling the town's secrets and dispelling the ominous shadow that clung to Gravewood.

Cameron took the lead, his heart thundering in his chest as a mix of fear and excitement coursed through his veins. With every cautious step they took, they delved deeper into the town's dark secrets.

"Watch your step," he warned the group as they navigated the narrow passageways. Their footsteps echoed throughout the tunnels, reminding them of how alone they were in this subterranean world.

"Guys, listen," Ellie said suddenly, stopping in her tracks. The others fell silent, straining their ears to catch any sound might give them a clue about what awaited them further down the tunnel.

"Is it just me, or does it feel like the air is getting heavier?" Ollie asked, his brow furrowed in concern as he wiped away beads of sweat from his forehead.

"Maybe it's just our nerves," Natalie replied, attempting to brush off her own growing unease. "We can't let fear get the best of us."

"Right," Cameron agreed, swallowing hard against the lump in his throat. "We have to stay focused and stick together."

"Let's keep moving," Ellie urged, her voice brimming with determination. "There has to be something here that can help us understand the curse."

As they resumed their cautious exploration, their flashlights casting eerie shadows on the ancient walls, a sense of awe at the power of friendship and the depths of courage lay within each of them. Together, they would face the darkness haunted their town for far too long.

As Cameron's heartbeat thudded in his ears, he couldn't help but notice the way each footstep echoed through the tunnels, bouncing off the damp walls. The sound was strangely hollow, as if the very earth was swallowing their presence.

"Ugh," Ellie muttered, her face scrunching up in disgust. "Is that... the smell of decay? Like something died down here?"

"Probably mold and mildew," Ellie replied, though the tremor in her voice betrayed her own doubts. "Nothing to worry about."

"Let's hope so," Ollie added quietly.

Cameron focused on the sensation of the cool, rough walls under his fingertips, trying not to let his imagination run wild with what might be lurking around each bend in the tunnel. He sensed the others doing the same, each of them clinging to whatever small comfort they could find in this unsettling environment.

"Guys, it's getting darker," Natalie whispered, her grip tightening on her camera. "Do you think we should turn back?"

"No," Cameron said, more confidently than he felt. "We've come this far. We can't give up now."

"Cam's right," Ellie chimed in. "We have to find answers for Gravewood and ourselves."

Deeper into the tunnels, they ventured, the darkness becoming more oppressive, as if it was a living entity attempting to smother them. The flickering light from their flashlights cast eerie shadows on the walls, making it appear as though sinister figures lurked beyond their reach.

"Stay close," Ollie advised, his voice barely audible over the steady drip of water echoing around them. "We don't want to get separated."

"Look at these markings," Natalie whispered, pointing her flashlight at some strange symbols etched into the stone. "What do you think they mean?"

"Maybe Millie would know," Ellie suggested, her eyes wide with curiosity. "She knows a lot about the town's history."

"I don't know," Ellie said, snapping a photo of the symbols with her phone.

Cameron swallowed hard, feeling a knot tightening in his stomach. The air grew colder, their breaths turning into puffs of white mist. He glanced at his friends, each of them now wearing expressions of unease that mirrored his own. How much farther could they go before the darkness swallowed them whole?

"Keep moving," he urged, his voice no more than a whisper. "I have a feeling we're close to something important."

"Let's hope it's something that can help us," Ollie murmured, his glasses fogging up from the chill. "And not something... worse."

As they pressed on, the tension in the air grew thicker, the shadows darker, and the silence more unnerving. Despite their fears, the team continued forward, driven by their determination to uncover the secrets hidden within the depths of the ancient tunnels.

The darkness presses in on them from all sides, suffocating and unyielding. The flickering glow of their flashlights cast distorted shadows that danced menacingly along the tunnel walls, giving life to the unimaginable.

"Guys, do you hear that?" Ollie whispered, his voice trembling with fear. They all stopped and listened carefully. A faint, otherworldly moan echoed through the tunnels, making the hairs on the backs of their necks stand on end.

"Wh-what was that?" Ellie stammered, her eyes wide with terror. She clutched her flashlight tightly, her knuckles turning white.

"Probably the wind," Cameron tried to reassure them, though even he couldn't hide the tremor in his voice. "Come on, let's keep going."

Their hearts raced as they continued down the seemingly endless passageways, each step bringing with it a new wave of dread and uncertainty.

"Maybe we should turn back." Natalie's voice quivered, betraying her growing unease. "This place gives me the creeps."

"Are you scared?" Cameron teased, trying to lighten the mood.

"Of course, I'm scared!" Natalie snapped back, her fear now palpable. "Aren't you?"

"Terrified," admitted Ellie, her face pale but determined. "But we have to find out the truth. We've come too far to turn back now."

"Ellie's right," Ollie chimed in, adjusting his fogged-up glasses. "We need answers. For ourselves...and for Gravewood."

As they ventured further into the inky depths, the supernatural energy intensified, like an unseen presence watching their every move. Suddenly, a gust of frigid air swept through the tunnel, extinguishing their flashlights and plunging them into total darkness.

"Everyone okay?" Ellie called out, her voice barely audible over the sound of their pounding hearts.

"Y-yeah," Ollie stammered, fumbling for his flashlight. "I think so."

"Something's here with us," Ellie whispered, her breath frosting in the freezing air. "I can feel it."

"Me too," Natalie agreed, her voice shaking. "But we can't let it stop us. We have to keep going."

"Alright." Cameron took a deep breath, trying to steady himself. "Let's find those answers and get out of here."

With renewed determination, they pressed on into the unknown, each step taking them further into the heart of the mystery that haunted Gravewood for centuries. Despite the terror clawing at their minds, they continued forward, driven by their unquenchable thirst for knowledge and the hope of finally breaking the curse that tormented their small town for far too long.

The air in the tunnel thickens as Cameron led the group deeper into the shadows, their flashlights casting eerie patterns on the walls. The darkness was alive, pressing in on them from all sides, but they couldn't let it consume them—not when there's answers to be found.

"Hey, guys," Ellie whispered, shining her flashlight on a crumbling section of the wall. "Look at this."

The others clustered around her, squinting at the strange symbols etched into the stone. They appeared ancient and almost otherworldly, twisting and writhing like serpents on the cold rock. Natalie raised her camera to take a picture, her hands trembling slightly.

"Could these... mean something?" Ollie asked, his voice cracking with uncertainty.

"Maybe," Ellie replied, studying the symbols with furrowed brows. "They could be connected to the curse or Gravewood' dark past."

"Whatever they are, we should keep an eye out for more of them," Cameron said, his heart pounding in anticipation. "Come on, let's keep moving."

As they continued down the tunnel, they stumbled upon a collection of dusty, forgotten artifacts scattered across the ground. Ellie picked up a tarnished locket, the metal cold and heavy in her hand, while Natalie examined a cracked porcelain doll with vacant eyes that followed her every move.

"Who would leave these things down here?" Ollie shivered, clutching his flashlight tightly.

"Maybe they belonged to someone who tried to break the curse before us," Ellie suggested, her eyes darting nervously between the artifacts. "Or maybe they're offerings to appease whatever force is behind all this."

"Either way, they're creepy," Cameron muttered, trying to shake off the feeling of being watched.

As they ventured further, they noticed the passageway narrowing, forcing them to walk single file. The sense of claustrophobia was suffocating, and Cameron struggled to catch his breath.

"Guys, I think we're approaching some kind of trap," he whispered, wiping sweat from his brow. "Look at those pressure plates on the floor."

"Good eye, Cam," Ellie replied, her eyes widening in alarm. "We need to find a way to get past this without setting it off."

"Maybe we can use those artifacts to weigh down the plates?" Natalie suggested, her voice strained with fear. "It's worth a shot."

"Good thinking, Nat," Cameron agreed. "Let's give it a try."

The group huddled together, studying the artifacts they had gathered. Each object held a unique aura, resonating with the supernatural energy that permeated the cave. After a brief but intense discussion, they devised a plan to place specific artifacts on the pressure plates strategically. Ellie, with her knowledge of the occult, suggested which artifacts might be more attuned to counteracting the arcane traps.

Working together, they carefully placed the artifacts on each pressure plate until the path ahead seemed safe. They held their breath as they cautiously stepped forward, hearts pounding in their chests. The intricate dance of collaboration and caution became a crucial aspect of their journey, each member playing a vital role in navigating the treacherous path toward unveiling Gravewood's secrets. They held their breath as they cautiously stepped forward, hearts pounding in their chests.

"Phew," Ollie exhaled, relief flooding through him once they all made it safely across. "That was close."

"Too close," Ellie agreed, shivering despite the cold sweat dampening her clothes. "But we did it. We overcame it, together."

"Right," Cameron nodded, feeling a surge of determination. "We can't let anything stop us. Not traps, not creepy symbols, not even our own fears. We'll find the answers we're looking for and break this curse once and for all."

"Let's keep going," Ellie said, her voice steady and resolute. "Together, we can unravel the mystery haunted Gravewood for centuries."

The team pressed onward, their flashlights casting eerie shadows on the damp tunnel walls. Cameron led the way, his pulse quickening with each step he took into the darkness.

"Hey, Cam," Ollie whispered, catching up to him. "I think I see a hidden door up ahead."

Cameron squinted at the spot Ollie pointed out and saw it too: a discernible outline of a door, cleverly camouflaged within the carved stone. His heart raced as he approached it, reaching out a trembling hand to touch the cool surface.

"It looks like we've found one of Gravewood's darkest secrets," Ellie said, her voice hushed with wonderment.

"Let's see what's inside," Natalie added, her camera at the ready.

With a collective deep breath, the group pushed the door open, revealing a hidden chamber lit by flickering torches lining the walls. Dust swirled through the air, stirred by the group's entrance, and the scent of ancient decay filled their nostrils. They stepped cautiously inside, their eyes taking in the unsettling scene before them.

"Whoa, look at this place," Ellie breathed, her gaze fixed on the elaborate mural painted across one wall. It depicted scenes of sacrifice and torment, displaying at a dark past they can only begin to imagine.

"Over here!" Ollie called, drawing their attention to a massive, tattered book chained to an altar-like table. The pages were filled with cryptic symbols and illustrations that made their skin crawl.

"Guys, this must be some sort of record of the curse," Ellie whispered, her blue eyes wide with disbelief. She reached for the book, her fingers tracing over the ancient symbols as she mumbled to herself. "These symbols, they're not just random. They represent elements of a binding spell—a dark magic that's been woven into the very fabric of Gravewood's existence."

As she spoke, her eyes scanned the pages, connecting the dots between the symbols etched on the cave walls, those found in the Gravewood Middle School, and the mysterious artifacts they had collected. "Each of these symbols corresponds to a different aspect of the curse. Look here," she pointed to a particular symbol, "this one signifies a containment, like a barrier that keeps the curse locked within the town."

A sudden gust of icy wind blew through the chamber, extinguishing the torches and plunging them into darkness. The group gasped, feeling a supernatural presence in the cold air. Ellie continued, her voice steady despite the unsettling turn of events, "We need to be cautious. The curse is aware of our presence, and every step we take in decoding its secrets brings us closer to the heart of the supernatural forces at play."

Determined, the group gathered around Ellie as she illuminated the ancient pages with a dim light, seeking to understand the dark magic that bound Gravewood and, hopefully, find a way to break free from its malevolent grip.

"Let's get some photos and get out of here," Ellie suggested, her voice strained. "I don't think we should linger."

Natalie snapped a series of pictures, capturing the images that might hold the key to breaking the curse. As they prepared to leave the chamber, an unearthly wail echoed through the tunnels, sending shivers down their spines.

"Wh-what was that?" Ollie stammered, glasses fogging up with fear. "That didn't sound... human."

"Whatever it is," Ellie said, feigning bravery, her voice betrayed by a quiver, "we can't let it stop us. We've come too far to turn back now."

"Ellie's right," Cameron agreed, determination steeling his resolve. "We have to keep going. For Gravewood, for ourselves, and for everyone who's been affected by this curse."

"Deep breaths, everyone," Ellie instructed, steadying herself. "We'll face whatever comes our way, together."

The weight of the curse was bearing down upon them as they stepped closer to unveiling the truth behind Gravewood's darkest mystery.

The dampness in the air grew thicker as the group ventured further into the tunnels, their flashlights flickering ominously. The sound of their heavy breathing filled the narrow passageway, mingling with the distant drip of water. Cameron's heart pounded in his chest as he led the way, his fear of isolation gnawing at him.

"Guys," Ollie whispered, his voice quavering, "do you feel that? Like, something's watching us."

"Ollie, don't start," Ellie snapped, her own anxiety making her tense. She paused, pressing a hand to her forehead. "Sorry, I didn't mean to snap at you."

"No, it's okay," Ollie replied, adjusting his glasses nervously. "I know we're all on edge."

"Let's keep moving," Natalie suggested, her camera ready to capture any potential clues. "We need to stay focused."

As they continued through the winding tunnels, ancient symbols etched into the walls pulsed with a sinister energy. Ellie traced her fingers over one such symbol, feeling an inexplicable surge of dread course through her veins.

"Careful, Ellie," warned Cameron, noticing her discomfort. "We don't know what these symbols mean or what power they hold."

"Right," Ellie agreed, pulling her hand away quickly, her fear of losing control surfacing.

Suddenly, the group stumbled upon a small chamber, its floor littered with fragments of broken pottery and discarded bones. A faint scent of decay lingered in the air, and Cameron felt an icy shiver run down his spine.

"Look!" Ellie exclaimed, pointing to an object half-buried in the dirt. She carefully unearthed it, revealing a rusted, ancient key with intricate engravings that seemed to tell a story of its own.

"Could this be...?" Natalie trailed off, snapping a photo of the mysterious artifact. The key's design mirrored some of the symbols they had encountered, suggesting a profound connection between this seemingly mundane object and the supernatural forces at play in Gravewood.

Ellie's eyes widened with recognition. "This key is more than just an artifact; it's a symbolic link. In ancient occult practices, keys often represented access or unlocking, like a bridge between realms. It could hold the key to unraveling the curse—perhaps a way to unlock the hidden truths of Gravewood."

As the group pondered the significance of the key, a sense of anticipation lingered in the air. Little did they know, this unassuming relic might be the key to unlocking the secrets that bound Gravewood in its supernatural grasp.

"Only one way to find out," Cameron replied, gripping the key tightly in his hand.

"Wait!" Ellie cautioned, her intuition flaring. "We need to be careful. The curse won't let us uncover its secrets without a fight."

"Agreed," Ollie chimed in, his fear of abandonment making him cling even more fiercely to his friends. "Let's stick together, no matter what."

As they turned to leave the chamber, a ghostly apparition materialized before them. Its hollow eyes bore into each of their souls, eliciting gasps of terror from the group.

"Wh-who are you?" Cameron demanded, trying to mask his fear with bravado.

The spectral figure did not respond and instead raised a skeletal hand and pointed down a dark, unexplored tunnel. Then, as quickly as it appeared, the phantom vanished, leaving behind an overwhelming sense of dread.

"It's like we don't have much choice but to follow," Ellie murmured, her fear of failure driving her to see the quest through to its end.

"Are we really going to trust a ghost?" Ollie asked hesitantly, looking to his friends for reassurance.

"Trust is a strong word," Cameron replied, his voice cracking slightly. "But we've come too far to back out now."

"Together," Natalie whispered, echoing their earlier promise.

"Right," agreed Ellie, taking a deep breath. "Together."

With a mix of determination and trepidation, the group ventured further into the tunnels, following the path laid out by the ghostly apparition. As they walked, the darkness grew more oppressive, and the air thick with anticipation and fear.

The damp, musty air weighed down on the group as they cautiously moved forward, their flashlights casting eerie shadows on the tunnel walls. The rough, uneven ground beneath them shifted with each step as if the earth trying to keep them away from the secrets hidden within.

"Did you hear that?" Natalie whispered, her voice audible above the sound of their footsteps. She hugged her camera close to her chest, her fear of the unknown manifesting in the subtle tremble of her hands.

"Probably our own echoes," Cameron replied calmly, though his eyes betrayed his uncertainty. The thought of any sound being amplified and distorted in the tunnels made him shudder, his deep-rooted fear of isolation urging him to stay close to his friends.

"Or maybe it's something else," Ellie offered, her imagination running wild. "Something we're not supposed to find."

"Let's keep our wits about us," Ollie suggested, rubbing his glasses nervously on the hem of his shirt. His fear of abandonment made him cling to the notion sticking together would keep them safe.

"Look at this!" Ellie exclaimed, her torchlight falling upon a cluster of strange symbols etched into the tunnel wall. She traced a finger along the ancient markings, her curiosity overriding her fear of failure. "These have to be connected to the curse somehow."

"Maybe they're warnings," Natalie mused, snapping a photo of the symbols. "Or directions to something important."

"Either way, we need to document this," Ellie agreed, pulling out a small notebook and sketching the intricate designs. As she worked, her fear of losing control over her life fueled her determination to decipher these cryptic messages.

"Guys, there's a fork in the path up ahead," Cameron called out, peering into the darkness. "Which way do we go?"

"Left," Ellie said without hesitation, her intuition guiding her. "It feels...right."

"Feels right? Seriously?" Cameron scoffed, but he couldn't deny the sense of unease that crept through him as he looked down the right-hand path.

"Follow your gut, Cameron," Ollie advised, his voice soothing despite his own apprehension. "Trust yourself."

"Fine," Cameron relented, taking the lead as they veered left. The tunnel narrowed as they continued, the darkness closing in around them like a suffocating embrace.

"Can't breathe," Ellie gasped, her chest constricting with panic.

"Deep breaths, Ellie," Natalie whispered, her hand on Ellie's shoulder. "We're all here with you."

"Thanks," Ellie managed, forcing herself to focus on her friends' reassuring presence.

As the group entered the chamber, a hushed reverence settled over them. The air was thick with an almost tangible energy, and the flickering torchlight cast dancing shadows on the stone walls adorned with ancient symbols. Ellie's gaze darted across the room, her eyes alighting on a series of murals depicting scenes from Gravewood's history. Each mural seemed to tell a story—a visual chronicle of the curse that had plagued the town for generations.

Natalie, camera in hand, began snapping photos of the murals, capturing the eerie scenes frozen in time. As the flash illuminated the chamber, the group caught glimpses of symbols intertwining with the narrative, reinforcing Ellie's earlier revelations. The key in Ellie's hand pulsed with a faint glow, resonating with the energy emanating from the room.

"Look at these carvings," Cameron exclaimed, tracing his fingers along the intricate patterns etched into the stone. "They match the symbols we found in the cave and the school. It's like the history of Gravewood is written in code."

Ellie, drawn to a dusty tome resting on a stone pedestal, opened it with care. The pages were filled with descriptions of rituals, incantations, and details about the curse's origins. As she translated the archaic text, the group realized they were uncovering the very foundation of Gideon Blackwell's dark legacy.

With bated breath, they continued to explore the chamber, discovering artifacts that mirrored those in Gideon Blackwell's scrapbook. Each object seemed to resonate with the supernatural forces at play, and the more they unearthed, the clearer the connection between the curse, the symbols, and their quest for a solution became.

The chamber became a nexus of revelation, a space where the echoes of the past whispered cryptic truths. The group, surrounded by the weight of history, knew they were on the brink of unraveling the curse that had ensnared Gravewood for centuries. As they meticulously documented their findings, a sense of purpose surged within them, propelling them toward the final leg of their enigmatic journey.

CHAPTER 9

The Gravewood Middle School library was a sanctuary of hushed whispers and the scent of aging paper. A warm, golden glow emanated from the antique lamps scattered throughout the room, casting shadows along the towering shelves. The only sounds breaking the silence were the soft rustling of pages turning and the occasional creak of an old wooden chair as someone shifted their weight.

Cameron, Ellie, Ollie, and Natalie gathered around a large oak table near the back of the library, deep in discussion. Their eyes darted between one another and the pile of research they'd accumulated on Gideon Blackwell's curse. Tension hung in the air, thick and palpable, as they whispered their theories and findings.

"Hey, guys," a friendly voice interrupted their conversation. The group looked up to find Tim Jenkins, a classmate known for his easy smile and laid-back demeanor. He had short, sandy blonde hair and freckles dusting his cheeks. "I couldn't help but overhear your conversation about Gideon Blackwell. That's some pretty interesting stuff."

"Uhm, thanks, Tim," Cameron replied cautiously, trying to gauge whether Tim was genuinely interested or simply poking fun at them. His fear of isolation gnawed at him, making it difficult to trust anyone outside their tight-knit group.

"Mind if I join you?" Tim asked, sliding into a vacant seat before anyone could object. He leaned in closer, apparently captivated by the aged newspaper clippings and scribbled notes strewn across the table. "I've always been kind of fascinated by Gravewood's history, too."

The group exchanged glances, a silent debate unfolding among them. After a moment, Cameron nodded, allowing Tim to join their huddle of conspiracy and ancient mysteries. As Tim delved into their research, genuine curiosity gleamed in his eyes, dispelling Cameron's initial reservations. Little did they know, this unexpected addition to their quest would play a crucial role in the unfolding events that awaited them.

Ellie, her piercing blue eyes narrowed with suspicion, shared a glance with the rest of the group. Tim appeared genuinely intrigued, and hope sparked within them at the idea that perhaps they'd found another ally in their quest to break the curse.

"Sure, Tim," Ollie said, his gentle voice laced with uncertainty. "We appreciate any help we can get."

As they continued their discussion, Cameron couldn't shake the feeling that something off. He watched as Tim's eyes flicked between each of them, a slight smile playing on his lips. Was he truly interested in their research, or did he have an ulterior motive? Only time would reveal the truth, but deep down, he couldn't help but fear what the truth might be.

"Alright, let's get back to work," Ellie said, directing her gaze to the pile of research materials. The hushed whispers and quiet rustling of pages resumed as the friends delved deeper into Gravewood's history. Tim appeared to be poring over a tattered map Natalie discovered in the library's archives, his fingers tracing the faded lines crisscrossed the yellowed paper.

Cameron glanced around the table, noting the furrowed brows and intense concentration on his friends' faces. He couldn't shake the nagging feeling that something was amiss, and he found himself watching Tim out of the corner of his eye.

"Guys, I think I found something," Ellie whispered excitedly, holding up an article she'd been reading. "This can be the key to breaking the curse."

"Really?" Ollie asked, leaning in to take a closer look. "What does it say?"

"Listen to this," Ellie began, her voice barely audible as she read aloud. "'It is believed that the spirit of Gideon Blackwell still haunts the town, seeking revenge for his untimely death. To break the curse, one must find the hidden talisman that Gideon used to wield his dark powers...'"

"Wait, there's a talisman?" Natalie interjected, her eyes wide with curiosity. "That could be the answer we've been searching for!"

As they continued to discuss their findings, Cameron noticed Tim's eyes darting between them and the article in Ellie's hand. His gut tightened, and a sudden sense of unease crept over him. Before he can voice his concerns, however, Tim made his move.

In one swift motion, Tim reached across the table and snatched the article from Ellie's grasp. The sudden movement startled her, causing her to drop the paper.

"Hey!" she exclaimed, her face flushed with indignation. "What do you think you're doing?"

"Sorry," Tim mumbled, feigning innocence as he handed back the article. "I wanted a closer look."

But as Ellie took it back and unfolded the paper, her eyes widened with disbelief. "The part about the talisman...it's gone!"

Cameron's heart raced as the pieces fell into place. Tim had been watching them all along, waiting for the right moment to strike. And now he'd stolen the one clue that could lead them to break the curse.

"Tim, what did you do?" Ellie demanded, her blue eyes flashing with anger.

"Nothing!" Tim insisted, although his voice betrayed a hint of panic. "I didn't do anything!"

As the tension in the library grew, so too did the sense of unease creeping over Cameron. They were running out of time, and with each passing moment, Gideon Black-well's spirit grew stronger, casting an ever-darker shadow over Gravewood. Outside the library's sanctuary, the town grappled with a series of unexplained phenomena. Strange whispers echoed through the narrow streets, and flickering lights cast eerie shadows on the facades of aging buildings.

Residents reported sightings of ghostly apparitions, adding fuel to the growing fear that Gravewood was on the brink of a paranormal upheaval.

Cameron, Ellie, Ollie, and Natalie felt the weight of their mission intensify, their determination fueled by the urgency of the supernatural events unfolding in the town. The once-bustling streets now bore an air of abandonment, with windows shuttered and doors locked as if the town itself held its breath, waiting for the group to unravel the secrets that bound it in a spectral grip.

Amid the chaos, Tim shared stories he had heard from other townsfolk. Tales of sleepless nights, unexplained noises, and unsettling visions fueled the group's sense of urgency. As they delved deeper into the curse's history, the ominous signs in Gravewood manifested in increasingly tangible ways, reinforcing the inescapable truth that time was running out for them to break the curse and free the town from its haunted past.

The missing section of the article—the part that detailed the talisman's location and purpose—like a beacon of hope snuffed out in an instant. It was the key to breaking Gideon Blackwell's curse—the very thing that drew the friends into the treacherous waters of Gravewood's dark history. Now, with it lost, their path forward was shrouded in uncertainty.

"Tim, give it back," Cameron pleaded, his voice shaking with urgency. "You don't know what you've done."

A flicker of doubt crossed Tim's face, but he quickly masked it with a defiant glare. "I didn't do anything!"

"Stop lying!" Ellie snapped, her hands clenched into fists at her sides. "We saw you take it!"

"Guys, we need to stay calm," Ollie interjected, his glasses slipping down his nose as he anxiously adjusted them. "Arguing isn't going to help us find what we need."

A heavy silence settled over the group, punctuated only by the distant rustling of pages and the stifled sobs of Natalie, who clutched her camera tightly to her chest as if a lifeline. The betrayal weighed on each of them, a jagged shard of ice lodged in their hearts.

"Fine," Ellie said finally, her eyes never leaving Tim's face. "If you won't give it back willingly, we'll have to find another way."

Cameron could see the resolve in her gaze, the steel in her spine refused to bend, even in the face of such treachery. They couldn't afford to lose hope now, not when they'd come so far.

"Right," he agreed, nodding determinedly. "We can still break the curse. We need to figure out how."

As they turned their attention back to the scattered papers and books, Cameron couldn't help but glance over at Tim. The boy's expression was unreadable, his eyes darting nervously between the group and the door. Despite his bravado, it was clear he didn't relish being caught in the crossfire of their battle against Gideon Blackwell's spirit.

"Whatever you're planning, Tim," Cameron said grimly, "I hope it's worth the price you'll pay for betraying us."

Cameron clenched his fists, the paper crumpling beneath his fingers as he looked into Tim's eyes. "Why, Tim?" he asked, his voice a whisper. "Why would you do this to us?"

Tim hesitated, his gaze darting around the library, before settling back on Cameron. "I'm sorry," he said, swallowing hard. "I didn't want to. But Gideon—he's too powerful. He threatened my family–" Tim's voice cracked, and he looked away. "I couldn't risk their safety."

"By betraying us?" Ellie spat, her face red with anger. "We're trying to protect everyone, Tim. Including your family."

"Maybe," Tim conceded, biting his lip. "But I can't wait for 'maybe.' Gideon was so insistent–" He shuddered involuntarily as though recalling something terrifying. "He promised that if I gave him the information, he'd leave my family alone. And I... I believed him."

"Even if it means putting the rest of us in danger?" Natalie accused, tears still streaming down her cheeks.

"Sometimes we have to make difficult choices," Tim whispered, his voice hollow. "I'm sorry. Truly."

Before anyone could respond, an eerie chill swept through the library. The friends exchanged uneasy glances, each sensing the impending arrival of Gideon Blackwell's spirit. A sudden gust of wind blew through the room, extinguishing all light and plunging them into darkness.

"Guys..." Cameron murmured, feeling a rising sense of dread. The air thickened, making it difficult to breathe. Somewhere in the distance, they heard the sound of books toppling from shelves as if the library itself protesting against Gideon's presence.

"Stay together," Ellie warned, grabbing onto Cameron's arm in the darkness. "Don't let him separate us."

As their eyes adjusted to the dim light filtering through the windows, they could see the faint outline of Tim standing a few feet away. He was rooted to the spot, unable to move or speak.

"Tim!" Natalie hissed, her voice trembling. "What have you done?"

"Please," he whispered, his eyes wide with fear. "I didn't know it would be like this."

"None of us did," Cameron replied grimly, feeling anger and pity warring within him. "But now we have to deal with the consequences of your actions."

"Tell me," Ellie said, steel in her voice as she stared at Tim, "do you think Gideon will keep his promise now that he has what he wants?"

"I... I don't know," Tim admitted, tears streaming down his face. "I have to hope so. For my family's sake."

"Hope won't be enough," Cameron thought as the library continued to tremble under Gideon Blackwell's growing power.

A heavy silence fell over the library as the group processed Tim's betrayal. It was at this moment that the true gravity of their situation began to sink in. Cameron clenched his fists, feeling a surge of adrenaline coursing through him. They had to act fast.

"Guys, we need to find those papers," he said urgently. "If Gideon gets hold of them..."

"Then we're all doomed," Natalie finished, her voice no more than a whisper. Her eyes darted around the dimly lit room, searching desperately for any sign of the stolen information.

"Tim, help us look," Ellie demanded, her voice wavering with determination. "You owe us that much."

"I... I'm sorry," Tim stammered, still rooted to the spot. "I didn't know what I was getting into."

"None of us did," Cameron replied, his voice tight with frustration. "But right now, we need to focus on finding those papers and stopping Gideon before it's too late."

As they spoke, they sensed the malevolent presence of Gideon Blackwell growing stronger. The air charged with energy, sending shivers down their spines. A book slammed shut on its own across the room, making them jump.

"Let's split up," Natalie suggested, her voice trembling. "We can cover more ground that way."

"Are you sure?" Ellie asked nervously, glancing at the shadows closing in around them.

"It's our best chance," Cameron agreed, swallowing hard. "Just remember to stay alert and call out if you find anything."

As they fanned out across the library, each one felt a growing sense of urgency. They rifled through stacks of books, pulled open drawers, and crawled under tables in search of the lost papers. The smell of old parchment filled their nostrils while the creaking of ancient wooden shelves echoed around them.

"Guys, I think... I think I found something!" Tim called out, his voice shaking. The others rushed to his side, hearts pounding in their chests.

"Is it the papers?" Natalie asked, her eyes wide with hope.

"I'm not sure," Tim replied, holding up a torn piece of parchment with trembling hands. "It looks old, and there's some writing on it. But it's only part of it."

"Can we use it?" Ellie asked, desperation edging into her voice.

"Maybe," Cameron said slowly, examining the fragment closely. "But we'll need to find the rest."

"Then let's keep looking," Natalie declared, her determination returning. "We can't give up now. Not when we're this close."

"Right," Cameron agreed, clenching his fists once more. "Let's do this. Together."

As they continued their frantic search, the supernatural events intensified. Books flew off the shelves as if possessed, and whispers echoed from every corner of the library. Time was running out, and they knew it.

"Okay," he began, taking a deep breath to steady himself. "We need to come up with a plan. We can't keep searching aimlessly."

"Right," Natalie agreed, her voice firm despite the tremble in her hands. "Let's think this through. What do we know so far?"

"Maybe there's something else hidden in this library," Ellie suggested, her brow furrowed in thought. "Something we've overlooked that could help us break the curse."

"Or perhaps," Cameron mused, rubbing his chin, "we can try to find out more about the traitor who took the information. They must have a reason for doing it, maybe we can get the papers back."

"Either way," Natalie said, clenching her fists, "we can't give up. We need to stay strong and fight this curse, for ourselves and for Gravewood."

"Agreed," the others echoed, a newfound resolve shining in their eyes.

As if responding to their determination, the library suddenly plunged into darkness. The flickering lights above them snuffed out like candles in a gust of wind, and an eerie silence descended upon the room.

"Wh-what was that?" Tim stammered, his voice barely audible in the sudden stillness.

"Stay close," Cameron whispered, reaching out blindly to grasp his friends' hands. "We need to get out of here."

"Wait," Natalie hissed, her grip tightening on Cameron's hand. "Do you hear that?"

In the darkness, a faint sound reached their ears—a distant, unearthly whisper came from everywhere and nowhere at once.

"Guys," Ellie whimpered, her voice shaking with terror. "I think Gideon Blackwell's spirit is trying to communicate with us."

Cameron's heart thudded in his chest as he strained to make out the words, his breaths coming in short, shallow gasps. The room was closing in on them, the oppressive presence of the malevolent spirit bearing down like a crushing weight.

"Listen closely," he whispered, his voice taut with fear. "This might be our only chance to find out what we need to do next."

As the whispers grew louder, Cameron strained to understand the message hidden within them. And then, as suddenly as they began, the whispers ceased, leaving a chilling silence in their wake.

The group exchanged terrified glances, wondering what horrors awaited them as they continued their desperate fight against an enemy more powerful than they had ever imagined.

CHAPTER 10

Cameron's heart pounded in his chest as he looked around the dimly lit room, taking in the faces of his friends. Their expressions mirrored his own—a mixture of determination and fear. They stood huddled close together as if proximity could protect them from the unknown horrors awaited.

The room itself eerie and foreboding, the flickering candlelight casting long shadows on the walls danced like malevolent spirits. The air carried a chill seeping into their bones, making Cameron shiver involuntarily. He glanced at Ellie, who shared a knowing look with him, sensing his unease. She always good at reading people, especially Cameron.

"Um, guys?" Ollie's voice trembled slightly as he spoke up, drawing their attention. "Are we really sure about this? I mean, confronting Gideon Blackwell's spirit sounds... terrifying."

Natalie stepped forward, her eyes focused and her voice steady despite the trepidation that clung to her words. "We have to face him, Ollie. It's the only way to lift the curse and save Gravewood."

"Nat's right," Ellie chimed in, her quiet strength offering a sense of calm amidst the tension in the room. "We can do this together. We're stronger than whatever Gideon throws our way."

Cameron swallowed hard, trying to push down the knot of anxiety settled in his stomach. They're right; they had no choice but to confront the malevolent specter that had haunted their town for generations. But the thought of facing something so ancient and so powerful made him feel small and vulnerable. And yet, he couldn't let his friends down. They were counting on him.

Cameron's gaze held steady on the dusty, leather-bound tome that lay open before them on the scarred wooden table. The flickering candlelight danced across the ancient script, casting eerie shadows that twisted and writhed upon the walls. The weight of the words bore down on him, as if they were a physical presence in the room.

"Alright," he said, forcing himself to focus. "We know Gideon Blackwell's spirit is bound to the basement. That's where we'll confront him." His voice was steady, belying the uncertainty gnawing at his insides.

"First, we need to establish a protective circle," Natalie suggested, her eyes scanning the text for any useful information. "That way, we can contain his power and keep ourselves safe."

"Great idea, Nat," Ellie agreed, nodding thoughtfully. Her quiet strength anchored them all, keeping their fears at bay. "I can bring some salt and incense that we can use for the circle. I read that this would help."

"Awesome. Ollie, can you research how to break the curse binding Gideon's spirit to this place?" Cameron asked, turning to the nervous boy, who paced back and forth, his hands fidgeting.

"Y-yeah, I can do that," Ollie replied, his eyes darting between the others apprehensively. "I-I'll start looking right away."

"Let's not forget about the artifacts we found," Cameron continued, his newfound confidence and knowledge guiding the group. "Each one must serve a purpose. We'll have to figure out how to use them against Gideon."

"Right," Natalie affirmed, determination shining in her eyes. "We'll study them closely and see if there's anything we've missed."

The room fell silent as each member of the group considered their role in the plan, their thoughts a whirlwind of anticipation and anxiety. Cameron can almost hear the pounding of his own heart, the blood rushing in his ears like the roar of a storm-tossed sea.

"Guys," he said finally, locking eyes with each of his friends in turn. "We can do this. We've come too far to back down now. Together, we'll face Gideon Blackwell's spirit and lift the curse that plagued Gravewood for generations."

They exchanged determined nods, their expressions resolute and unwavering. And though fear still clawed at the edges of his mind, one thing for certain: together, they're stronger than anything the darkness can throw their way.

Cameron's heart pounded in his chest as he looked around the dimly lit room, the flickering candlelight casting eerie shadows on the walls. The air thick with tension, and each of his friends shared the same mix of determination and fear.

"Okay, let's be honest," Ellie whispered, her voice wavering slightly. "We're all scared, right? I mean, facing Gideon Blackwell's spirit, it's not exactly a walk in the park."

"More like a walk through a haunted graveyard," Ollie added, attempting a weak joke. He rubbed his sweaty palms on his jeans, unable to meet anyone's eyes.

"Ellie's right," Natalie admitted, her gaze steady but showing vulnerability. "But we have to face our fears if we want to save Gravewood. This is bigger than us."

Cameron swallowed hard, feeling the weight of their mission pressing down on him. He clenched his fists at his sides, fighting back the urge to run. Instead, he focused on the shimmer of determination in his friends' eyes, the unspoken promises they made to each other.

It was then that Ellie stepped forward, her piercing blue eyes shining with unwavering belief. "We can do this," she said firmly, her voice clear and strong. "We've faced challenges before, and we've always come out stronger on the other side. We have the knowledge, the tools, and, most importantly, each other. Together, we'll defeat Gideon Blackwell's spirit and protect our town."

Her words sparked something within the group, like a flame igniting their resolve. They exchanged glances, nodding solemnly, drawing strength from one another.

"Alright," Cameron said, his voice steadier now. "We need to prepare ourselves mentally and emotionally. We need to be ready for anything."

"Let's do it," Natalie agreed, determination once again coloring her features. "We'll show Gideon Blackwell that he chose the wrong town to haunt."

Cameron sensed the power of their unity as they stood together in the dimly lit room, each of them willing to face their fears for the sake of Gravewood. And though doubts still lingered in the shadows, their collective courage burned brighter, casting a light even the darkest of spirits could not snuff out.

Ollie's glasses slipped down his nose as he paced back and forth, his hands fidgeting with the hem of his shirt. His heart pounded like a drum in his chest, each beat echoing the doubts that plagued him. He tried to focus on the muffled sound of his sneakers against the wooden floor, but he couldn't even drown out the thoughts racing through his mind.

"Ollie," Natalie called, her voice steady and determined. She looked at him with her brown eyes focused, a reassuring contrast to the flickering candlelight casting eerie shadows on the walls. "We need you with us."

He stopped pacing, his gaze meeting hers. At that moment, Ollie felt a flicker of hope, like a tiny flame refusing to be extinguished in the darkness. He nodded, swallowing hard, and joined the group huddled around the table.

"Alright," Natalie said, her voice strong as she began outlining their plan. "We know Gideon Blackwell's spirit is tied to the basement, but we don't know how powerful he has become. We need to be prepared for anything."

"Right," Cameron agreed, his newfound confidence shining through. "We'll need salt to create a circle of protection around us. And holy water, just in case."

"Got it," Ellie murmured as she jotted down their list of necessities.

"Is there anything else?" Ollie asked, trying to steady his voice. He wasn't alone in feeling fear, but they needed him to be strong. They all had to be strong if they were going to face Gideon Blackwell's spirit.

"Stay together, no matter what," Natalie added, her eyes never leaving Ollie's. "We're stronger together. We've got each other's backs."

Ollie nodded, taking a deep breath. The weight of their friendship and the unbreakable bond they shared. It was a lifeline amidst the fear and uncertainty that threatened to consume him.

"Alright," he whispered, his hands finally stilling. "We can do this. Together."

"Exactly," Natalie replied, her determination unwavering. "Now, let's get everything we need and put an end to Gideon Blackwell's reign of terror over Gravewood."

As the group dispersed to gather supplies, Ollie took another deep breath, focusing on the steady rhythm of his friends' movements around him. Though fear still gnawed at the edges of his thoughts, together, they were unstoppable. And with each step they took, they're one step closer to facing the supernatural force haunting their town, ready to shine a light into the darkness and reclaim their home.

Ellie stood by the window, her petite frame casting a shadow on the floor, her curly red hair like an ember in the flickering candlelight. She didn't pace or fidget like the others, but her presence was enough to ground them in the midst of their fear.

"Okay," Cameron began, his voice calm and determined. "We need to gather everything necessary for this confrontation. Each item has a specific purpose, so let's make sure we have them all."

Ollie reached for a small leather pouch containing various protective herbs. His hands shook slightly, but he managed to tightly clasp it shut. "I've got the herbs for purification," he announced, trying to sound more confident than he felt.

"Good," Natalie said, nodding in approval. She picked up an old book with a cracked spine, its pages filled with incantations. "I'll be in charge of the spells. We need to make sure we recite them correctly."

"Right," Ellie chimed in, grabbing a box filled with candles of varying sizes and colors. "We'll set these around the basement to create a protective circle."

Cameron looked over at Ellie, who remained silent throughout their preparations. Though she appeared small and fragile, there was an undeniable force behind her eyes—a quiet strength that spoke volumes without uttering a word.

"Ellie," he said softly, "do you think you can handle the charms and emulate?"

She nodded, her eyes never leaving his. "Of course," she replied, her voice steady and unwavering. She picked up the assortment of charms and amulets, each one imbued with a different power, her small hands carrying the weight of their collective resolve.

"Thanks," Cameron whispered, feeling a surge of gratitude for her quiet resilience. It was as if her presence reassured them that they were strong enough to face whatever lay ahead.

As the group moved around the room, gathering their tools and artifacts, Ellie heart swelled with a mixture of fear and determination. They're about to face an unimaginable evil, but they're stronger together. Together, they can confront the darkness and reclaim their town from the grip of Gideon Blackwell's spirit.

Cameron's fingers grazed the cold metal of an old pocket watch, its ticking heartbeat a reminder of time slipping away. Ollie's hands shook as he tried to steady the compass that would guide them through the shadows. Natalie clutched her camera, ready to capture the unseen with a single click.

"Cam," Ellie whispered, her voice thick with tension, "how do we know this will work?"

Cameron glanced around at his friends, their faces etched with a mixture of determination and fear. He swallowed hard, feeling the weight of their trust on his shoulders. "We don't," he admitted quietly. "But we have to try, don't we?"

A heavy silence settled over the room as they stared at one another, each lost in their own thoughts and fears. The flickering candlelight cast eerie shadows on the walls, making it seem as if the darkness was closing in around them.

Finally, Ellie spoke up, her voice soft yet resolute. "We can do this," she said, looking into each of their eyes. "Together."

Cameron felt a surge of gratitude for her quiet confidence. It was as if she reached into his chest and gave his heart a reassuring squeeze. "Yeah," he agreed, nodding. "Together."

"Let's take a moment to prepare ourselves mentally and emotionally," suggested Ollie, his voice wavering slightly. "This confrontation is going to test us in ways we've never imagined."

They closed their eyes, taking deep breaths as they each tried to steady their nerves and gather their strength. Cameron focused on the sound of his own heartbeat, letting the steady rhythm anchor him in the present moment.

"Everyone, join hands," said Natalie, her voice firm and steady. They reached out, forming a circle, and shared a silent moment of solidarity. Their hands were clammy and trembling, but together, they felt an unbreakable bond.

As they stood there, united in their determination to face Gideon Blackwell's spirit, a wave of emotion washed over Cameron. Fear, yes, but also something more powerful: love.

For his friends, for his town, and for the future they're fighting to protect.

"Let's go," he whispered, squeezing their hands one last time before releasing them. "Together."

They nodded, their eyes meeting in silent agreement as they prepared to step into the darkness that awaited them.

With a final nod, the group stepped out of the dimly lit room and into the empty hallway. The air heavy, thick with anticipation and unspoken fears. Cameron led the way, his footsteps echoing off the walls, each step a drumbeat in their journey toward the unknown.

"Remember what Millie said?" Ellie murmured, her voice steady despite the tremor in her hand. "Gideon Blackwell's spirit will be at its strongest down there. We need to be ready for anything."

Cameron swallowed hard, feeling the weight of his responsibility as the leader of the group. "We're ready," he assured her, though his own doubts swirled like shadows in his mind. Would they truly be able to face such an ancient and powerful force?

Ollie's nervous energy radiated through the group as he fidgeted with the hem of his shirt, his glasses slipping down his nose. He tried to hide his fear behind a shaky laugh. "You know, I never was a fan of basements before this whole thing started. Now, I'm pretty sure they'll give me nightmares for the rest of my life."

"Focus, Ollie," Natalie urged, her eyes locked onto the floor below, her camera dangling from her neck like a protective talisman. "We need to stay sharp."

"Right, sorry." Ollie took a deep breath, trying to slow his racing thoughts.

As they reached the top of the basement stairs, Ellie hesitated for a moment. Her small frame drew inward as if she was steadying herself against the waves of darkness rising up from below. But then, she clenched her fists and squared her shoulders, her quiet strength shining through the shadows.

"Here we go," Cameron whispered, placing his hand on the railing and beginning the descent into the depths below. The wooden stairs creaked beneath their feet, each groaning a haunting reminder of the terrors awaited them.

"Be careful," Ellie warned, her eyes scanning the darkness for any sign of danger. "We don't know what could be down here."

The sound of their hearts pounding in their chests nearly drowned out the whispers of doubt threatened to overtake their minds. Each step brought them closer to the final showdown, and an icy shiver ran down Cameron's spine as he realized there was no turning back now.

"Stay close," he instructed, his voice barely audible above the persistent creaking of the stairs. "We're stronger together."

Their footsteps were slow and measured, each one bringing them closer to the confrontation with Gideon Blackwell's spirit. As they neared the bottom of the stairs, Cameron took a deep breath, steeling himself for the battle that lay ahead.

"Let's do this," he said, determination glinting in his eyes. "For Gravewood, for our families, and for ourselves."

At the bottom of the stairs, Cameron's hand hovered over the cold, iron handle of the basement door. His heart pounded furiously, its beats reverberating through his entire body. As he glanced back at his friends, he searched their faces for any sign of doubt or fear.

"Are we ready?" he asked, swallowing hard. Their eyes met his, each gaze filled with determination and resolve.

"We've come this far," Ellie said, her voice steady despite the tremor in her hands. "We can't back down now."

"Right," Ollie agreed, taking a deep breath to calm his racing thoughts. He adjusted his glasses nervously, the lenses fogging up as he exhaled. "We're stronger together, remember?"

Natalie nodded, gripping her camera tightly. It was their only means of capturing a photograph of Gideon Blackwell's spirit, and she couldn't afford to let her fears get the better of her. "Once we're inside, I'll start snapping pictures to keep him distracted."

"And I'll be ready with the salt circle," Ellie added, clenching her fists around the small pouch she carried. Her knuckles turned white, but she refused to let her fear show. "We'll trap him, no matter what."

Cameron took one last look at his friends, feeling a surge of gratitude and pride swell within his chest. They had come so far and faced unimaginable horrors, and yet they still stood by his side, ready to fight. With a deep breath, he turned the handle and pushed the door open.

The darkness beyond the threshold beckons them, reaching out with icy tendrils that send shivers down their spines. The air, thick with the scent of damp earth and something more sinister, a sickly-sweet odor, made their stomachs turn. But they refused to be deterred, stepping forward into the shadows as one.

"Stay close," Cameron whispered, his voice barely audible above the distant drip of water and the creaking floorboards overhead. "We don't know what's waiting for us in there."

"Let's hope our plan works," Ellie murmured, her eyes scanning the darkness before them. As they moved further into the basement, the weight of their task pressed down on them, threatening to crush their spirits.

But then Ollie reached out and grasped Cameron's hand, his own fingers trembling with fear. One by one, the others followed suit, forming a circle of strength and unity amidst the chilling atmosphere. They shared a silent moment of solidarity, drawing courage from each other's presence.

"Whatever happens," Cameron said softly, his breath leaving his lips in a cloud of vapor, "we'll face it together."

He released his friends' hands and stepped forward, leading them deeper into the darkness. Their hearts pounded in unison, fueled by adrenaline and the unwavering conviction that they would succeed. And as the door closed behind them, sealing them off from the world outside, they knew there was no turning back.

"Here we go," Cameron whispered, determination glinting in his eyes. "For Gravewood, for our families, and for ourselves."

CHAPTER 11

The cold wind howled through the empty halls of Gravewood Middle School, making the building like a mausoleum rather than a place of learning. Cameron leaned against his locker, arms crossed, as he waited for Ellie and Ollie to join him. He shivered involuntarily, his breath forming wispy clouds in the chill air.

"Can you believe this weather?" Cameron muttered to himself, his voice audible above the whistling gusts. "It's like the school is turning into a giant icebox."

"Tell me about it," Ellie said, approaching with her arms wrapped tightly around herself. "I can't remember the last time it this cold." Ollie trailed behind her, rubbing his hands together for warmth.

"Let's get going before we freeze to death," Ollie suggested, adjusting his glasses. The trio set off down the hallway, their footsteps echoing ominously in the near-empty school. As they rounded a corner, Cameron halted abruptly, causing Ellie and Ollie to collide with him.

"Hey, what's the big idea?" Ellie demanded, rubbing her arm where she'd bumped into Cameron.

"Shh, listen," Cameron whispered, holding up a hand for silence. All three strained to hear above the wind's moans, and then they caught it: the faintest hint of an eerie whisper, seemingly coming from everywhere and nowhere at once.

"Did you guys hear that?" Ollie asked, his voice wavering. Cameron nodded, his eyes wide with disbelief.

"Sounds like..." Ellie began, but she couldn't find the words to describe the unsettling noise.

"Like someone's whispering our names," Cameron finished, his mind racing with fear and curiosity. The whispering grew louder and more insistent, sending a shiver down their spines.

"Should we... should we follow it?" Ollie asked hesitantly, looking to his friends for reassurance.

"There's only one way to find out what's going on," Cameron said, trying to sound braver than he felt. "Come on." He led the way, following the source of the whispers as they navigated the dimly lit corridors.

As they moved deeper into the school, shadows dance around them, and the temperature continued to plummet. Suddenly, a row of lockers slammed shut in unison, making them jump in fright. Ellie gasped, instinctively grabbing Ollie's hand for support.

"Okay, that was... not normal," she stammered, her heart pounding in her chest.

"Something strange is definitely happening here," Cameron agreed, feeling a knot form in the pit of his stomach. The whispers grew more urgent, beckoning them onward. Despite their fear, the trio knew they had no choice but to confront whatever supernatural force at work within their school.

Cameron led the way, trying to keep his steps steady despite the shadows creeping closer with every passing second. The eerie whispers echoed around them, growing more intense as they continued down the darkened hallway.

"Guys?" Cameron called out, turning back only to find himself alone. Panic surged through him, his heart pounding like a drum in his chest. He hated being alone; the fear of isolation gnawed at him like a relentless specter. "Ellie? Ollie? Where are you?"

"Cam! We're here!" Ellie's voice reached him from behind a corner, her tone both relieved and anxious. "We got separated for a moment. Don't worry, we're right here."

The relief washed over Cameron palpable, even as he chastised himself for letting his fears sabotage his courage. "Okay," he said, swallowing hard. "Let's keep going. We need to find out what's happening."

As they cautiously proceeded, Ellie couldn't help but feel the weight of her own fear pressing down on her. She had always been terrified of failure, and the thought of not uncovering the truth behind these supernatural events only fueled fear. Her eyes scanned their surroundings, trying to spot any clue might aid their investigation.

"Look!" she whispered suddenly, pointing to a dusty, old bookshelf that appeared to be untouched for years. "Maybe there's something useful in those books."

Her nimble fingers skimmed the spines of the ancient tomes, searching for anything that might shed light on the chilling occurrences plaguing their school. She pulled out an old leather-bound volume, its pages yellowed with age, and began to flip through it.

"Anything?" Ollie asked, watching her intently.

"Nothing yet," Ellie responded, frustration creeping into her voice. "But we can't give up. There has to be something here."

Cameron watched Ellie's determination with a mixture of admiration and concern. She was struggling with her fear. "Ellie, it's okay if we don't find anything right now. We'll keep looking," he reassured her.

"Thanks, Cam," she replied softly, forcing a smile. "I feel like we're running out of time."

As they continued their search, the supernatural events grew more intense. Objects moved on their own, shadows shifted and morphed around them, and the whispers became increasingly persistent. Through it all, Cameron, Ellie, and Ollie clung to one another, determined to face their fears and uncover the truth.

A chill in the air as Ollie trailed behind Cameron and Ellie, his heart pounding with unease. The dimly lit hallway, thick with an unnameable tension, clings to every surface, making each step forward a battle against his own fear.

"Guys, wait up," Ollie called out, his voice smaller than he would have liked. He adjusted his glasses nervously, trying to shake the feeling of being watched.

Cameron and Ellie paused, waiting for him to catch up. "Sorry, Ollie," Cameron apologized, giving him a reassuring smile. "We didn't mean to leave you behind."

But even with their reassurances, Ollie felt left out as they resumed their search for answers. They moved from room to room, opening long-forgotten cabinets and scanning the dusty shelves while Ollie hung back, uncertain of his place within the group. He watched them closely, his thoughts racing.

"Is there anything I can do? Am I even helping?" he wondered, his anxiety mounting. "What if they solve this mystery without me? What if they don't need me anymore?"

His thoughts were interrupted by a sudden, bone-chilling gust of wind swept through the hallway. The doors slammed shut, and the whispers grew louder, filling the air with a sinister cacophony of what?

"Did you guys hear that?" Ollie asked, his eyes wide with terror.

"Stay close, Ollie," Cameron instructed, gripping his friend's arm tightly. "We'll figure this out together."

As they pressed on, the supernatural events intensified. Shadows danced along the walls, taking on grotesque shapes and reaching out towards them. An unseen force rattled the lockers, causing the metallic clangs to echo throughout the hallways.

"Something's definitely not right," Ellie whispered, her voice wavering. "These occurrences are getting worse."

"Maybe we should turn back," Ollie suggested hesitantly. "I don't know how much more of this I can take."

"Ollie, you're stronger than you think," Cameron reassured him. "We're all in this together."

"Right," Ollie mumbled, nodding his head. But deep down, he still couldn't shake the feeling he expendable—a tagalong who added little to their investigation.

As they continued down the ominous hallway, Ollie took a deep breath and summoned every ounce of courage he could muster. He knew he had to face his fears for the sake of his friends, even if it meant confronting the possibility of being left behind. With a renewed sense of determination, he vowed to prove his worth to himself and the others, no matter what challenges lay ahead.

Cameron, Ellie, and Ollie huddled together in the dimly lit library, their faces drawn with fear and exhaustion. The flickering lights cast eerie shadows on the worn bookshelves that loomed over them like silent guardians. A distant howl echoed through the room, making Ollie shiver involuntarily.

SHADOWS IN GRAVEWOOD

"Guys, we need to talk about what's going on," Cameron said, his voice cracking slightly. "These supernatural events are getting worse, and they're messing with our heads."

"Agreed," Ellie whispered, her piercing blue eyes scanning the room as if searching for an unseen threat. "It's like these occurrences are targeting our deepest fears."

"Then it's important for us to share those fears with each other," Ollie chimed in, his glasses fogging up from his nervous breaths. "That way, we can support one another and be better prepared for whatever comes next."

"Alright, I'll go first." Cameron took a deep breath, trying to steady his racing heart. "I'm... I'm terrified of being alone. When I got separated from you guys earlier, I thought I was going to lose my mind."

"Thanks for sharing, Cameron," Ellie said softly, reaching out to squeeze his hand. "And for me, I've always been afraid of failing. That's why I push myself so hard, even when it's not necessary. I can't stand the thought of letting anyone down."

Ollie swallowed hard before speaking up. "My fear is being abandoned by the people I care about. Sometimes, I feel like I don't really belong in this group and that you guys would be better off without me."

"Ollie, that's not true at all," Cameron protested, looking at him with concern. "You're as important as any of us, and we'd never leave you behind."

"Thanks, guys," Ollie said, his voice trembling slightly. "It means a lot to hear that."

"Okay," Ellie said decisively, her eyes narrowing with determination. "Now that we've put our fears out in the open, let's come up with a plan to stand up to these supernatural forces. We can't let them control us any longer."

"Right," Cameron agreed. "We need to confront the next event head-on, no matter how terrifying it may be."

"Agreed," Ollie muttered, clutching his backpack straps tightly. "But how do we know when or where it will happen?"

"Easy," Ellie replied, pulling out a wrinkled map of the school from her pocket. "We'll cover as much ground as possible and stay vigilant. If we stick together and communicate openly, I believe we can overcome whatever is thrown at us."

"Then let's do this," Cameron declared, determination shining in his eyes. "For ourselves and for everyone else in this school."

As the trio stood, their hearts pounded with a mix of fear and resolve. They were facing something far beyond their wildest nightmares. But with their shared courage and unwavering friendship, they were ready to face the darkness head-on.

Cameron's heart pounded in his chest as he scanned the dimly lit hallway, the shadows stretching out like tendrils. The air thick with tension, the weight of their fears bearing down on them. It was as if the very walls of the school turned against them, trapping them in a nightmare they couldn't escape.

"Did you guys hear that?" Ollie whispered, his eyes wide with terror. In the distance, a faint sound echoed through the corridor, like nails scraping against a chalkboard.

"Stay close," Ellie warned, her voice quivering despite her best efforts to remain composed. The three friends huddled together, each taking slow, measured steps as they followed the unnerving sound.

As they rounded a corner, Cameron gasped. His locker door swung open violently, spewing his belongings all over the floor. He stared at the chaotic scene, feeling the icy fingers of isolation grip his chest. The supernatural force singled him out, as he'd feared.

"Whatever this thing is, it knows our fears," Ellie said, her brow furrowed in concentration. She glanced down at the scattered papers on the floor, searching for any clue that might help them understand the curse plaguing their school. But each time she reached for a promising lead, it slipped from her grasp, feeding her fear of failure.

Ollie stood slightly apart from the others, his gaze fixed on an unseen presence. As Cameron and Ellie focused on the unfolding chaos, he couldn't shake the feeling he was being left behind. His insecurities gnawed at him, amplifying his fear of abandonment.

"Guys, I think we're running out of time," Ollie murmured, his voice audible over the eerie sounds echoing through the hallways. "We need to face this... thing."

"Ollie's right," Cameron agreed, his voice cracking with emotion. "We can't let this force control us any longer. It's time to stand up to our fears and fight back."

Ellie took a deep breath, her chest swelling with determination. "Okay, on the count of three, we face our fears head-on. One... two... three!"

Cameron stepped forward, staring down at the supernatural force as it continued to ransack his locker. As the icy grip of isolation loosened, it was replaced by the warmth of his friends standing beside him. "You don't scare me," he growled, defiance burning in his eyes.

Ellie kneeled among the scattered papers, her hands trembling as she picked up an old history book. With every fiber of her being, she forced herself to accept some answers might remain hidden, but she refused to let fear hold her back. "I won't be defeated," she whispered, clutching the book tightly.

Ollie moved closer to his friends, feeling their unwavering support and loyalty. He realized even when he felt left out or overlooked, they were still there for him. "I am not alone," he declared, his voice steady and resolute.

As the trio faced their fears, the supernatural force lost its grip on them. The eerie sounds ceased, and the atmosphere in the hallway shifted, becoming less oppressive. But the relief short-lived, as a blood-curdling scream echoed through the school, sending a shiver down their spines.

"Wh-what was that?" Ollie stammered, the hairs on the back of his neck standing on end.

"Whatever it is, it's not over yet," Cameron replied, steeling himself for whatever new horror awaited them. "But we're ready for it. Together, we'll face whatever comes next."

The friends braced themselves, their courage and determination holding strong. But as they prepared to confront the unknown, they couldn't help but wonder what terrifying revelation awaited them in the darkness.

Cameron's heart pounded in his chest as he exchanged nervous glances with Ellie and Ollie. The silence followed the scream deafening, amplifying their shared dread. They stood at the threshold of the darkened library, its shadowy depths seeming to swallow all light and hope.

"Are we really going in there?" Ollie whispered, his voice trembling.

"Y-yeah," Cameron stammered, trying to sound braver than he felt. "We can't ignore what's happening."

Ellie gripped a flashlight tightly, her knuckles turning white. "We've come this far," she said, her voice firm despite her fear. "We can't back down now."

As they stepped into the library, the heavy door creaked shut behind them, plunging them into darkness. Ellie switched on the flashlight, its beam slicing through the blackness like a knife. Shadows danced on the walls, creating monstrous shapes leering at them from every corner.

"Stay close," Cameron warned, his eyes darting around nervously. "We can't afford to get separated."

"Agreed," Ollie said, swallowing hard. "I-I don't want to be alone in here."

"None of us do," Ellie added, her gaze never wavering from the path ahead. "But we're stronger together, remember?"

In the eerily quiet library, the trio cautiously navigated through rows of towering bookshelves. The musty scent of old paper filled the air, mingling with an inexplicable odor of decay. Cameron could feel the cold, clammy grip of fear tightening around him, but he fought to keep it at bay.

"Listen," Ellie said suddenly, stopping in her tracks. A low, guttural growl echoed through the library, sending chills down their spines.

"Wh-what is that?" Ollie stammered, his eyes wide with terror.

"Only one way to find out," Cameron said, forcing himself to take a step forward. "We have to confront it."

As they turned the corner, the flashlight beam fell upon a grotesque figure hunched over a book—Gideon Blackwell. His hollow cheeks and dark eyes were even more sinister in the dim light. The growling stopped as he slowly raised his head, locking his gaze on the three friends.

"Y-you," Cameron choked out, his voice barely audible. "What do you want from us?"

"Your fear has given me strength," Gideon rasped, a twisted grin spreading across his gaunt face. "But now I crave somet hing... more."

"Stay away from us!" Ellie shouted, her voice trembling with rage and fear. "We're not afraid of you!"

"Really?" Gideon taunted, his eyes flicking between them. "I can taste your terror... It's delicious."

"Leave us alone!" Ollie yelled, clenching his fists. "We won't let you win!"

"Brave words," Gideon sneered, rising to his full height. "But ultimately futile."

The library suddenly shook, books flying off the shelves and hurtling towards the trio. As they scrambled for cover, Cameron's eyes locked onto Gideon's, vowing silently he would do whatever it took to protect his friends.

"Find a way to stop him!" Cameron yelled, dodging a heavy tome. "Together, we can do this!"

"Look for anything that might help!" Ellie shouted back, narrowly avoiding a barrage of books.

"Right behind you!" Ollie cried, determination surging through him as he plunged into the chaos.

CHAPTER 12

The flickering flame from the single candle cast eerie shadows on the walls of the middle school basement as the group huddled together, their faces illuminated by the faint glow. They were surrounded by the relics and artifacts they unearthed throughout their harrowing investigation: a dusty leather-bound book, its pages brittle with age; an old locket, tarnished and cold to the touch; and a stack of yellowing photographs depicting Gideon Blackwell in various stages of his life.

"Guys, we're so close," whispered Ellie, the fear evident in her voice. "We've got to be on the brink of figuring out how Gideon fits into all of this."

"Agreed," said Ollie, his fingers nervously playing with the frayed edge of one of the photographs. "This ritual has been haunting Gravewood for centuries, and we're the only ones who can break it. We can't let Gideon's tormented spirit continue to roam our town."

"Okay, let's go over what we know about the ritual one more time," urged Ellie, her eyes darting between her friends and the relics scattered around them. "And then, maybe, maybe, we'll find that final piece of the puzzle."

As they began to discuss their findings and theories, the air in the basement grew colder and heavier. There was an almost palpable sense of anticipation and urgency, as if the spirits lingered in Gravewood, watching and waiting for them to uncover the truth.

"According to the book," said Ollie, running his finger along the ancient text, "the ritual performed to gain power and control over the forces of nature. But something went wrong. The balance was upset, and now Gravewood is paying the price."

"Right," added Ellie, "and. Gidon Blackwood is in all of these photos, and it's like his eyes are trying to tell us something."

As their theories wove together, a chilling picture of Gideon Blackwell's connection to the ancient ritual and the weight of their task bore down on them. As if the walls of the basement were closing in, urging them to solve the mystery before it's too late.

"We have to break this curse," Ollie declared, determination burning in his gaze. "For Gideon, for Gravewood... for all of us."

A chill ran down Camerson spine as he gazed around the dim basement. The air thick with dust, and the faint smell of mildew hung in the atmosphere. Shadows danced on the walls, cast by the flickering light of the single, bare bulb dangling from the ceiling. The group huddled together, surrounded by artifacts and relics they collected during their investigation. Each object held a piece of the dark mystery that haunted Gravewood.

Cameron's fingers brushed against an old, dusty book hidden beneath a pile of ancient relics. Its tattered leather cover vibrated with energy as if it held secrets waiting to be unleashed. The golden embossed lettering on the spine caught his eye: "Rituals of the Ancients." He carefully pulled it out, feeling its weight in his hands.

"Guys," he said, his voice a whisper, "I think I found something important."

A hush fell over the group as they gathered around him, anticipation evident in their wide eyes. Ellie leaned in, her curiosity piqued, while Ollie adjusted his glasses to get a better look at the mysterious tome. Natalie raised her camera, capturing this pivotal moment, and Ellie stood on her tiptoes, eager to see what lay within the pages.

As Cameron opened the book, an aging piece of parchment slipped from between the pages and fluttered to the floor. It was covered in strange symbols and elaborate diagrams, accompanied by a chilling illustration of the ritual they had been investigating.

"Look at this," Oliver gasped, snatching up the parchment. "These symbols... they match the ones we've seen all over town!"

"Wait," Ellie breathed, leaning closer to examine the document, her heart pounding. "This diagram... it shows the steps needed to perform the ritual. And here"—she pointed at the chilling illustration—"is Gideon Blackwell, right in the center of it all."

The air in the basement grew colder as if the very presence of the document summoned an icy chill. Each of them stared wide-eyed at the parchment, realizing the gravity of what they discovered. Cameron's palms grew clammy as he gripped the ancient book tighter.

"Does this mean..." Natalie hesitated, her voice wavering. "Gideon, the one who performed the ritual? The one responsible for all of this?"

"It looks like it," Cameron replied, his voice barely audible. "No wonder his spirit is cursed."

"Guys, this is huge," Ellie whispered, her eyes darting between the parchment and her friends. "We finally know what happened. And now we have a chance to fix it."

"Right," Ollie agreed, his expression resolute. "But first, we need to understand these symbols and diagrams. Only then can we figure out how to reverse the ritual and break the curse."

As they pored over the parchment, their excitement and curiosity mingled with an underlying sense of horror. The basement was now charged with the weight of this revelation. They're standing on the precipice of truth, with the key to saving Gravewood in their hands.

"Let's not waste any time," Ellie urged, determination shining in her blue eyes. "We've come so far—we won't let fear hold us back now. Together, we'll decipher this document and save our town."

"Agreed," the others echoed, their voices strong and united.

With renewed resolve, the group bent over the parchment and the ancient book, determined to unlock the secrets within and put an end to the evil haunting Gravewood. As they delved into the mysteries before them, the shadows around them grew darker, as if the spirits of the town watched and waited.

Ellie's heart raced as she traced her finger over the parchment, carefully following the intricate diagrams. "According to this ancient book, the ritual meant to summon and bind a powerful entity from another realm," she said, shivering at the thought of such an ominous force existing within their quiet town.

"Binding an entity?" Ollie frowned, his eyes narrowing in concentration. "So, what are the steps?"

"First, they had to draw a circle with these symbols around it," Ellie pointed out, indicating the complex markings on the parchment. "Then there's the incantation, which must be repeated three times. It says each participant must offer a personal item as a sacrifice, and finally, one of them performs a blood offering."

"Does it mention why they would want to summon such an entity?" Ellie asked, her voice a whisper.

"The book hints at gaining power and control," Ellie replied, her stomach knotting at the implications. "But it also suggests that those performing the ritual might have been desperate for some sort of solution or salvation."

As the group absorbed this information, their thoughts turned to Gideon Blackwell, the gaunt man whose dark eyes follow them even now from the old photograph.

"Guys," Ollie said, his voice heavy with realization. "I think I understand Gideon's connection to all of this. Look at this passage." He pointed to a section of the ancient book. "It says the one who offers their blood becomes a vessel for the entity, but something went wrong during the ritual."

"Wrong? What do you mean?" Ellie asked, fear creeping into her voice.

"Instead of binding the entity to their will," Ellie continued, swallowing hard, "it seems Gideon became bound to the entity itself. A curse born from the failed ritual, trapping him between worlds—unable to leave our realm but also unable to fully exist in it."

"Is that why he's been haunting Gravewood all these years?" Ellie questioned, her eyes wide with horror.

"Seems so," Ollie responded grimly. "And every time the entity gains strength, Gideon's spirit becomes more tormented.

It's like he's slowly being consumed by the very force he tried to control."

"Then we have to help him," Ellie declared, her heart pounding with determination. "We can't let this continue any longer. Not when we know the truth."

"Agreed," the others echoed, their faces set with resolve. They had to uncover the secrets within the ancient ritual and find a way to free Gideon Blackwell from his eternal torment.

As they continued to study the parchment and ancient book, the atmosphere in the basement grew heavier with the knowledge of what they must do. The dim light flickered across their focused faces, casting eerie shadows on the walls as they delved deeper into the mystery before them. Each heartbeat and breath amplified, echoing through the quiet space as if the air charged with anticipation for what was to come.

The weight of the revelation settled upon them like a thick, oppressive fog, suffocating their hopes and dreams of a normal life in Gravewood. They sat there, huddled together in the dimly lit basement, surrounded by artifacts that whispered secrets from the past. The air heavy with anticipation and dread.

SHADOWS IN GRAVEWOOD

"Guys!" Ellie's voice trembled as she spoke, her eyes never leaving the dusty pages before her. "We really have to help Gideon break free from this curse. But how can we even begin to reverse a ritual that's so ancient and powerful?"

"First, we need to understand it better," Ollie said, his fingers tracing the old, faded ink on the parchment they found. "There must be something we've missed—some key to unlocking its true nature."

"Maybe there's a counter-ritual or something," Ellie suggested, her face pale as she considered the enormity of what lay before them. "Something to undo the damage that's been done."

"Even if there is," Caleb added, his voice laced with anxiety, "how do we know we're capable of performing it? This isn't exactly amateur-hour stuff we're dealing with here."

Ellie's heart was pounding in her chest, her palms growing slick with sweat as she glanced around at her friends. Their faces were etched with determination but also fear—a potent mix of emotions threatened to tear them apart even as it bound them together. Yet, within the maelstrom of feelings, a fierce resolve began to take shape.

"Look," Ellie said, her voice steady despite the turmoil inside her. "I know we're scared. I'm scared, too. But we're the only ones who can do this. We're the only ones who even know about this curse and how Gideon Blackwell is suffering because of it."

"Ellie's right," Ollie chimed in. "We owe it to Gideon and to Gravewood to at least try. We can't sit back and watch as our town is consumed by this darkness."

"Besides," Ellie added, her eyes shining with determination, "we've already come so far. It's not like we haven't faced challenges before, and we've always managed to find a way through them."

"Then it's settled," Caleb said, his voice firm with resolve. "We'll do whatever it takes to break this curse. Together."

They each nodded in agreement, their faces set with determination. As they began to pore over the ancient texts once more, Ellie could feel the bond between them strengthening—a connection forged from shared experiences and a common goal.

"Alright," she whispered, her fingers tightening around the edges of the ancient book. "Let's do this. For Gideon. For Gravewood. For all of us."

And together, they delved deeper into the shadows of the past, searching for the key that would unlock the door to redemption—or damnation.

The air grew colder as they continued to study the ancient texts, each word feeling like a heavy stone dropped into their minds. The shadows in the basement grew longer, snaking around the artifacts and relics surrounding them. Ellie shivered, not from the chill but from the creeping sense of dread settling over her like a suffocating cloak.

"Listen to this," Ollie said, his voice wavering slightly. "It says here to reverse the ritual, we need to face Gideon's spirit directly. We have to confront him at the exact location where the original ritual took place."

"Are you serious?" Caleb asked, his eyes wide with shock. "That place is probably crawling with dark energy. Who knows what can happen if we go there?"

As the others exchanged uneasy glances, Ellie clenched her fists. "We don't have a choice, Caleb. If we want to break this curse, we have to do whatever it takes."

"Right," Ellie whispered, her heart pounding against her ribcage. She tried to silence the fear gnawing at her insides, focusing instead on the determination burned within her and her friends. They're Gravewood's last hope, and she couldn't allow herself to falter now.

"According to this map, the ritual site should be somewhere deep within the woods. We need to find it before the

next full moon, or we'll be too late, according to the book,"
Ollie said, his voice barely audible over the sound of his own
rapid heartbeat.

"Then we'll leave first thing tomorrow morning," Ellie announced, her voice resolute. "We can't afford to waste any
more time."

"Agreed," Caleb said, nodding grimly. "But we should prepare ourselves for whatever we might encounter out there.
We're stepping into the unknown, and I don't think any of
us can predict what we'll find."

"Alright, everyone. Gather whatever you think will be useful and meet back here in the morning," Ellie instructed.
"We'll need all the help we can get."

As they dispersed to gather their supplies, Ellie's thoughts
raced with images of dark forests, ancient rituals, and the
haunting figure of Gideon Blackwell. She wondered how
much more horror they would have to face before these
nightmares were over.

The sun had risen when they met at the entrance to
the Gravewood forest, their backpacks heavy with protective charms and research materials. Despite the cool breeze

rustling through the trees, a layer of sweat coated Ellie's palms, and her heart thudded in her chest.

"Are you guys ready?" she asked, looking around at her friends. Their faces were etched with determination, but she could see the fear lurking in their eyes. They knew the dangers that awaited them, but they also understood the magnitude of their mission.

"Ready as we'll ever be," Ollie replied, his jaw set as he took the first step into the woods.

As they ventured deeper into the forest, the light grew dimmer, swallowed by thick branches overhead. The air was heavy with the scent of damp earth and decay, and every snap of a twig or distant rustle echoed with sinister intent.

"Wait!" Caleb suddenly shouted, stopping dead in his tracks. The others froze, their breaths caught in their throats as they waited for an explanation.

"Look," he said, pointing at the ground before him. The dirt had been disturbed, revealing the faint outline of a symbol—the same one they had seen in their research on the ritual.

"Is this...?" Ellie started, her voice shaking.

"Welcome to the ritual site," Ollie confirmed grimly.

A sudden gust of wind whipped through the trees, sending a shiver down Ellie's spine. Her pulse quickened as the immense weight of their task settled on her shoulders.

"Alright, let's do this," Ellie said, her voice steely with determination. "Let's break this curse and save Gravewood."

As they gathered in a circle around the symbol, preparing to confront the spirit of Gideon Blackwell, an eerie silence fell over the woods. As if the very air held its breath, waiting for the battle would decide the fate of Gravewood and the souls bound by the ancient curse.

"Here goes nothing," Ellie whispered, her voice over the pounding of her heart.

They began the ritual which would either save them all or seal their doom.

Cameron's heart raced as he stared at the ancient symbol etched into the ground, its twisted lines seemingly pulsating with an energy that sent shivers down his spine. The air was thick with anticipation, and the shadows cast by the trees close in around them like sinister hands reaching out to grasp their prey.

"Okay," Ellie said, "according to the ritual instructions we found, we need to stand at each point of the symbol and recite the incantation together."

"Are we sure this is going to work?" Natalie asked nervously, clutching her camera tightly as if it could protect her from the unknown.

"We have to try," Ollie replied, adjusting his glasses with shaky hands. "It's our only chance to break the curse and save Gideon's spirit."

Cameron saw the fear in his friends' eyes but also their determination. They came this far, and there was no turning back now. He took a deep breath, focusing on the task at hand, and stepped forward to take his place on the symbol.

As they each positioned themselves, the wind picked up once more, causing the leaves to rustle and whisper like ghostly voices urging them on. Cameron glanced around at his friends, their faces bathed in the pale moonlight filtered through the branches above.

"Ready?" Ellie whispered, her blue eyes meeting each of theirs in turn.

"Ready," they echoed in unison, their voices a blend of trepidation and resolve.

"Alright," she continued, "on the count of three, we'll start the incantation. One, two, three..."

Together, their voices rose, the words of the ancient ritual rolling off their tongues like a haunting melody. "In lumine tuo videbimus lumen, Lux et tenebrae, in aeternum connex-ae." Each syllable resonated with an ancient power.

As they spoke the arcane phrases, the air crackled with energy, and Cameron felt a cold sweat breaking across his forehead while goosebumps prickled his skin. The surround-ings seemed to respond to the invocation as shadows danced and flickered in the dim candlelight, and the room pulsated with an otherworldly force. The weight of the ritual hung in the air, intensifying the suspense as they continued to recite the ancient words, their fates intertwined with the mystical incantation.

"Please work," he thought, his chest tightening with anxiety as they continued to chant.

Suddenly, the ground beneath them began to vibrate, send-ing a jolt of fear through Cameron's body. His heart pounded in his ears, drowning out the whispered incantation and the rustling leaves above.

"Guys!" Ellie cried out, her voice quivering, "Something's happening!"

"Keep going!" Ellie urged, her eyes wide with both terror and determination. "We can't stop now!"

As they pressed on, the tremors intensified, and the dark presence of Gideon Blackwell drew near. The air grew colder, and an oppressive weight settled over them—a sinister force threatened to crush their spirits.

"Almost there," Ollie muttered through gritted teeth, beads of sweat dripping down his forehead.

"Stay strong," Cameron told himself, locking eyes with Natalie for a brief moment of reassurance before returning his focus to the incantation.

With one final powerful recitation, a blinding flash of light erupted from the center of the symbol. Stunned, they shielded their eyes, waiting for the intensity to subside. When they finally dared to look, they gasped at what they saw standing within the symbol.

"Did we... did we do it?" Ellie stammered, her eyes wide with disbelief.

"Be careful," Ellie warned, her voice shaking. "We don't know if the ritual worked or not."

Cameron's heart raced, the outcome of their desperate attempt now hanging in the balance. The weight of their actions, the impact on Gravewood, and the fate of Gideon Blackwell's tormented spirit all rested on their shoulders, leaving them no choice but to face the consequences head-on.

"Let's find out," he said, swallowing hard and taking a step closer to the spectral figure before them.

The spectral figure wavered before them like a heat haze, its edges shimmering and indistinct. Its eyes, once dark and piercing, burn with an inner light flickered like the last embers of a dying fire. Cameron's heart hammered against his ribcage, his pulse pounding in his ears as he studied the apparition. He senses other eyes on him, their breaths held hostage by fear and anticipation.

"Who are you?" Cameron asked, his voice shaking despite his best efforts to sound confident. The figure regarded him silently, its hollow gaze burrowing into his soul. Then it opened its mouth and spoke, the words echoing through whispers from the grave.

"Once... I was Gideon Blackwell," the spirit rasped, its voice a haunting blend of sorrow and regret. "But now, I am but a shadow of the man I used to be."

Cameron swallowed hard, trying to ignore the icy tendrils of fear creeping down his spine. "We performed the counter ritual," he said, his eyes never leaving the ghostly visage. "To break the curse and set your spirit free."

Gideon's spectral form shuddered as if struck by an unseen force. A tortured moan escaped his lips, sending chills down Cameron's back.

"Are you... free?" Ellie asked hesitantly, her fingers twisting around the edge of one of the ancient scrolls they found.

"Not yet," Gideon replied, his voice no more than a whisper. "One final step remains."

The weight of responsibility settles on Cameron shoulders like an iron yoke. "Tell us what we need to do," he demanded, his hands curling into fists at his sides. "We'll finish this."

"Resolute words," Gideon's ghost murmured, a faint, sad smile touching his transparent lips. "But be warned, the path before you is fraught with danger. Your courage will be tested, as will your loyalty to one another."

"Whatever it takes," Ellie declared, her voice firm and unwavering. "We're not leaving Gideon's spirit trapped here any longer."

"Nor will we allow the curse to continue harming Gravewood," Ollie added, his glasses reflecting the eerie glow emanating from Gideon's form.

"Very well," Gideon sighed, his spectral figure growing more transparent by the second. "Within the heart of Gravewood lies a hidden chamber, sealed for centuries. There, you will find an ancient relic—the key to breaking the curse. But beware, for once the seal is broken, the true extent of the darkness plagued this town will be revealed."

Natalie's fingers tightened around her camera, capturing the ghostly image of Gideon Blackwell as he faded away, leaving them in darkness once more. The air felt heavy and oppressive, thick with secrets and unspoken fears.

"Whatever lies ahead," Cameron said, his voice filled with determination, "we'll face it together. We've come too far to back down now."

"Agreed," Ellie replied, her blue eyes steely and resolute. "For Gravewood."

"For Gravewood," they echoed, their voices mingling in a chorus of unity and resolve.

As they prepared to embark on the final leg of their journey, Cameron couldn't shake the sense of foreboding gnawed at the edges of his mind. They came so far and unearthed so many dark truths—but could they truly be prepared for what awaited them in the heart of Gravewood? Only time would tell.

CHAPTER 13

The old school clock's ticking echoed through the empty classroom, punctuating the tense silence as the group of friends huddled together in a corner. Cameron Hawthorne chewed on his lower lip, his mischievous grin replaced by a determined scowl. He locked eyes with each of his friends, silently assessing their strengths and weaknesses.

"Alright, guys," he said, his voice a whisper. "We need to gather everything required to reverse this ritual. We've all got unique skills, so let's use them."

Natalie nodded, her eyes filled with resolve. "I'll research the history behind the artifacts we find. Maybe that will give us some clues about how to break the curse."

"Good idea," Ellie chimed in. "I'm not afraid of those creepy spirits, so I'll face them head-on if we encounter any."

"Nice one, Ellie," Cameron grinned, feeling a surge of pride for his brave friend. "Ollie, you can use your tech skills to decipher any cryptic symbols or codes we come across. And Ellie, your intuition is like a sixth sense. You'll guide us when things get... weird."

"Okay, but where do we start looking for these materials?" Ollie asked, pushing up his glasses nervously.

Cameron hesitated, his brow furrowing in thought. A memory flickered in his mind—a rumor he'd heard from older students about hidden rooms in the middle school basement. It felt like a long shot, but it was worth a try.

"Let's search the basement," he suggested, trying to sound more confident than he felt. "There might be hidden rooms or compartments down there with the stuff we need."

The others exchanged glances, uncertainty, and fear momentarily clouding their expressions. But Cameron had a knack for finding what they needed, even in the most unlikely places. His impulsiveness has gotten them into trouble before, but it has also been the key to their survival.

"Alright," Natalie said, her voice steady. "Let's do this."

A mixture of dread and excitement as Cameron and the others prepared to embark on their mission. The dangers lurked in the shadows and the supernatural obstacles they would face. But they're stronger together, a team united by friendship and determination.

With one last glance at his friends, Cameron led them out of the classroom, his heart pounding in his chest. The basement awaited them—a dark and mysterious realm held the key to breaking the curse.

Cameron led his friends down the dimly lit hallway, the flickering overhead lights casting eerie shadows on the walls. The creaking floorboards echoed their every step as if the building itself was warning them to turn back. Despite the unsettling atmosphere, Cameron's curiosity and determination drove him forward, refusing to let fear get the better of him.

"Are you guys sure we should be doing this?" Ellie whispered nervously, her eyes darting around the dark corners of the corridor.

"Trust me, I've got a feeling about this," Cameron replied with a hint of apprehension in his voice. They're delving into dangerous territory, but a risk they had to take.

As they descended further into the depths of the basement, the air grew colder and more oppressive, sending shivers down their spines. An unspoken sense of foreboding hung heavy in the air as if being watched by unseen eyes.

"Guys, look!" Ellie called out, her voice trembling slightly as she pointed to an inconspicuous door hidden away in the darkness. The rusty lock and dust-covered surface hinted at secrets long forgotten and buried beneath years of neglect.

"Great find, Ellie!" Cameron exclaimed with enthusiasm as he retrieved the key they had discovered earlier. His fingers deftly played with the small metal object, the gleam of anticipation in his eyes. With a deliberate motion, he inserted it into the lock, the distinct clicks of the tumblers resonating through the hushed atmosphere of the basement.

"Can you hurry up, Cam? I don't like this place," Ollie muttered, his eyes scanning the shadows warily. Cameron heard the uneasiness in his friend's voice, and he shared the sentiment. But they didn't have time to waste.

"Got it!" Cameron exclaimed, feeling a small surge of pride as the lock finally gave way. With bated breath, they pushed open the door, revealing a hidden room filled with ancient artifacts and relics. Their eyes widened in awe as they took in the dusty shelves lined with mysterious objects that defy time and logic.

"Whoa," Natalie whispered, her historian's instincts kicking in as she examined the artifacts with fascination. "This can be exactly what we need."

"Let's hope it's enough to break the curse," Cameron thought to himself, his heart pounding in his chest. As they began to carefully explore the hidden room, he couldn't help but feel they were one step closer to finding the answers they so desperately sought.

Natalie cautiously stepped into the hidden room, her eyes drawn to the artifacts beckoning her. The air was heavy with the scent of decay and whispers of long-forgotten memories, making the hairs on the back of her neck stand on end. She reached out a trembling hand to pick up an intricately carved wooden box adorned with ancient symbols.

"Look at this," Natalie said, her voice hushed as if speaking too loudly would disturb the past. "These symbols are from a time long before our middle school was built. They hold great power."

Ollie, his glasses perched precariously on the tip of his nose, observed the mysterious objects that filled the room. A shiver ran down his spine as he realized they surrounded by the remnants of powerful rituals and dark history. With furrowed brows and a determined glint in his eyes, Ollie set to work deciphering the cryptic markings on the artifacts, running his fingers over their surfaces as he concentrated on unlocking their secrets.

"Guys, I think I've found something," Ollie announced quietly, holding up a crumbling parchment covered in symbols. "This is an ancient language, but I recognize some of these characters from my studies. I believe this can be a key piece of the puzzle."

"Are you sure?" Cameron asked, his voice wavering with uncertainty.

"Positive," Ollie replied, his focus unwavering as he traced the symbols with a steadier hand than any of them expected. "Give me a moment. I just need to... there! I think I understand it now." His words carried a mix of excitement and trepidation as if understanding the text equal parts triumph and curse.

"Tell us what it says, Ollie," Ellie urged, her hands wringing anxiously.

"According to this," Ollie began, his voice steady despite the weight of his discovery, "the ritual we need to reverse is tied to these artifacts. We must use them in a specific order to break the curse."

"Then let's start," Natalie said, her determination shining through her fear. "Together, we'll put an end to this once and for all."

As they gathered around the ancient parchment, the weight of history pressed down on them. The room breathed with anticipation, as if it had been waiting centuries for someone to finally unravel its secrets. But despite the supernatural aura that clung to the air like spiderwebs, this was their only chance to save their school—and themselves. They would face whatever darkness lay ahead, united by courage and the unbreakable bond of friendship.

As the friends inspected the mysterious objects, they couldn't shake an eerie feeling blanketing the room. Ellie, her keen intuition heightened, noticed a cold draft brushing against her skin, making her shiver involuntarily. "Do you guys feel that?" she asked, rubbing her arms for warmth.

"Feel what?" Ollie inquired, his focus still on deciphering the cryptic symbols.

"Something's not right," Ellie whispered, her piercing blue eyes scanning the dimly lit chamber. A low, guttural growl filled the air, and a pungent odor of decay assaulted their nostrils.

"Did you hear that?" Natalie questioned, her face pale as she clutched one of the ancient artifacts tightly.

"Stay close," Ellie commanded, her voice calm despite her racing heart. The group huddled together, moving cautiously through the hidden room.

The oppressive atmosphere grew heavier with each step, the once distant whispers now echoing inside their heads, disorienting and frightening them. Their hands trembled as they reached out to touch the cold stone walls, only to retract at the sensation of something slimy and alive beneath their fingertips.

"Ellie, I'm scared," Ellie admitted, her voice over the cacophony of unsettling sounds.

"Me too," Ellie replied, swallowing hard. "But we have to keep going. We're so close."

Then, a spectral figure materialized before them, blocking their path to a crucial artifact. It was a chilling sight; the figure appeared to be made of smoke and shadows, its hollow eyes boring into their very souls. Ellie stepped forward, her courage surging. "We need that artifact," she said, staring down at the ghostly apparition.

"Leave this place," the spirit hissed, its voice sending shivers down their spines.

"Please, we just want to break the curse," Ellie implored, her determination unwavering. "Let us pass."

"Your quest will bring only suffering," the spirit warned, its form flickering like a dying flame.

"Maybe, but we have to try," Ellie insisted, her voice strong and resolute. "We won't give up. We can't."

For a tense moment, the friends held their breath, uncertain of the spirit's reaction. Then, with a mournful wail, it vanished, leaving them trembling but undeterred. Ellie took a deep breath, steadying herself before she reached for the Enchanted Runestones they so desperately needed. "Together, we'll put an end to this nightmare," she vowed, her eyes shining with fierce resolve.

"Alright, everyone," Cameron said, his voice steady despite the lingering tremors running through his body. "We've made it this far, and we'll make it through whatever else comes our way. We can do this."

Ollie nodded vigorously, adjusting his glasses as he clutched the artifact Ellie gathered. Despite his fear, he found solace in the knowledge they were all in this together.

"Cam's right," Natalie chimed in, her camera strap wrapped tightly around her wrist like a lifeline. "We're stronger together."

Ellie took a deep breath, inhaling the musty scent of ancient relics and the faint whiff of something cold and metallic—something otherworldly. She straightened her shoulders and focused on the task at hand. "Let's get to work," she declared, her voice filled with determination.

As they moved cautiously through the hidden room, they discovered more artifacts, each one shrouded in an aura of mystery and power. The dim light flickered across the surfaces of these objects, casting eerie shadows that danced and twisted along the walls.

"Look at this," Ollie whispered, his fingers tracing the intricate markings etched into a small, golden amulet. As he concentrated, his mind began to unravel the cryptic symbols, revealing clues about the artifact's purpose. His heart was racing, but he pushed past his fear, determined to decode the ancient language.

"Good work, Ollie," Ellie encouraged, her blue eyes scanning the rest of the room for any additional items they might need. "Keep going."

"Hey, I think I found something!" Cameron exclaimed, holding up a dusty old book. Its leather cover cracked and worn, but the pages within held secrets crucial to their mission. They huddled around him, eager to uncover its contents.

"Be careful with that, Cam," Ellie warned, her red curls bouncing as she leaned in for a closer look. "We don't want to trigger anything dangerous."

"Got it," he replied, gingerly turning the fragile pages.

As they deciphered the book's contents, each friend relied on their unique skills and knowledge to make sense of the information. They discussed theories, pieced together puzzles, and reassured one another when doubts or fears threatened to overwhelm them.

"Guys, I think we're getting close," Natalie said with a hint of excitement, snapping a photo of a particularly ominous-looking page. "We might actually be able to reverse this ritual."

"Imagine if we can put an end to all of this," Ollie mused, his eyes filled with hope as he continued to analyze the amulet in his hands.

"Let's not get ahead of ourselves," Ellie cautioned, her intuition telling her more obstacles surely awaited them. "But you're right—we're making progress. We have to stay focused."

"Absolutely," Cameron agreed, closing the book with a determined nod. "We won't let Gideon Blackwell win. Not this time."

With each relic they discovered and every mystery they unraveled, the friends felt a growing sense of hope and determination. The air around them crackled with anticipation and excitement as they realized they were one step closer to breaking the curse haunted that Gravewood. Together, they knew they had the power to change everything, and they wouldn't let fear stand in their way.

The air in the hidden room grew colder, and an icy chill crept up the spines of the gathered friends. Shadows danced unnervingly across the walls, and an oppressive weight descended upon them.

"Guys," Ellie whispered, her eyes wide with fear. "I don't think we're alone anymore."

The temperature plummeted further, and the friends huddled together for warmth. Suddenly, a dark presence manifested before them, filling the room with a malevolent energy suck the life from the air. Gideon Blackwell's spirit appeared, his hollow cheeks and piercing eyes a terrifying sight to behold.

The spirit in front of them looked different, its ethereal form distinct enough for them to discern that they were now face-to-face with the entity that looked like Gideon. A subtle chill ran down their spines as they realized the gravity of the encounter.

"Your efforts are in vain," entity hissed, his voice echoing through the chamber. The spirit's words carried a weight that seemed to penetrate the very fabric of reality. "You cannot hope to undo what has been done."

The children exchanged uneasy glances, the subtle difference in the spirit's appearance confirming their suspicions. The air around them grew heavy with a mix of trepidation and determination as they prepared to confront the entity.

"Watch us," Ellie shot back, her bravery shining through despite the spectral manifestation before them. Her heart pounded wildly in her chest as she stared down at the vengeful spirit. "We've come too far to be stopped by you."

"Indeed," Natalie agreed, her knowledge of history fueling her resolve. "Evil never triumphs forever, Gideon. We'll find a way to break your curse."

"By all means, try," Gideon taunted, his dark eyes filled with malice. "But know this: even if you succeed, there is something far worse awaiting you—a truth more horrifying than you can possibly imagine."

As the friends exchanged worried glances, Ollie's determination took over. He refused to let Gideon's ominous words

STEPHANIE TYO

derail their mission. "Whatever it is," he said resolutely, "we'll face it together."

"Very well," Gideon sneered, and in an instant, the air around them crackled with renewed intensity. The friends braced themselves, prepared to use their unique skills and quick thinking to outsmart the vengeful spirit.

"Get ready!" Cameron shouted, and with a collective surge of courage, the friends confronted Gideon Blackwell's spirit head-on. The room became a whirlwind of supernatural energy as each friend called upon their strengths to battle the dark force that threatened to consume them.

The friends found themselves locked in a relentless battle against the malevolent presence that had ensnared Gideon. The air crackled with energy as the clash between good and evil played out in the chamber.

Cameron, the agile and quick-witted among them, darted around the periphery, utilizing his nimble movements to distract the entity. With every nimble step, he drew the malevolent force's attention away from his comrades, creating openings for the others to exploit.

Natalie, possessing a keen intellect and a talent for deciphering ancient texts, delved into her bag of mystical artifacts. She unearthed a talisman passed down through generations,

214

its protective energies pulsating with an ethereal glow. With a flick of her wrist, she unleashed a wave of protective magic, forming a barrier that shielded her friends from the dark entity's malevolence.

Meanwhile, Ellie, known for her unwavering strength and courage, confronted the possessed Gideon head-on. Muscles tensed and determination etched on her face, Ellie grappled with the malevolent force, resisting its attempts to overpower her. Her sheer physical prowess became a formidable obstacle for the entity.

Ellie, the empathetic and intuitive member of the group, closed her eyes and tapped into the latent mystical energies within the chamber. Sensing the emotional core of the malevolent presence, she channeled her empathic abilities to weaken its resolve. Her connection to the emotional essence of the entity provided a crucial advantage, disrupting its focus and sowing discord within its essence.

With each passing moment, the synergy of their individual strengths began to unravel the malevolent presence. The tide turned in their favor as a collective surge of hope infused their efforts. The chamber echoed with the sounds of clashing energies and determined voices, creating a crescendo that reverberated through the enchanted space. The friends, unified by their unique abilities, pressed on relentlessly, their unwavering resolve driving back the darkness that had threatened to consume them. Hope blossomed anew within their hearts as they harnessed their strengths to overcome the malevolent force that had gripped their friend's soul.

But as victory was within their grasp, Gideon unleashed one final, desperate attack. The world around them shattered, and the friends found themselves engulfed in darkness.

"Wait! Look at this!" Ellie cried, her voice above the chaos. In her hands, she held a torn piece of parchment—a clue been hidden in plain sight among the ancient artifacts.

"Could this be the missing piece of the puzzle that will help us finished this once and for all?" Ollie wondered, his mind racing to decipher the cryptic symbols scrawled across the page.

"Only one way to find out," Ellie whispered, her intuition guiding her as the friends regrouped and prepared for the final battle lay ahead.

With the revelation of the mysterious parchment, they're on the brink of uncovering a shocking secret—one thing could change everything. But as the darkness closed in around them, they also realized their greatest challenge still awaited them. And so, with hearts pounding and determination burning like fire within their souls, they stepped forward into the unknown, ready to confront whatever horrors Gideon Blackwell's spirit had in store for them.

CHAPTER 14

A cold shiver ran down Cameron's spine as he gazed at the deserted streets of Gravewood, an unsettling sensation gnawing at the edges of his consciousness. The group, in the midst of grabbing ice cream from the truck, couldn't shake the feeling that something was amiss. The air around them felt heavy and charged, reminiscent of the moments before a thunderstorm. Cameron couldn't quite put his finger on it, but the atmosphere was undeniably tinged with an eerie energy.

"Guys, do you feel that?" he asked, turning to face his friends. Ellie glanced up from her history book, her piercing blue eyes meeting his with concern.

"Yeah," she said softly, her intuition picking up on the same foreboding energy. "It feels like... something's coming."

The group shared worried glances, each of them sensing the impending threat hanging over the town like a dark cloud. Ollie adjusted his glasses nervously, his gentle demeanor belying the courage that resided within him. "Whatever it is, we need to be ready," he stated, his voice steady despite the anxiety etched on his face.

Gravewood appeared deceptively tranquil, bathed in the warm glow of the setting sun. The quaint shops lining the cobblestone streets closed for the evening, their windows casting long shadows stretched across the deserted town square. In the distance, the ancient clock tower loomed ominously, its weathered bricks and moss-covered stones whispering tales of secrets long buried.

"Everything looks normal, but it doesn't feel right," Natalie murmured, her camera hanging limply in her hands as she surveyed the scene before her. Her artistic soul could sense the subtle shift in the atmosphere, as if the essence of Gravewood had been tainted by an unseen force.

"Maybe we're imagining things," Ellie suggested, though her voice lacked conviction. She knew better than anyone that the supernatural forces they'd encountered in the past were anything but imaginary. Fear of losing control wrestled with her determination to do what was right.

"Cam, do you think it's Gideon?" Ellie asked, clutching her history book tightly to her chest. The name Gideon Blackwell sent a ripple of unease through the group, as trouble always followed in his wake.

Cameron hesitated, biting his lip as he considered the possibility. His fear of isolation battled against his innate curiosity and the need to protect his friends. "I don't know," he admitted, "but we should be prepared for anything."

As the sun dipped below the horizon, casting Gravewood into shadow, the group of friends braced themselves for the unknown. Little did they know darkness was not only descending upon their town but also on their lives, as they faced an enemy more powerful and terrifying than they could ever imagine.

The silence befallen Gravewood, unnatural and unsettling, like the calm before a hurricane. The wind ceased its gentle whistle, and the leaves stopped their playful dance in the breeze. As if the town itself held its breath, waiting for an impending catastrophe.

Ellie shivered, pulling her cardigan tighter around herself. Her eyes darted nervously from one shadow to the next as though expecting some malevolent force to emerge from the darkness at any moment.

Suddenly, an icy chill cut through the air, sending shivers down their spines. The spirit of Gideon Blackwell, his terrifying visage twisted with malice, materialized out of the shadows. His hollow eyes bore into them, his gaunt face a horrifying testament to the centuries he'd existed in this purgatorial state between life and death.

"Run!" Cameron shouted, panic seizing hold of him as he realized they're no match for the vengeful spirit before them. But even as his legs propelled him forward, he couldn't help but wonder what had driven Gideon Blackwell to unleash such fury upon the town.

"Cam, what do we do?" Ellie gasped, sprinting beside him. The desperation clawed at her chest, threatening to overwhelm her rationality. Would they be able to protect Gravewood against this ancient evil?

"Stay close and stick together!" Cameron called back, hoping his fear of isolation wouldn't hinder their chances of surviving the night.

As the spirit of Gideon Blackwell began his assault on Gravewood, the air crackled with an unnatural energy. Windows shattered, sending shards of glass flying like deadly projectiles. Streetlights flickered and died, plunging the town into darkness. The howling wind returned with a vengeance, carrying the anguished cries of terrified townsfolk as they scrambled for safety.

"Look out!" Ellie screamed, her keen senses alerting her to the danger in time. Cameron dove to the side, narrowly avoiding the toppled lamppost that crashed to the ground where he'd been standing moments before.

"Thanks," Cameron breathed, his pulse racing from the adrenaline surge. He glanced at Ellie, her eyes wide with terror but also filled with determination. At that moment, they couldn't let fear control them; they had to fight back against Gideon's spirit if they wanted to protect their town and each other.

But as the destruction around them intensified, Cameron couldn't shake the nagging feeling this was only the beginning of a long and terrifying night, filled with dangers and challenges they could never have anticipated.

Cameron's heart pounded in his chest as he led the group toward the middle school. The air reeked of acrid smoke and burnt wood, a signal of Gravewood's impending doom. With every step they took, Gideon's malevolent presence grew stronger, like an oppressive weight bearing down on them.

"Everyone, remember our plan," Cameron said, clutching the charm bracelet Ellie made to boost their abilities. "We need to protect this place at all costs."

"Right," Ellie replied, her face pale but resolute. She focused her attention on the ground.

"Whatever you say, fearless leader," smirked Ollie, grabbing a baseball bat.

"Ollie, don't!" Ellie hissed, her eyes scanning the surroundings for any signs of danger. As the group's lookout, her keen vision had already spared them from disaster more than once.

"Sorry, I was just trying to lighten the mood," Ollie muttered, looking sheepish. He raised the bat defensively, ready for whatever horrors awaited them.

As they approached the school, the wind picked up, howling like a pack of angry wolves. Suddenly, a swarm of shadowy figures emerged from the darkness, their distorted faces twisted into snarls of hatred. Gideon's minions arrived.

"Everyone, brace yourselves!" Cameron shouted, gripping his own crowbar tightly. His palms slick with sweat, but there's no time for doubt or fear.

The battle began in earnest, with the group employing every ounce of skill and determination they possessed. Ellie utilized her keen vision to pinpoint weaknesses in their foes. She shouted out instructions to maximize the group's effectiveness. Meanwhile, Ollie wielded his bat with skill and precision, striking down the shadowy figures one by one. The combined efforts of the team showcased their regular strength and resourcefulness in the face of adversity.

"Ollie, aim for their heads!" she cried as another wave of minions approached.

The approaching wave of minions was like a surreal blend of whimsy and menace. Standing just under three feet tall, these peculiar creatures resembled animated clusters of shimmering, iridescent bubbles. Their bodies seemed to ripple with a playful luminescence, shifting through a spectrum of vibrant colors as they moved. Each minion had a spherical head adorned with a pair of mischievous, oversized eyes that gleamed with an otherworldly intelligence. Instead of distinct limbs, they possessed a dynamic, amorphous form that allowed them to undulate and flow like living liquid.

Their unique appearance defied conventional expectations, challenging anyone to define their true nature. While their demeanor exuded a childlike curiosity, their eyes betrayed an eerie focus as they locked onto their targets. Ollie, the courageous defender, braced for the encounter, realizing that these minions were not to be underestimated. As he prepared to confront the incoming wave, he couldn't help but marvel at the strange and captivating spectacle of these enigmatic beings that blurred the lines between fantasy and menace.

"Got it!" he replied, swinging his bat with renewed vigor, shattering the shadows like glass.

Cameron, fueled by adrenaline and a fierce protectiveness for his friends, fought tooth and nail alongside them. Every time he felt himself faltering, he would glance at Ellie's charm bracelet that she created from the box of amulets, feeling a surge of strength and resolve flow through him.

But despite their best efforts, the tide of battle was insurmountable. The minions were relentless, their numbers seemingly endless. For every shadow they vanquished, two more took its place. Gideon's spirit proved to be an ever-looming presence that wouldn't be ignored or defeated so easily, and they couldn't keep this up forever.

"Guys, we need to find another way!" he yelled over the din of battle, desperation clawing at his throat. "We can't keep fighting like this!"

"Agreed!" Ellie shouted back, sweat pouring down her face as she unleashed another shockwave. "But what do we do? We're running out of options!"

Cameron gritted his teeth, scanning the battlefield for any sign of hope. Shadows continued to close in around them, and time was running out. The fate of Gravewood hung in the balance.

Cameron's heart pounded in his chest as he looked around the battlefield, the cacophony of shrieks and yells echoing in his ears. This was a nightmare come to life, and the very air vibrated with malevolence.

"Stay close!" Ellie shouted through the chaos, her face a mask of determination. "We can't let them divide us!"

"Right," Ollie agreed, gripping his baseball bat tight enough for his knuckles to turn white. "Stick together, no matter what!"

The three friends formed a triangle formation, their backs against one another. They were surrounded by flickering shadows, the eerie glow of Gideon's spirit casting twisted shapes on the asphalt beneath them. The odds were stacked against them, but they refused to back down.

"Come on, then!" Cameron yelled defiantly at the encroaching darkness. "You want a fight? You've got one!"

"Let's take these things down, once and for all!" Ellie added, her eyes blazing with a fierce light.

"Here they come!" Ollie warned, his bat ready to strike.

As the first wave of minions crashed against their defenses, Cameron's mind raced. If they didn't find a weakness soon, the battle would be lost. But how could they defeat a force as powerful as Gideon Blackwell's spirit?

"Watch out!" Ellie cried suddenly, sending a shockwave, narrowly deflecting a shadowy tendril reaching for Cameron.

"Thanks!" he gasped, wiping sweat from his brow.

"Anytime," she replied through gritted teeth, her focus unwavering.

Cameron felt a deep bond between them, forged through shared adversity. They're more than friends – they're warriors, fighting side by side against an ancient evil.

"Ellie! Ollie!" he called out. "We can do this! Together, we're stronger than any spirit!"

"Right!" they responded in unison, their determination renewed.

With a surge of adrenaline, Cameron attacked the shadows with newfound ferocity. He channeled his fear and desperation into each blow, refusing to let Gideon's spirit gain the upper hand.

Cameron's heart pounded in his chest as he analyzed the battlefield, his eyes darting between the minions and Gideon's spirit. With every second that passed, the cold grip of dread tightened around him, but he refused to let it consume him. He needed a plan—a strategy—to turn the tide.

"Ollie, Ellie!" he shouted, his voice above the cacophony of the battle. "We need to create a barrier!"

The three friends moved quickly into position, their backs pressed against one another. Cameron closed his eyes, focusing all his energy on creating a barrier of light around them.

"Keep them at bay!" Ellie yelled, her hands crackling with electricity as she sent bolts of energy at the shadowy figures surrounding them.

"Got it!" Ollie replied, his bat swinging with deadly precision, cutting through the darkness like a scythe.

"Okay," Cameron muttered under his breath, sweat beading on his forehead. "We can't defend ourselves forever. We need to strike back and weaken Gideon's spirit."

"Maybe if we combine our powers?" Ellie suggested, her voice strained from the effort of maintaining her attacks.

"Let's do it!" Ollie agreed, his eyes full of determination.

Cameron nodded, his heart racing. "On my count... One, two, three!"

The trio unleashed a torrent of energy—a brilliant fusion of light, electricity, and raw force—hurtled toward Gideon's spirit. The impact shook the foundations of Gravewood

Middle School, sending shockwaves rippling through the air. For a moment, as though they succeeded, Gideon's spirit faltered, and the minions recoiled in fear.

But then the unthinkable happened.

Gideon's spirit roared with fury, its dark form growing larger and more menacing than before. A vortex of shadows swirled around it, consuming everything in its path and hurling debris through the air.

"Get down!" Cameron screamed, diving to the ground as a jagged piece of metal whizzed past his head.

"Ollie, are you okay?" Ellie cried out, her voice laced with panic.

"Y-yeah," Ollie stammered, blood trickling from a gash on his forehead. "But I don't know how much longer we can keep this up."

As the battle raged on, the friends found themselves facing losses they did not anticipate. Their barrier weakened, allowing more minions to slip through, and their exhaustion grew with each passing minute. Gideon's spirit grew stronger, feeding off their fear and despair.

"Guys, we need to find a way to stop him!" Cameron shouted, his desperation evident in his voice. "We can't let Gravewood fall!"

"Any ideas?" Ollie panted, his strength waning.

"None yet," Cameron admitted, gritting his teeth as he struggled to hold the barrier together. "But we can't give up. Not now."

"Never," Ellie agreed, her eyes blazing with determination, even as tears streamed down her face. "We fight to the end."

A bone-chilling gust of wind swept through the devastated middle school grounds, ruffling Cameron's hair as he stared at the ominous figure of Gideon Blackwell's spirit. Despite their best efforts to outmaneuver and weaken the malevolent force, their struggle was in vain.

"Nothing's working!" Ellie cried, her voice cracking with frustration as she hurled another surge of energy at the darkness surrounding Gideon. The attack only enrageed the spirit further, causing it to lash out with even more intensity.

"Keep trying!" Ollie shouted, his eyes darting from one side of the battlefield to the other, searching for any possible advantage they could exploit. He gritted his teeth as he focused his thoughts on the barrier holding back Gideon's minions. "We can't let Gravewood fall!"

"Guys," Cameron muttered, his heart pounding in his chest. "I can't shake the feeling that we're missing something important. Something crucial can turn the tide."

Ellie's gaze met his. "What do you mean?"

"Think about it—" Cameron's words cut off as a sudden explosion rocked the area, sending them all sprawling onto the debris-strewn ground. He groaned, pushing himself up and grimacing at the fresh scratches and bruises that covered his body. "Gideon's been around since the 1860s. There has to be some way to defeat him we haven't tried yet."

"Like what?" Ollie asked, his breath coming in ragged gasps. "We've thrown everything we've got at him, and nothing's worked!"

"Maybe we need to dig deeper into the town's history," Ellie suggested, wiping away tears mixed with sweat and blood. "Look for clues that might help us figure this out."

"Sounds like a plan," Cameron agreed, his voice trembling with the weight of their situation. "But first, we need to survive this battle."

"Everyone, focus!" Ollie commanded, clenching his fists and feeling the last remnants of his energy flow through him. "We can't afford to let doubt cripple us now!"

As they resumed their assault on Gideon's spirit, a gnawing sense of unease settled in Cameron's gut. He couldn't shake the feeling they were fighting a losing battle, and with each passing moment, the specter of defeat loomed closer. Despite their bravest efforts, doubts and insecurities began to worm their way into Cameron's thoughts.

"Is this it?" he wondered, his heart heavy with dread. "Are we going to lose Gravewood to Gideon Blackwell's dark reign?"

"Stay strong!" Ellie urged, her voice above the chaos and destruction. "We can't give up!"

"Never," Cameron whispered, the word more than a breath as he steeled himself against the encroaching darkness. "For Gravewood. For our families. For ourselves."

With a deafening crash, the roof of the middle school gymnasium caved in under Gideon's relentless assault. The group exchanged frantic glances, finally understanding they couldn't continue to fight like this any longer.

"Retreat!" Ollie yelled, his voice hoarse with desperation. "Get out now!"

The group scrambled to escape the collapsing building, leaping over debris and dodging falling beams. Cameron's heart pounded in his chest as he glanced back at the chaos behind him. He saw the terror etched on the faces of his friends, their resolve wavering beneath the crushing weight of defeat. They had given their all, but it hadn't been enough.

"Where do we go now?" Ellie gasped as they stumbled into the daylight outside, the dust from the ruined gymnasium choking the air.

"Somewhere safe," Cameron replied, his eyes scanning the devastated town around them. "We need to regroup and figure out a new plan."

"Look at this place," Ellie whispered, her gaze following Cameron's. Gravewood was a shadow of its former self, reduced to rubble and wreckage by Gideon's malevolent fury. The once-thriving community now lay in ruins, a grim testament to the spirit's insatiable lust for destruction.

"Is there even anything left to save?" Ollie questioned, his voice heavy with despair.

"Of course, there is," Ollie insisted, his jaw clenched in determination. "We can't let Gideon win. We have to keep fighting, no matter the odds."

"Ollie 's right," Ellie agreed, wiping away the grime and tears streaking her face. "We owe it to everyone who's lost something—lost someone—to this battle."

Cameron nodded, his thoughts racing as he considered their options. "We need to find out more about Gideon and uncover his weaknesses. There has to be something we've missed—a key to defeating him."

"Then let's get to work," Ellie said, her voice firm despite the tremor of fear still running through her. "We're not giving up on Gravewood—not now, not ever."

As the group moved cautiously through the streets, Cameron felt the weight of their responsibility. The town's fate rested in their hands, and the only way to save it was to vanquish Gideon's dark presence once and for all. But how could they hope to stand against such an overwhelmingly powerful force?

"Stay strong," Cameron whispered to himself, his knuckles white as he clenched his fists at his sides. "For Gravewood. For our families. For ourselves."

Cameron's heart raced as they moved further away from the wreckage of their town, desperately trying to come up with a new plan. The air was thick with the acrid smell of burnt wood, and the cries of frightened townspeople echoed in the distance.

"Wait," Ellie whispered, stopping in her tracks. Her piercing blue eyes scanned the area, her intuition telling her something amiss.

"Wha—?" Cameron began but was silenced by a wave of Ellie hand.

"Listen," she urged them, her breaths shallow. The group held still, straining their ears for any sign of danger. And then they heard it— faint, sinister laughter sent shivers down their spines.

"Is that... Gideon?" Ollie asked, his voice trembling as he clutched the strap of his backpack.

"Must be," Ellie muttered, gripping her camera tightly as if preparing for a confrontation.

"Okay," Cameron said, trying to keep his voice steady despite the terror coursing through him. "We need to be smart about this. Gideon knows we're here, so we have to stay one step ahead."

"Right," Ollie murmured, swallowing hard. "But how do we do that?"

"Divide and conquer," Cameron suggested, his mind racing with strategies. "If we split up, we'll have a better chance at finding information on Gideon's weaknesses and catching him off guard."

"Are you sure that's a good idea?" Ollie asked skeptically, his glasses slipping down his nose.

"Ollie's right," Ellie agreed. "What if we get cornered by Gideon or his minions? We'd be sitting ducks."

"Then we'll have to rely on each other," Cameron insisted, his fear of isolation momentarily forgotten. "We'll have to trust that we can hold our own until help arrives."

"Alright," Ellie said, taking a deep breath. "Let's split up and meet back here in an hour. And remember—no matter what happens, we won't give up on each other or Gravewood."

"Agreed," the others whispered, their determination evident in their eyes.

The group reluctantly separated, each heading off into the eerie darkness of the ruined town. Cameron's heart pounded in his chest as he ventured alone, the shadows swallowing him whole. The laughter grew louder with each step, filling him with dread.

"Stay strong," he repeated his earlier mantra to himself, trying to block out the menacing sound. "For Gravewood. For our families. For ourselves."

And then, as he turned a corner, he saw it—a flickering light in the distance, illuminating what appeared to be a hidden passageway. His curiosity piqued, and Cameron cautiously approached, only to find a cryptic message scrawled on the wall:

"Your darkest fears hold the key..."

As he read the words, a sudden gust of wind extinguished the light, plunging him into total darkness. The sinister laughter echoed even louder now, ringing in his ears like a twisted symphony of doom.

"Guys!" Cameron shouted.

CHAPTER 15

The moon hung low in the sky, casting an eerie glow over Gravewood's twisted branches while Cameron and his friends huddled together in a secluded clearing. The air was thick with tension as they tried to ignore the unsettling whispers of the wind carrying secrets from the shadows.

"Alright," Cameron started, his voice rising above the ghostly rustling of leaves. He clenched his fists, trying to conceal the tremble in his hands. "We need to talk about what happened." His messy brown hair fluttered in the cold breeze, and even with the mischievous grin he usually wore, his eyes looked weary.

"Yeah, that... That didn't go as planned," Natalie mumbled, her gaze fixed on the ground as she shuffled her feet nervously.

Ellie stood beside her, arms crossed and jaw set, a defiant glint in her eyes.

"Look, we lost this battle, but it's not over yet," Cameron continued, his voice growing stronger. He had always been the daring one in the group despite the fear of isolation that lurked beneath his surface. "Gideon Blackwell's spirit is still out there, and we can't give up now."

"Cam's right," Ellie chimed in, her voice calm and steady. "This isn't the end. We've faced setbacks before, and we've always come back stronger."

Cameron nodded at her encouraging words, feeling a renewed determination surge within him. He glanced around the circle, meeting the eyes of each of his friends, their faces illuminated by the pale moonlight. "You guys are my family," he confessed, swallowing hard as he fought the lump in his throat. "I can't do this alone, and I don't want to."

"Of course you're not alone, Cam," Ellie assured him, placing a hand on his shoulder. "We're in this together, no matter what."

"Exactly," Natalie agreed, finally looking up from the ground. "We'll find a way to stop Gideon Blackwell's spirit. We need to regroup and figure out our next move."

Cameron took a deep breath, letting the crisp air fill his lungs as he surveyed the dark forest around them, feeling the weight of the supernatural forces that threatened their town. Their journey was far from over, but with his friends by his side, they will face whatever horror lay ahead.

"Alright," he said, forcing a smile as he tried to rally their spirits. "We won't let fear or defeat hold us back. We're going to fight until Gravewood is safe again."

A shiver ran down Cameron's spine as the wind rustled through the trees, their branches casting eerie shadows on the forest floor. The moon above fought to break through the dense canopy of leaves, offering only a faint glow to guide their way. Ellie shifted her weight from one foot to another, her piercing blue eyes scanning the group before she spoke.

"Guys, we can't do this alone," she said, her voice filled with an urgency that echoed the looming threat of Gideon Black-well's spirit. "We need help. Our classmates, our neighbors, everyone in Gravewood has to stand together if we want to have a chance at defeating him."

Cameron nodded, his heart pounding in agreement as he imagined their small town united against the supernatural forces haunting them. Determination coursed through his veins, fueled by the knowledge they weren't alone in this fight.

"Alright," he said, clenching his fists as he envisioned their plan taking shape. "Let's split up and get the support we need. We'll get our classmates and go from there. I'll focus on the middle school students, while Ellie, you get the high school kids."

"Sounds like a plan," Ellie replied, her wavy blonde hair fluttering in the breeze. She looked around the group, her gaze lingering on each of their faces as she silently acknowledged the gravity of their task. "We have to make them understand that we need them now, and this isn't about us; it's about protecting our entire town from evil."

"Absolutely," Cameron agreed, feeling the weight of responsibility settle on his shoulders.

"Let's do this," Ellie chimed in, determination etched across her features. "We'll rally the town and stand together against Gideon Blackwell's spirit. We won't let him win."

Cameron watched as his friends dispersed, each heading off to fulfill their assigned tasks. As he made his way toward the middle school, he couldn't help but feel a mix of fear and hope for what lay ahead. The quiet sounds of the night whisper around him, reminding him he wasn't alone, they're all in this together.

And so, Cameron pressed on, his heart pounding with equal parts dread and anticipation. Their fight was far from over, but with each step he took, he felt more and more certain they had a chance to succeed.

For Gravewood, for his friends, and for himself, Cameron Hawthorne was ready to face whatever horrors awaited them.

The sun dipped behind the horizon, painting the sky with hues of orange and pink as Natalie and Ellie walked side by side through the quiet streets of Gravewood. The fading light cast eerie shadows on the houses they passed, a chilling reminder of the supernatural forces looming over their town.

"Alright," Natalie said, taking a deep breath as she approached the first door. "Here goes nothing." She rapped her knuckles against the wooden surface, her heart pounding in her chest. Beside her, Ellie clutched a handful of flyers detailing the community meetings they planned.

"Hi there!" Natalie greeted the woman who answered the door, forcing a smile onto her face despite her nerves. "We're organizing some meetings for the town to discuss the recent events happening in Gravewood."

The woman eyed them warily but took the flyer, scanning it quickly. "Sounds important," she remarked, her voice laced with concern. "I'll make sure to attend."

"Thank you," Ellie replied, relieved. "Please spread the word. We need everyone's help."

Meanwhile, at the middle school, Cameron stood in front of a sea of curious faces, the second gymnasium buzzing with hushed whispers that they have. He gripped the microphone tightly, his palms slick with sweat. This was the moment of truth.

"Good morning, everyone," he began, his voice wavering slightly. "As you all know, strange things have been happening in Gravewood lately. Things that can't be explained by science or logic."

He hesitated, glancing around at the students, who stared back at him with wide eyes. Taking a deep breath, he continued. "My friends and I have been investigating these occurrences, and we've discovered something terrifying. A malevolent spirit named Gideon Blackwell is responsible for the chaos that's been unfolding in our town."

Whispers rippled through the crowd, with some students exchanging skeptical glances while others appeared genuinely frightened. Cameron pressed on, recounting the chilling encounters they'd had with Gideon Blackwell's spirit and emphasized the danger he posed to all of Gravewood.

"Every one of us has a role to play in stopping this menace," Cameron concluded, his voice steadier now. "We need to stand together—students, teachers, parents—to protect our town and our loved ones. I'm asking you to join us in this fight."

As he stepped down from the stage, Cameron's heart raced with uncertainty. Had his words been enough? Would they rally behind him? Only time would tell.

Back on the streets, Natalie and Ellie moved from door to door, their determination unwavering as they spread the word about the supernatural threat that had befallen Gravewood. The shadows grew longer, but so did the list of people pledging to attend the community meetings.

"We're making a difference," Natalie whispered to Ellie as they walked toward another house, her voice tinged with exhaustion but also hope. "We're not alone in this."

"Right," Ellie agreed, her chin lifted in defiance. "We'll face this evil together, and we'll win."

As the last remnants of daylight vanished, the weight of the impending battle hangs over Gravewood like an oppressive fog. Yet, beneath it all, a spark of hope flickered—an ember waiting to ignite into a powerful blaze as the townspeople united against the darkness threatening to consume them.

Cameron watched his classmates' reactions. Their eyes widened, and murmurs rippled through the assembly hall. It cleared the gravity of the situation and finally hit home.

"Cam, I—I never knew it was this bad," stammered a boy from the front row, his voice shaking with newfound fear. "What can we do to help?"

"Me too," chimed in another classmate, her hands trembling as she clutched at her backpack. "We can't let Gravewood fall prey to this... this monster."

Cameron looked out into the sea of determined faces, his heart swelling with hope. "We need everyone's help. We must research Gideon Blackwell's history, find weaknesses, anything that will give us an edge in this battle." The students nodded, their resolve hardening like iron.

"Count me in," declared a girl with short black hair, her eyes burning with determination. "I've got access to my dad's library. There's loads of old newspapers and town records in there."

"Great!" Cameron beamed, his fear of isolation momentarily forgotten. "Let's meet after school and start working together. We'll need all the help we can get."

As the middle school students dispersed, their hearts heavy but filled with purpose, Ellie stood outside the high school gymnasium, her throat dry with anticipation. Convincing the older students wouldn't be easy, but she couldn't let her fear of failure hold her back now.

"Hey, listen up!" she called out, her voice echoing through the cavernous space. "We need your help. Gravewood is in danger—danger brought upon us by Gideon Blackwell's spirit."

Skeptical glances were exchanged among the high school students, but they fell silent, giving Ellie a chance to make her case. She recounted the chilling encounters with Gideon Blackwell's spirit, the eerie whispers haunting their dreams, and the dread settled over their town.

"Time is running out," she warned, her blue eyes imploring them to believe. "We have to unite against this supernatural threat."

A tall boy with a football jersey stepped forward, his brow furrowed in thought. "What's your plan, then?"

"Research and knowledge are our weapons," Ellie replied, her voice firm. "We'll work alongside the middle school students to uncover Gideon Blackwell's past and find a way to defeat him once and for all."

"Count us in," declared another student, her arms crossed defiantly. Soon, more and more voices joined in until the gymnasium echoed with pledges of support.

As the high school students filed out of the gym, a new-found sense of unity and determination took root within each of them. Gravewood might be facing its darkest hour, but its people would not go down without a fight. Together, they would stand against the ominous shadow of Gideon Blackwell's spirit, refusing to let fear rule their lives any longer.

A canopy of dark clouds shrouded the sun as Natalie and Ellie approached the worn-down house on the edge of town. The air was thick with the scent of damp earth, leaves crunching underfoot as they knocked on the weathered door. It creaked open to reveal a middle-aged woman with graying hair and stern eyes.

"Good afternoon, ma'am," Natalie began, her voice wavering only slightly in spite of her pounding heart. "We're here to talk about the strange occurrences happening in Gravewood."

The woman's mouth tightened, suspicion flaring in her gaze. "What's it to you, children?"

"Please," Ellie interjected, her small frame radiating determination. "We believe these events are connected to Gideon Blackwell's spirit, and we need your help to stop him."

For a moment, silence hung heavy between them. Then, the woman's expression softened, and she gestured for them to come inside. As they entered, the musty smell of old books filled their nostrils, and the faint sound of wind chimes echoed from somewhere within the dimly lit house.

"Alright," the woman sighed, folding her hands in her lap. "Tell me what you know."

As Natalie and Ellie shared their experiences, the woman listened intently, her concern growing more evident with each passing word. By the time they finished, she had made up her mind.

"Count me in," she declared, her voice firm with resolve. "And I'll gather some friends who won't shy away from the fight either."

Relief washed over Natalie and Ellie like a warm wave. Every ally counted in this battle, and they're grateful for the support.

Days later, the group reconvened in their secret spot deep within Gravewood, the shadows of tall trees casting eerie patterns on the ground. Each member shared their progress, the air electric with a mixture of excitement and trepidation.

"Thanks to your speeches, we've got the middle school and high school students on board," Cameron said, his eyes sparkling with pride. "And Natalie and Ellie managed to recruit a group of townspeople who are willing to help us."

"Even Mrs. Thompson, who's always been skeptical of the supernatural, agreed to join our cause," Ellie added, her voice brimming with astonishment.

As they discussed their growing number of allies, uncertainty flickered in Natalie's brown eyes. Each person they enlisted faced the terrifying unknown, yet she couldn't shake the feeling that this was their only chance to save Gravewood from Gideon Blackwell's malevolent grip.

"Are we sure about this?" she asked, her voice a whisper. "We're putting so many people at risk."

"Defeating Gideon Blackwell is our responsibility," Cameron reminded her gently, his gaze unwavering. "But we can't do it alone. We need everyone's support to stand a chance."

"Besides," Ellie chimed in, her fiery curls bouncing as she nodded resolutely, "we're all in this together now. And together, we'll protect our town from whatever horrors lie ahead."

As they stood there, united by their common goal, the dark clouds overhead began to part, revealing slivers of sunlight pierced through the oppressive gloom. It was as if the very sky itself acknowledged the strength of their resolve, offering a glimmer of hope in the face of the darkness threatened to consume them all.

Huddled around a worn, wooden table in the dimly lit room, Cameron and his friends began to discuss the logistics of their upcoming battle against Gideon Blackwell's spirit. The damp air hung heavy with anticipation, and shadows danced upon the walls as the flickering candlelight cast an eerie glow across their faces.

"Alright," Cameron said, taking a deep breath and brushing a hand through his messy brown hair. "We've got classmates from both middle and high school on board, and Natalie and Ellie have rallied a number of townspeople to our cause. It's time we figure out how to organize everyone for this final showdown."

Ellie nodded, her blue eyes reflecting determination. "I agree. We need to assign specific roles to everyone so we can maximize our collective strength."

"Let's start with the students," suggested Cameron, tapping his fingers nervously on the table. "What do you think they should be responsible for?"

"Maybe they can help with research?" chimed in Natalie. "You know, dig up more information about Gideon Black-well and any potential weaknesses we might exploit."

"Good idea," agreed Ellie, her fiery curls bouncing as she spoke. "And some of the older students, like Ellie's high school friends, can join us on the front lines during the battle."

Cameron's mind raced, trying to process all the information and strategize the best way to utilize everyone's skills. He glanced around the table at his friends, feeling the weight of their trust in him. He couldn't let them down.

"Exactly," he said, his voice firm with resolve. "The high schoolers will be crucial in helping us face whatever supernatural forces Gideon throws at us. As for the townspeople, I think it's important that they support us in any way they can—whether it's providing supplies, offering shelter, or even being there to lend a hand when we need it."

As they continued to devise their plan, the energy in the room shifted. The uncertainty and fear that plagued them earlier were gradually being replaced by hope and determination. It was a testament to the power of unity and teamwork—something they would need in order to defeat Gideon Blackwell's spirit.

"Listen up, everyone," Cameron began, his eyes locked on each of his friends as he spoke. "I know this won't be easy. We're going to face things we've never seen before, and we'll be tested in ways we can't even imagine. But I truly believe our collective strength is what will ultimately prevail against Gideon Blackwell's spirit."

"United, we are unstoppable," he continued, his words gaining momentum. "We have a chance to save Gravewood from the darkness that threatens it, but only if we stand together—classmates, townspeople, all of us. Remember, no matter how tough it gets or how scared we might be."

The candlelight flickered, casting shadows to mimic the unwavering determination etched onto their faces. It was clear Cameron's words struck a chord, uniting them more closely than ever before. They're ready for the battle ahead, armed with the knowledge they're stronger together than they ever be apart. And as they prepared to face the supernatural forces that threatened Gravewood, they would not back down.

Cameron looked around at the faces illuminated by the flickering candlelight, a sea of determination and courage spread across the makeshift assembly in the heart of Gravewood. Fear lingered at the edges of their expressions, but it was overshadowed by the fierce resolve that bound them all together.

"Thank you all for being here," Cameron said, his voice steady despite the churning anxiety inside him. "We're about to face something bigger than ourselves, something that haunted this town for generations. But I know that if we stand united, there's nothing we can't overcome."

A murmur of agreement rippled through the crowd, echoing softly amidst the rustling leaves and crisp autumn breeze. The scent of damp earth and burning candles mingled with the faint undercurrent of fear tinged the air.

"Remember," Ellie interjected, her blue eyes intense as she surveyed their gathered allies, "each of us plays a crucial role in this battle. Our strength lies in our numbers and in the bonds we share with one another."

Cameron nodded, feeling the weight of their mission settle onto his shoulders like a heavy cloak. He locked eyes with his friends—Ollie, Natalie, Ellie, and Ellie—and drew comfort from their unwavering support. Despite his fear of isolation, in his heart, they would never abandon him, as he would never forsake them.

"Gravewood needs us now more than ever," he continued, his voice gaining confidence as he spoke. "Are you ready to face the darkness? Are you prepared to fight for our town and protect our loved ones?"

A resounding chorus of "Yes!" erupted from the gathering, filling the air with a palpable energy crackle with electricity. The hairs on the back of Cameron's neck stood on end as a surge of adrenaline coursed through his veins.

"Then let's stand together," he declared, his voice echoing through the trees. "Together, we will defeat Gideon Blackwell's spirit and free Gravewood from its grip."

As one, they raised their fists in solidarity, and their voices united in a battle cry. The shadows of the forest recoiled from the power of their unity, retreating into the darkness as they prepared to face an evil lurking within Gravewood for far too long.

Cameron glanced at his friends once more, their faces etched with determination as they stood shoulder-to-shoulder with their classmates and townspeople. Their collective strength shone like a beacon amidst the encroaching darkness, a testament to the power of unity and the unwavering human spirit.

There would be no turning back now. They're ready to confront the supernatural forces that threatened their town, and they would not rest until Gravewood was safe once more. With a deep breath, Cameron tightened his grip on the resolve that bound them all together and stepped forward into the unknown.

CHAPTER 16

The dimly lit basement of Gravewood Middle School was a place where shadows loomed large, and the past clung to the air like damp fog. The flickering, yellow glow of bare bulbs swayed above them, casting eerie pools of light onto the dusty concrete floor. A cacophony of creaking floorboards echoed throughout the space as if restless spirits whispered from every corner.

"Are we really doing this?" Cameron asked, his voice over the unsettling sounds surrounding them. His unruly brown hair framed a face filled with both fear and determination. Despite the shiver running down his spine, he couldn't let his friends down now—not when they were all counting on him.

"Of course," Ellie replied, her piercing blue eyes searching the darkness as she clutched an old book to her chest. "We've come this far, and it's time for us to face Gideon Blackwell's spirit once and for all." Her love for history drove her to uncover the truth about the town's supernatural mystery, but now she feared failing her friends in their most desperate hour.

Ollie adjusted his glasses and nodded, his gentle demeanor masking a fierce loyalty to the group. The timidity in his eyes belied the courage that lay beneath. "We can do this, guys," he said, his voice quivering with conviction. "We need to trust in each other and follow the plan."

Natalie, with her dark brown hair falling around her shoulders, gripped her camera tightly. Her artistic nature allowed her to capture moments others might miss, but this situation was unlike anything she had ever faced. She tried to focus on documenting the supernatural occurrences, even as her fear of the unknown threatened to overwhelm her.

"Right," Ellie agreed, her curly red hair framing her petite figure. She took a deep breath, channeling her sense of justice into the task at hand. "We're going to break this curse and set Gideon's spirit free. We won't let him control us any longer."

The five friends formed a tight circle, their hearts pounding in unison as they braced themselves for the confrontation looming ahead. They were determined to vanquish the evil haunted Gravewood, no matter how terrifying the ordeal might be.

"Here goes nothing," Cameron whispered, his voice trembling with a mix of excitement and dread. The others nodded, each one silently vowing to give their all in the battle against Gideon Blackwell's malevolent spirit. With the fate of their town at stake, they had no choice but to confront the darkness head-on—and hope they emerged victorious on the other side.

The air in the basement grew colder as an unseen force settled over them. Shadows flickered along the walls, and a sudden gust of wind swept through the dimly lit space as if to announce the arrival of something sinister.

"Guys," Cameron whispered, his eyes wide with fear as he stared at the empty spot before them. "I think... I think he's here."

As if on cue, a tall, gaunt figure materialized in front of them, its hollow cheeks and piercing dark eyes emanating an aura of malevolence, sending shivers down their spines. Gideon Blackwell's spirit arrived.

"Wh-what do we do now?" Ollie stuttered, his hand shaking as it grasped the candle lighter. He glanced nervously at his friends, seeking reassurance in their determined expressions.

"Stay strong," Ellie urged, her voice wavering but resolute. "We can't let him intimidate us. We have the power to break this curse."

Ellie clenched her fists, her gaze locked on Gideon's menacing form. She was ready to face whatever supernatural forces he might unleash upon them. "We've come this far," she said quietly. "We can't back down now."

As though he sensed the group's resolve, Gideon's spirit unleashed his powers. Objects around the basement began to levitate, their forms twisting and distorting as if under some unnatural influence. The shadows on the walls came alive, swirling menacingly around the room like a dark storm. The chilling wind intensified, howling through the basement as if attempting to snuff out the flickering candles.

"Keep going," Natalie encouraged, her camera raised to capture the supernatural energy in a single photograph. "We can do this. Together."

Cameron's heart pounded in his chest, his thoughts racing as he focused on the task ahead. They had to break Gideon's hold on their town, but the sheer malevolence radiating from the spirit threatened to shatter his resolve. Gathering his courage, he stepped forward and addressed Gideon directly.

"Your reign of terror ends now," he declared, his voice strong despite the fear gripping him. "You won't control us any longer."

The other friends joined Cameron in facing down Gideon's spirit, each one playing a vital role in the battle against the darkness that consumed their town for so long. As they stared into the depths of Gideon Blackwell's dark eyes, they refused to let their fears dictate their actions. They united in their determination, ready to risk everything to save Gravewood from its haunted past.

Cameron clenched his fists, sweat beading on his brow, as he focused on the incantation scribbled hastily on the crumpled sheet of paper. The air around them grew colder, and the stench of rotting wood and damp earth filled their nostrils. He glanced at his friends, each one bracing themselves for their respective roles in the ritual.

"Ready?" he whispered, the sound over the cacophony of Gideon's supernatural fury. His friends nodded, their determined gazes meeting his own, and Cameron took a deep breath to steady himself.

Cameron's eyes flickered with a mix of trepidation and determination as he traced the ancient text within the worn pages of the book. The air seemed to thicken with anticipation as he carefully enunciated each word, his voice resonating with a resonance that hinted at a power long dormant. Symbols and glyphs adorned the pages, coming alive with an ethereal glow as if responding to the cadence of the incantation.

"Absum ab terra, exstinguere ignem," he began, his voice quaking with both fear and determination. "Discede a tenebris, ad lumen redire."

As the words left his lips, the basement trembled in response. The levitating objects began to shake violently, threatening to crash down upon them. But Cameron continued, unwavering in his resolve. He couldn't let his friends down—not now, not when they were so close to saving Gravewood.

"Libera nos a malo, dissolvi catenas," he recited, his voice growing stronger with each word. "Gideon Blackwell, ab hoc mundo discedas!"

Ellie joined in, her powerful chant harmonizing with Cameron's recitation. The air vibrated with energy, and the oppressive atmosphere began to lighten ever so slightly. The power of the ancient ritual worked its way through the foundation of the basement.

"Is it working?" Ollie asked nervously, scanning the room for any signs of change. His eyes darted from corner to corner, scrutinizing every shadow danced across the walls.

"Focus, Ollie," Ellie warned, her gaze locked on the formation of artifacts she carefully arranged earlier. "We can't afford any mistakes."

"Give it time," Natalie murmured, her camera ready to capture the essence of the curse as it broke. "It has to work."

Cameron felt the weight of their expectations on his shoulders, but he couldn't falter now. He came too far and risked too much. With a final surge of determination, he raised his voice, drowning out the howling wind and the haunting whispers that threatened to overpower him.

"Absum ab terra, exstinguere ignem! Discede a tenebris, ad lumen redire!" he shouted, his voice echoing throughout the basement as the air crackled with supernatural energy.

He only hoped it would be enough to break Gideon's curse and set them all free.

Ellie's fingers moved with precision, her intuition guiding her as she placed each artifact and relic in a specific pattern on the cold basement floor as the book instructed. The dim light flickered overhead, casting eerie shadows dancing along with her movements. Her heart raced in her chest, but she refused to let the fear of failure consume her.

"Okay, Ellie," Cameron said, his voice laced with both concern and admiration. "What's next?"

"Ollie, we need you to light the candles now," Ellie instructed, her blue eyes locked onto the intricate design she created. The pattern held the key to breaking the curse, and her hands remained steady despite the intensity of the moment.

"Got it," Ollie replied, his gentle nature shining through even as he battled his own insecurities. He took a deep breath and began lighting the candles placed strategically around the basement. As the flames flickered to life, they cast haunting shadows on the walls, creating an atmosphere both mesmerizing and terrifying.

"Is this really going to work?" Ollie asked, his voice wavering as his glasses slipped down his nose. He pushed them back up nervously, watching the flames dance in the darkness.

"We have to believe it will," Ellie responded, her determination unwavering. She sensed the powerful energy coursing through the room, and if they all played their parts correctly, they might stand a chance against Gideon Blackwell's spirit.

As Ollie finished lighting the last candle, the room came alive with supernatural energy. Shadows swirled around them, and a chilling wind blew through the basement, sending shivers down their spines.

Natalie's fingers tightened around her camera, her dark eyes scanning the shadowy basement for the perfect shot. Capturing the essence of the curse was vital to their plan, and she couldn't afford to falter now. Her heart raced as she noticed the way the candlelight flickered across the artifacts Ellie arranged, casting eerie shadows dancing with malicious intent.

"Okay, Natalie, you can do this," she whispered to herself, her voice above the howling wind surging through the basement. Taking a deep breath, she raised her camera, her artistic eye homing in on the swirling darkness that enveloped the room.

"Ellie, are you ready?" Natalie asked, her voice wavering slightly.

"Ready as I'll ever be," Ellie replied, her petite frame tense as she prepared to recite the powerful chant that would help them break the curse. Her curly red hair whipped wildly around her face, but her green eyes remained focused and determined.

The moment hung suspended, the air thick with anticipation and fear. And then, without warning, Natalie pressed the shutter button as Ellie began to chant.

"Ex tenebris lux surgat," Ellie's voice rang out, strong and unwavering despite the chaos surrounding them. "Ignis purgat omne malum."

Natalie could almost feel the supernatural energy pulsating within the photograph she'd captured, the image of the curse seemingly alive with malevolence. She fought back the urge to shudder, knowing she needed to remain focused on their mission.

"Stay strong, everyone," she thought, watching as Ellie continued to chant, her voice growing louder and more powerful with each word. "We can do this together."

"Per potentiam veritatis, liberemur a vinculis obscuritatis," Ellie intoned, her voice echoing throughout the dimly lit basement.

As the chant filled the air, a sudden surge of hope went through Natalie. They were finally confronting the curse that haunted Gravewood for so long, and she couldn't help but feel a sense of pride in their bravery.

"Keep going, Ellie," Natalie urged silently, her grip on the camera tightening as she prepared to capture more images of the supernatural energy at work. "We're almost there."

The wind howled louder, the shadows grew darker, and the very air electrified with power. But through it all, Ellie's voice remained strong and unwavering, her words acting as a beacon of light amidst the darkness.

"Per ardua ad astra, vincemus tenebras," Ellie finished, her final words ringing out like a battle cry.

The air in the basement held its breath as the last echoes of Ellie's chant faded away. A sudden stillness swept through the room as if the atoms around them paused to listen. Natalie's heart pounded against her ribcage, anticipation and fear mingling within her chest like a volatile potion.

"Is it... working?" Cameron whispered.

Natalie held the camera tightly in her hands, willing herself to remain focused on capturing any sign of change. Around them, the eerie manifestations began to subside. The objects that had been levitating crashed back to the floor, the shadows retreated into their corners, and the chilling wind ceased its relentless howl as though the supernatural forces gripped the basement were gradually losing their power.

"Look!" Ollie exclaimed, pointing towards the center of the room where Gideon Blackwell's spirit stood. His gaunt figure, once radiating malevolence, now appeared to waver and shimmer like a mirage.

"I think we did it, guys," Ellie breathed, awe evident in her voice.

"Stay focused," Natalie reminded her friends as she snapped another photograph, the flash briefly illuminating the tall figure before them. "We need to make sure Gideon's spirit is truly released."

Gideon's eyes, once dark and piercing, were now distant and almost mournful. As they watched, his form began to dissipate, the edges blurring and fading into the dimly lit air of the basement. His once-menacing presence softened, leaving behind an ethereal glow filling the room with a sense of calm and peace.

"It's happening..." Ollie muttered, awestruck.

"Remember what we learned," Cameron said, his voice firm but laced with empathy. "Gideon was once a man like any of us. He doesn't deserve to be trapped like this."

As the last remnants of Gideon's spirit vanished, Natalie felt a strange surge of relief mixed with sadness. They had done it; they freed him from his vengeful state. But she couldn't help but wonder what kind of life he lived before becoming the tormented figure they encountered.

"Gravewood is finally free of this curse," Ellie whispered, her eyes glistening with unshed tears. "We did it, guys. We really did it."

The last wisps of Gideon's spirit dissolved into the air, leaving the basement bathed in a newfound tranquility. The once dim room now glowed with a sense of restored balance as if the darkness that plagued it for so long was finally vanquished.

"Is it... over?" Ollie asked hesitantly, his glasses fogging up from the lingering chill.

Cameron nodded, his face flushed with relief and triumph. "We did it. We broke the curse."

As the reality of their success settled in, an infectious wave of elation took hold of the group. They huddled together, arms around one another, their laughter reverberating through the now peaceful basement. Even Ellie, who often kept her emotions under wraps, allowed herself a rare grin as she squeezed Ellie's hand.

"Can you believe we actually did it?" Natalie exclaimed, her voice quivering with excitement. "Gideon's spirit is free, and Gravewood can finally start healing."

"Who would've thought that we'd be the ones to break a century-old curse?" Cameron added, his mischievous grin making a triumphant return. "I guess we're not a bunch of ordinary kids after all."

"Ordinary? Speak for yourself, Cam," Ellie teased, her eyes sparkling with pride. "We're anything but ordinary. And don't forget, our journey isn't finished yet."

"Ellie's right," Ollie chimed in, his own insecurities momentarily forgotten as he basked in the shared victory. "We may have won this battle, but there's still so much more to uncover in Gravewood."

"Let's enjoy this moment for now," Ellie suggested, her blue eyes gazing at each of her friends in turn. "We'll need our strength for whatever lies ahead. But tonight, we celebrate."

Cameron raised an imaginary glass, a playful glint in his eyes. "To us, the Gravewood curse breakers!"

"Cheers!" they all echoed, their laughter and joy filling the once-eerie corners of the basement.

For a fleeting moment, the weight of the supernatural world fell away, replaced by the simple warmth of friendship and shared accomplishment. They stood together as one, a formidable force against whatever darkness still lingered in the shadows of Gravewood. And although uncertainty awaited them beyond the basement's walls, they would face it together.

As the laughter subsided, Cameron looked around at his friends, their faces a mixture of joy and exhaustion. The basement, once a place of terror, was now a sanctuary of victory. The flickering lights dance in celebration, casting a warm glow over the group.

"Alright," Natalie finally spoke up, her fingers still tightly gripping her camera. "What's next? We've broken this curse, but there's more out there. I can feel it."

Cameron nodded, his eyes narrowing in determination. "Yeah, there's definitely more to Gravewood than meets the eye," he agreed, recalling the countless other strange occurrences they stumbled upon throughout the town.

Ellie began pacing the floor, her thoughts racing as she considered the possibilities. "We should probably start by investigating some of the other unsolved mysteries in town," she suggested, her blue eyes alight with excitement. "I know Millie mentioned a few cases that have never been solved."

"Sounds like a plan," Ellie chimed in, her small stature belying her fierce determination. "But first, we need to rest. We can't tackle any more supernatural forces if we're running on empty."

"Ellie's right," Ollie agreed, pushing his glasses up the bridge of his nose. "Besides, we've earned a little break after all this." He gestured around the basement, a smile tugging at the corner of his mouth.

"Okay," Cameron acquiesced, knowing his friends were right. "We'll regroup tomorrow and figure out our next move. But for now, let's enjoy this moment."

"Cameron's right," Natalie said, snapping one last photo of the group, their triumphant smiles caught forever in time. "We'll face whatever comes next together, like we always have."

The group slowly made their way upstairs, leaving the now peaceful basement behind. As they stepped out into the dimly lit hallway, an unspoken promise hung in the air—a vow to protect Gravewood and its people from the darkness lurked within.

As they walked down the corridor towards the exit, Cameron couldn't help but feel a sense of hope and anticipation swelling inside him. The mysteries of Gravewood were far from solved, but one thing was certain: as long as they had each other, there was nothing they couldn't overcome.

CHAPTER 17

The morning sun cast long shadows across Gravewood, illuminating the scars left by the supernatural events that plagued the town. Cameron Hawthorne stood at the edge of the shattered town square, his mischievous grin replaced by a look of somber disbelief as he surveyed the wreckage. Windows shattered like broken teeth, and once-sturdy brick buildings now leaned precariously as if they'd been built by children with trembling hands.

"Can't believe this," Cameron muttered, kicking a shard of glass that skittered across the pavement. He took a deep breath, inhaling the scent of burnt wood and damp earth; remnants of the storm accompanied the nightmarish chaos.

"Hey, Cam!" called out Ellie, her wavy blonde hair fluttering in the breeze as she approached him. "We're gathering in front of Millie's library to help clean up. You coming?"

Cameron glanced over at his friend, noting the determination in her piercing blue eyes. She was shaken as him but unwilling to let fear hold her back. With a nod, he joined her, and together, they walked to where the townspeople congregated.

Millie Finch, the elderly librarian, directed groups of volunteers as they worked tirelessly to remove debris and shore up weakened structures. Her gray hair was pulled into a tight bun, and her spectacles perched on her nose as she consulted a clipboard. A group of middle schoolers, including Ollie Thompson, Natalie Martinez, and Ellie Grayson, worked together to clear rubble from the street.

"Alright, everyone!" Principal Warren's voice rang out, rallying the crowd. "Let's work together and get Gravewood back to its former glory!"

Cameron couldn't help but admire the principal's courage despite knowing how much he feared the supernatural. The townspeople, united in their determination, began the arduous task of rebuilding their beloved town.

"Watch your step, Cam," Ellie cautioned as they approached a pile of debris. They heard the sounds of hammers and saws mingling with the distant murmur of conversation.

"Thanks, Ellie," Cameron said, wiping the sweat from his brow. He looked around at the people working side by side, their individual fears momentarily forgotten in the face of collective resolve. As he picked up a piece of broken wood, he couldn't help but wonder what lay ahead for Gravewood and its inhabitants. The shadows have been cast over the town have not quite banished; they lingered at the edges, waiting for an opportunity to strike again.

"Let's do this," Ellie said, her voice resolute. "Together."

Cameron nodded, his heart swelling with pride. Despite the darkness surrounded them, the spirit of Gravewood unbreakable. And as long as they faced the unknown together, there was nothing they couldn't overcome.

Cameron's gaze drifted across the bustling scene, eventually landing on a lone figure standing at the edge of the crowd. Mrs. Eleanor Hawthorne, his own mother, looked like a pale ghost amidst the chaos. Her eyes were wide and haunted, and her hands were wringing the hem of her cardigan nervously. It was clear the traumatic events they had all experienced struck a particular chord within her, leaving her hesitant to join in the efforts to rebuild.

"Mom," Cameron called out, approaching her with concern. "Are you okay?"

Mrs. Hawthorne jumped slightly at the sound of her son's voice. She forced a weak smile and nodded, though the fear evident in her trembling hands. "Oh, yes, dear. I'm just... worried, I suppose.

"About what?" Cameron asked gently, sensing there was more to her hesitation.

"About everything," she admitted, her voice barely audible. "What if those awful things come back? What if we can't stop them this time?"

"Hey," Cameron said softly, placing a comforting hand on her shoulder. "We faced down the darkness once, and we'll do it again if we have to. But right now, we need to focus on rebuilding. We can't let fear hold us back."

Mrs. Hawthorne hesitated, her eyes lingering on the destruction around them. "I know you're right, but... I'm not sure I have the strength to face it all again."

"None of us are sure," Cameron replied, understanding her concerns. "But we don't have to do it alone. We have each other, and that's what makes us strong."

A moment passed as Mrs. Hawthorne considered her son's words. With a deep breath, she straightened her spine, determination flickering in her eyes. "You're right, Cameron. We can't let fear rule our lives."

"Exactly," he said, his heart swelling with pride. "Now, let's go help the others. Together, we can overcome anything."

As they walked towards the crowd of townspeople, Cameron couldn't help but feel a sense of hope amidst the ruins. No matter what challenges lay ahead, they would face them as one, united by their shared experiences and the knowledge they're stronger when they stood together. The darkness may still linger at the edges, but the light of their collective courage would keep it at bay, pushing back against the shadows that sought to consume them all.

As the townspeople continued to work together, clearing debris and making repairs, Mrs. Hawthorne found herself standing on the outskirts of the cemetery, staring at the now-closed crypt that had been one of the epicenters of the supernatural events. The earth was still disturbed from when the spirits had risen, and the air was thick with a lingering chill. Her heart raced in her chest as she remembered the terrifying apparitions and the eerie whispers that haunted her dreams.

"Mom?" Cameron's voice broke through her reverie. "Are you sure you're ready for this?"

She glanced back at her son, who stood a few steps behind her, concern etched on his face. Swallowing her fear, she nodded. "I have to be. We can't move forward if we don't confront what happened."

Cameron offered her a small smile and stepped up beside her. "We'll do it together."

Taking a deep breath, Mrs. Hawthorne forced herself to take one step, then another, slowly moving closer to the crypt. Each footfall felt like a victory against the fear gripped her, even as her pulse pounded in her ears.

"Remember," Cameron murmured, sensing her struggle, "you're not alone."

"Thank you," she whispered, her voice shaking slightly. "Your support means the world to me."

They reached the entrance of the crypt, its once-ominous door now cracked and broken from the force of the supernatural outburst. Mrs. Hawthorne hesitated, her hand hovering over the cold iron handle. Taking another steadying breath, she grasped it and pushed the door open, revealing the dark interior.

The smell of damp earth and mold assaulted her nostrils, and she shivered involuntarily. Cameron squeezed her hand reassuringly, and together, they stepped inside. As they ventured further into the crypt, the darkness pressed in on them, but Mrs. Hawthorne refused to let it stop her.

"Look," Cameron whispered, pointing to the far corner where a single beam of sunlight pierced the gloom, illuminating a small patch of ground. "Even in the darkest places, there's still light."

Mrs. Hawthorne smiled, tears pricking at the corners of her eyes as the weight of her fear lifted slightly. "You're right. We can't let the darkness win."

Though her heart still raced and her palms slick with sweat, she took another step forward, each movement a testament to her newfound determination. The crypt may have been a place of horror and despair, but together, they would reclaim it from the shadows that once held sway.

As they left, Mrs. Hawthorne couldn't help but feel a sense of accomplishment. There would be more challenges ahead, moments when fear threatened to overwhelm her once again. But with Cameron by her side and the power of their love and friendship, she was certain they could face whatever came next.

"Thank you," she told her son as they stood outside the crypt, hand in hand. "I couldn't have done it without you."

Cameron grinned, his eyes shining with pride. "We're in this together, Mom. Always."

The sun was beginning to set, casting a warm glow over the town of Gravewood. The air filled with the scent of sawdust and freshly turned earth as the townspeople continued their rebuilding efforts. Amid the bustling activity, Natalie sat alone on a bench outside the school, her camera hanging limply in her hands.

"Can't get inspired?" Ellie asked, taking a seat beside her friend. Natalie's eyes remained glued to the ground, her fingers tracing the intricate patterns etched into the camera's metal casing.

"Ever since everything happened... I can't seem to find the beauty in anything anymore," Natalie admitted, her voice over the distant sounds of hammers and drills.

Ellie reached out, placing a comforting hand on Natalie's shoulder. "It's okay to feel that way, you know. We've all been through a lot."

"I know, but..." Natalie sighed, lifting her gaze to meet Ellie's. "Photography has always been my escape, my way of making sense of the world. And now, it's like I've lost that connection."

"Maybe you're looking at it from the wrong angle," Ellie suggested, gently nudging Natalie with her elbow. "Instead of trying to find beauty in what's left of Gravewood, think about the strength and resilience it took for this town to come together and rebuild."

Natalie considered Ellie's words, her brow furrowed in thought. As she glanced around the schoolyard, she noticed a group of children laughing and playing amidst the debris, their youthful energy undiminished by the recent events.

"See?" Ellie said, following Natalie's gaze. "They're making the best of a difficult situation. And even though their world changed, they're still finding joy in the simplest things."

"Maybe you're right," Natalie conceded, raising her camera to her eye and focusing the lens on the children's smiling faces. The shutter clicked, capturing a moment of pure, unadulterated happiness in the midst of chaos. "Maybe I needed a new perspective."

"Sometimes that's all it takes," Ellie agreed, beaming at her friend. "Remember, we're all in this together. We can lean on each other when things get tough."

"Thanks, Ellie," Natalie said, her spirits lifting as she continued to snap photos, each image a testament to the strength and resilience of the human spirit.

As the sun dipped below the horizon, painting the sky with vibrant hues of orange and purple, Natalie felt a renewed sense of purpose coursing through her veins. There would be more challenges ahead, moments when her motivation waned and inspiration elusive. But as long as she had her friends by her side and the power of their love and support, she was certain they could face whatever came next.

As the sun began to set, casting long shadows across Gravewood, Ollie found himself struggling with his own personal challenge. Despite trying to focus on helping the others restore the town, he couldn't shake the constant worry that gnawed at him like a ravenous beast. His fear of abandonment was a heavy weight, threatening to drag him under.

"Ollie," called Cameron, noticing his friend's distant expression. "You okay, buddy?"

"Uh... yeah," Ollie mumbled, forcing a smile that didn't quite reach his eyes. "Just thinking."

Cameron frowned, concern etched into his youthful features. "About what? You've been quiet all day."

"Nothing important," Ollie lied, unwilling to burden his friends with his insecurities. He busied himself by picking up pieces of broken glass from a shattered window.

"Hey, if it's bothering you, it's important," Cameron insisted, placing a hand on Ollie's shoulder. "You can talk to me, you know."

"Thanks," Ollie whispered, feeling the warmth of Cameron's touch seeping through his shirt. The connection offered a momentary sense of stability amidst the chaos. "I just... sometimes I feel like everyone's going to leave me behind."

"Leave you behind?" Cameron echoed, his brow furrowing in confusion. "Why would you think that?"

"Because..." Ollie hesitated, swallowing the lump in his throat. "People sometimes do."

"Ollie, we're not going anywhere," Cameron promised, his voice firm and unwavering. "We're a team, remember? We stick together, no matter what."

"Even when things get really hard?" Ollie asked, searching Cameron's eyes for reassurance.

"Especially then," Cameron declared, offering a genuine grin. "Now, how about we find something to help get your mind off things? Maybe you can try doing something new. What's something you've always wanted to do?"

"Actually," Ollie admitted, a spark of excitement igniting within him, "I've always been curious about woodworking. I love the idea of creating something beautiful from a simple piece of wood."

"Then let's make it happen!" Cameron exclaimed, his enthusiasm contagious. "We can talk to Jasper. I bet he knows a thing or two about woodworking."

Over the next few weeks, Ollie threw himself into learning the art of woodworking under Jasper's watchful eye. He discovered solace in shaping raw materials into intricate designs, each stroke of the chisel driving away his fears and apprehensions.

"Remember, patience is key," Jasper instructed as they worked together in his cluttered workshop. "Woodworking isn't a race; it's a journey."

"Thanks, Jasper," Ollie said, carefully carving a delicate flower pattern into the side of a small wooden box.

Ollie found himself growing in confidence. The once-crippling fear of abandonment still lingered, but with each completed project, it loosened its vice-like grip on his heart. And whenever doubt threatened to resurface, Cameron and the others were there to offer unwavering encouragement, reminding Ollie he was never truly alone.

"Hey, look at this!" Ellie exclaimed one day, holding up a wooden figurine Ollie carved—a miniature version of herself, complete with her curly red hair and fierce determination etched into every line.

"Wow, Ollie! That's amazing!" Natalie gushed, admiring the tiny statue. "You're really talented."

"Thanks," Ollie replied, feeling his cheeks warm with pride. "It's all thanks to you guys. You believed in me."

"Of course we did." Ellie smiled, placing a gentle hand on Ollie's shoulder. "We'll always believe in each other."

As they stood together in Jasper's workshop, surrounded by wood shavings and the scent of freshly carved timber, Ollie knew he had found more than a hobby—he discovered a way to heal his heart and strengthen the bond between himself and his friends. And through it all, he was learning the power of community could help him face even his darkest fears.

The sun set over Gravewood, casting a warm glow on the town's now-battered buildings. The once-peaceful streets lined with debris from the supernatural events that shook the community to its core. Yet, even amidst the destruction, the townspeople banded together, determined to reclaim their home from the lingering darkness.

"Alright, team!" Principal Warren called out, his voice surprisingly steady despite his secret fear of the supernatural. "We've got a lot of work ahead of us. Let's get to it."

As Cameron and his friends joined the clean-up efforts, they couldn't help but notice the ripple effect their actions had on the community. Mrs. Hawthorne, who had once been paralyzed by fear, now worked alongside her son to remove debris from their front yard. Millie Finch, the kindly librarian, organized a book drive to restock the library's damaged shelves.

"Cam," Ollie whispered as they lifted a fallen tree branch together. "Do you think we're making a difference?"

"Of course we are," Cameron replied, grunting under the weight of the branch. "Look around. Everyone's facing their fears, like us."

"Hey there, kiddos," Jazz called from across the street, waving a hammer in their direction. "Need a hand with that?"

"Thanks, Mr. Whittaker." Ellie smiled, appreciating the historian's newfound involvement in the community. "Any help is welcome."

As the days turned into weeks, the town slowly began to rebuild. Everywhere, people found the courage to face their own challenges, inspired by the determination of Cameron and his friends. Mrs. Sinclair, Ellie's mother, took up painting again after years of neglecting her passion. Natalie's younger brother, John, finally began therapy to address his anxiety.

"See?" Ellie said one afternoon, wiping sweat from her brow as she surveyed their progress. "We're making a real difference here."

"Yep," Natalie agreed, snapping photos that would later fill the pages of her scrapbook. "And the best part is, we're doing it together."

"Exactly," Ellie chimed in, her fear of failure momentarily forgotten. "Together, we can face anything."

As the sun dipped below the horizon, casting long shadows across the now-revitalized streets of Gravewood, a sense of hope and renewal filled the air. Buildings once reduced to rubble now stood tall once more, and laughter echoed through the town square as children played without fear.

"Look at what we've accomplished," Ollie marveled, his eyes shining with pride. "I never thought we could come this far."

"Neither did I," Cameron admitted, clapping Ollie on the back. "But we did it. Together."

The resilience of the human spirit shone brightly in the faces of every person who called Gravewood home. And as they stood side by side, united by courage and determination, the town's once-broken heart began to beat anew.

As the group of friends stood in the town square, basking in the warm glow of their collective accomplishments, Cameron's gaze fell upon an old, crumbling building at the edge of town. He couldn't help but feel a chill run down his spine as he stared at its darkened windows and weathered bricks. It was a stark reminder not all of Gravewood been restored, and perhaps not all scars can be healed.

"Hey," Ellie said, following Cameron's gaze to the dilapidated structure. "That place gives me the creeps."

"Me too," Ollie admitted, pushing his glasses up his nose nervously. "But I guess we can't fix everything, right?"

As they spoke, a gust of wind blew through the square, carrying with it a faint, eerie melody emanating from the direction of the old building. The sudden shift in atmosphere sent a shiver down Natalie's spine, her camera shaking slightly in her hands.

"Did you guys hear that?" she asked, her voice a whisper.

"Probably the wind," Ellie offered, trying to sound convincing despite the unease settled over them like a heavy fog.

But Cameron wasn't so sure. As the haunting melody drifted on the breeze, a growing sense of dread deep within him—a feeling told him that their troubles far from over. "I don't know," he said, his eyes never leaving the building. "Maybe there's more to this town than we thought."

"Look," Ellie said, trying to dispel the tension that hung in the air. "We've done a lot of good here. We should focus on that."

"Right," Ollie agreed, forcing a smile. "We'll deal with whatever comes our way together. We always do."

The group exchanged nervous glances, each silently acknowledging the gnawing uncertainty that lay beneath the surface of their newfound hope. As they turned to leave the square, the wind picked up once more, carrying with it a whispered warning echoing through the very bones of Gravewood.

"Be careful," it hissed, like a thousand voices speaking as one. "The darkness is never far away."

And as the last remnants of daylight slipped away, casting the town in a cloak of shadows, the friends couldn't shake something sinister lurking beyond their reach, waiting for the perfect moment to strike.

CHAPTER 18

The sun cast a warm glow over the serene clearing in Gravewood, where Cameron Hawthorne and his friends gathered to enjoy the newfound peace that enveloped their town. They sat in a circle on the soft grass, a gentle breeze rustling through the trees above them. Cameron's mischievous grin was even brighter than usual as he basked in the tranquility, feeling the weight of the curse lift from him and his friends.

"Can you guys believe it?" Cameron asked, his brown eyes sparkling with excitement. "We did it! Gravewood is back to normal!"

As if on cue, a chorus of laughter echoed through the streets beyond the clearing, reaching the ears of the group. The once-dreary town had been transformed into a vibrant haven now that the curse had been lifted. Children played in the parks without fear, their joyful shrieks blending harmoniously with the songs of the birds above. Couples strolled hand-in-hand, pausing to admire the brilliant blossoms adorned every tree and bush. The scent of freshly cut grass and fragrant flowers filled the air, a stark contrast to the musty odor that once permeated Gravewood.

"Look at all those flowers," marveled Ellie as she gestured towards a nearby flowerbed. "I've never seen such vivid colors before. It's like the whole town come back to life."

Cameron nodded in agreement, his gaze wandering over the bustling town. He couldn't help but feel a sense of pride swelling within him, knowing he and his friends played a crucial role in saving Gravewood. They faced their deepest fears and emerged victorious, and now they can finally enjoy the fruits of their labor.

"Remember how dark and gloomy this place used to be?" Cameron mused, plucking a blade of grass from the ground and twirling it between his fingers.

"Everything feels lighter now," agreed Ollie, another member of their tight-knit group. "Even the air seems fresher like we can finally breathe again."

"Let's not forget how far we've come," Cameron said, his voice laced with determination. "We've grown stronger, braver, and more resilient than ever before. And we're not going to let anything stand in our way again."

As Cameron spoke, energy coursed through him, fueling his adventurous spirit. There were still many mysteries lurking in the shadows of Gravewood, and he couldn't wait to uncover them all with his friends by his side. For now, though, they would savor the peace and beauty surrounding them, grateful for the chance to rebuild their beloved town and forge a brighter future together.

The sun dipped low in the sky, casting long shadows across the park where Cameron and his friends gathered. A warm breeze rustled through the leaves of the towering trees, carrying with it the scent of blooming flowers and the distant laughter of children playing nearby. They lounged on the grass, their faces touched by the fading golden light, and for a moment, they felt at peace.

"Guys," Ellie began, her voice soft. "I can't believe how much we've changed since this all started. I mean, think about who we were before we discovered the curse."

They fell silent for a moment, each lost in thought, reflecting on their individual journeys. The memories of fear, determination, and triumph swirled together like a kaleidoscope of emotions.

Cameron sat up, resting his arms on his knees. "You're right, Ellie. We've come so far, and not just in the adventures we've had, but in ourselves too." He looked around at his friends, seeing the growth in each of them.

Ellie nodded, brushing a strand of blonde hair from her face. "Before all this, I was always so afraid of failing, of not being good enough. But now, I know it's okay as long as we learn from them."

Ollie adjusted his glasses and cleared his throat. "I used to feel so insecure, like I didn't belong anywhere. But you guys...you made me realize I do have a place right here with all of you."

Natalie glanced down at her camera, cradled in her lap. "I've learned sometimes the most important thing is to trust my instincts. To see beyond what's right in front of me and look for the hidden truths."

Ellie's eyes sparkled with determination. "I know now that I can trust others to help me, and that's not a sign of weakness."

As they spoke, Cameron's heart swelled with pride. He had grown as well, learning to face his fear of isolation by leaning on his friends for support in their darkest moments.

"Guys," he said, looking at each of them in turn, "we've come so far together, and it's because we've been there for each other every step of the way. We've faced our fears head-on, and we're better for it. And now, we're ready for whatever new challenges Gravewood might throw at us."

They nodded in agreement, their faces lit with excitement and determination. The breeze picked up, carrying with it the echo of laughter and the promise of more mysteries waiting to be uncovered. And as the sun dipped below the horizon, casting the park in twilight shadows, Cameron and his friends knew together they were ready for anything.

Cameron's gaze drifted away from his friends, settling upon a peculiar object partially buried beneath the roots of an ancient oak tree. The fading sunlight glinted off its surface, catching his eye. Curiosity piqued, and he stood and walked over to investigate.

"Hey guys, check this out," Cameron called as he carefully extracted the mysterious artifact from its resting place. His friends gathered around, their faces etched with curiosity.

The object was an intricately carved wooden box no larger than the palm of his hand. Its surface was adorned with elaborate runes and symbols that danced before their eyes. A sense of foreboding emanated from the box, causing the hairs on the back of Cameron's neck to stand on end.

"Whoa, it looks ancient," Natalie remarked, her brown eyes wide with awe as she reached out to trace the enigmatic symbols delicately with her fingertips.

"Maybe there's something inside," Ollie suggested, pushing his glasses up the bridge of his nose nervously. "You know, like a secret message or something."

"Only one way to find out," Ellie said, her voice brimming with excitement. She gently took the box from Cameron and examined it closely, searching for an opening mechanism.

As the wooden box creaked open, a musty smell wafted through the air, stirring memories of long-forgotten secrets. Inside lay a single, aged piece of parchment, folded neatly in half. The group exchanged anxious glances before Ellie unfolded the paper, revealing a cryptic message written in an elegant, looping script.

"Listen to this," Ellie began, her voice wavering slightly with anticipation. "'When darkness falls and shadows rise, seek the truth that lies beneath Gravewood's skies.'"

"What does it mean?" Ellie asked, her red curls bouncing as she leaned forward to get a better look at the parchment.

"Maybe it's a clue," Natalie mused, her eyes narrowing in thought. "Like, there's some kind of hidden truth we need to find."

"Or maybe it's another supernatural mystery," Cameron added with a mischievous grin. The prospect of diving back into the unknown sent a thrill down his spine. "After all, that's what we're good at, right?"

His friends nodded, their faces a mixture of excitement and determination. Gravewood taught them much about fear, courage, and the power of friendship. And now, armed with their newfound strength, they're ready to face whatever this enigmatic message might lead them to.

"Alright then, let's do this," Ollie said, clapping his hands together resolutely. "Together, we can solve any mystery that comes our way."

As the group gathered their belongings and prepared to leave the park, the shadows lengthened around them, casting eerie patterns on the ground. In the distance, an owl hooted as if heralding the arrival of yet another dark and mysterious chapter in the lives of Cameron and his friends.

Cameron's heart raced as they approached the Gravewood Library, the familiar scent of old books and dust filling his nostrils. The formidable building loomed before them, its stone façade seemingly encroached upon by creeping ivy twisted and writhed like a living thing.

"Are you guys ready?" he asked his friends, gripping the mysterious parchment tightly in his hands.

"Definitely," Natalie replied with a determined nod, her eyes gleaming with the prospect of uncovering hidden secrets. "Millie might have some answers for us."

They pushed open the heavy wooden doors, the creaking hinges echoing throughout the hushed library. The dim interior was illuminated by flickering candles, casting dancing shadows on the rows of books lining the walls.

"Ah, here she is," Ollie whispered, gesturing toward the back of the library, where Millie Finch sat at a cluttered desk, her gray hair pulled back into a tight bun.

"Millie," Cameron called softly, not wanting to disturb the library's quiet atmosphere. She looked up from her book, her spectacles perched precariously on the edge of her nose, and smiled warmly at the group.

"Hello, dear children," she greeted, beckoning them to join her at the table. "What can I help you with today?"

"Actually, we found this," Ellie said, handing over the parchment. Millie's eyes widened behind her glasses as she examined the cryptic message.

"Curious," she murmured, tracing a finger over the words. "I've never seen anything quite like it. Let's see what we can find in the archives, shall we?"

As Millie led them through the labyrinthine library, Cameron couldn't shake the feeling of unseen eyes watching their every move. He glanced back at his friends, who were equally uneasy but determined to press on.

"Here we are," Millie announced, stopping before a dusty bookshelf containing the oldest and most fragile volumes. "These books hold more records of Gravewood's history and supernatural occurrences."

"Wow!" Natalie breathed, her fingers hovering over the cracked leather spines. "I didn't even know these existed."

"Many don't," Millie replied with a knowing smile. "But you've proven yourselves capable of handling such knowledge."

For hours, they delved into the dusty tomes, poring over ancient accounts of ghostly apparitions, cursed artifacts, and other supernatural phenomena. Cameron's mind raced as he read about strange rituals once practiced in the woods surrounding Gravewood, wondering if they could be connected to the message on the parchment.

"Guys, listen to this," Ollie said suddenly, his voice hushed but urgent. "It says here that there was once a powerful artifact hidden somewhere in Gravewood—an object said to reveal hidden truths and grant its possessor great power."

"Could this be what the message is leading us to?" Ellie asked, her brow furrowed in thought.

"Perhaps," Millie mused, her eyes flitting back to the mysterious parchment. "But remember, with great power comes great responsibility. You must tread carefully, for the darkness that lies beneath Gravewood's skies is not to be trifled with."

Cameron swallowed hard, a shiver running down his spine. Despite the chill of fear settled in his chest, they came too far to turn back now. They would face whatever awaited them in the dark heart of Gravewood—together.

Cameron's heart pounded as he led his friends deeper into the shadowy woods, following the cryptic clues they discovered in the library. The sun was setting, casting an eerie orange glow through the trees. A shiver ran down his spine as if Gravewood itself was warning them against venturing further.

"Are you sure about this, Cameron?" Ollie whispered, his voice quivering with fear. He pushed his glasses up on his nose and looked around nervously.

Cameron hesitated, feeling the weight of responsibility bearing down on him. "We have to find out the truth," he said, trying to sound braver than he felt. "We've come too far to turn back now."

Ellie tightened her grip on the ancient map they had found, her blue eyes scanning their surroundings. "According to this, we should be close to... something. But what?"

"Maybe it's that." Natalie pointed to a gnarled old tree standing alone in the clearing, its twisted branches clawing at the darkening sky. A strange symbol was carved into its trunk, barely visible beneath layers of moss.

As they approached the tree, Ellie let out a gasp. "Guys, look!" She crouched down, brushing aside dead leaves to reveal a small, weathered wooden box half-buried in the earth.

"Could this be the artifact Millie told us about?" Cameron wondered aloud, his curiosity piqued. He reached for the box, but Ellie grabbed his arm, stopping him.

"Wait," she cautioned. "We don't know what's inside or what it can do. We need to be careful."

"Right," Cameron agreed, swallowing hard. "Let's open it together, then. On three."

"One..." Ellie began, her fingers trembling as she joined Cameron and Ellie in gripping the box.

"Two..." Ollie added, his voice a whisper.

"Three!" They lifted the lid in unison, and a cold gust of wind erupted from within, extinguishing their flashlights. In the sudden darkness, Cameron felt a chill.

"Wh-what just happened?" Natalie stammered, her voice shaky.

"Maybe we should close it," Ollie suggested nervously, but Ellie was already reading the inscription inside the lid, illuminated by the faint moonlight filtering through the trees.

"Listen," she said, her voice hushed and urgent. "It says that this box contains the power to summon spirits – both good and evil."

"Summon spirits? Are you kidding?" Cameron's mind raced, torn between curiosity and fear. What if they unleashed something dangerous on Gravewood?

"Should we really be messing with this?" Ellie asked, echoing Cameron's concerns. "I mean, I know we wanted to uncover the town's secrets, but this... this seems like it can be more than we can handle."

"We have a choice," Ellie said solemnly, looking each of her friends in the eye. "We can either close the box now and walk away, leaving Gravewood's mysteries unsolved... or we can see what lies beyond the veil, no matter the risks."

Cameron hesitated, then nodded resolutely. "We'll face it together. Whatever happens, we won't let fear hold us back."

As one, they prepared to delve deeper into Gravewood's history and confront the supernatural forces that remained hidden for centuries. With newfound courage, they stood united, ready to face whatever challenges awaited them in the darkness.

The moon cast a silvery glow over the ancient tombstones in Gravewood Cemetery, casting eerie shadows. Cameron Hawthorne stood at the edge of an open grave, his heart pounding in anticipation as he peered into the darkness.

"Are you guys sure about this?" Ollie asked, his voice no more than a whisper. His eyes widened behind his glasses, and Cameron can see the fear mingling with excitement deep within them.

"Absolutely," Ellie replied, her blue eyes gleaming with determination. "We've come too far to turn back now. We need to find out what's going on in this town."

"Besides," Natalie added, her camera strap wrapped tightly around her wrist, "we're not the same kids we were when all this started. We've grown stronger and braver. We can handle whatever's down there."

Cameron nodded, his earlier fears temporarily banished by his friends' resolve. He took a deep breath, inhaling the scent of damp earth and decaying leaves, and climbed down the rickety ladder into the open grave.

As his feet touched the ground, a chill ran up his spine. The air was colder here, heavy with the weight of secrets long buried. He looked up to see Ellie descending the ladder, her red curls bouncing as she made her way down.

"Remember," she whispered as she joined him, "we stick together. No matter what happens."

"Right," Cameron agreed, feeling the familiar rush of adrenaline coursing through his veins. "Let's do this."

Together, they ventured deeper into the darkness, their flashlights casting pools of light on the crumbling walls of the underground tunnel. As they walked, they discussed their theories about Gravewood's history, their voices echoing through the narrow passage.

"Maybe it's a hidden society," Ollie suggested, his voice wavering slightly. "Living beneath the town, controlling everything from the shadows."

"Or it can be a gateway to another world," Natalie mused, her brown eyes wide with wonder. "A place where the laws of nature don't apply."

"Whatever it is," Ellie said firmly, "we're going to get to the bottom of it. Gravewood deserves to know the truth."

As they continued through the tunnel, Cameron couldn't help but marvel at how far they come. Once frightened by the mere mention of the supernatural, they now embraced the unknown with open arms, determined to solve the mysteries that has been haunting their town for generations.

"Hey, look at this!" Ellie called out suddenly, pointing to an ancient symbol etched into the stone wall. It pulsed with an otherworldly energy, as if alive and aware of their presence.

"Can that be a clue?" Ollie asked, his curiosity momentarily overcoming his fear.

"Only one way to find out," Cameron replied, his hand brushing against the cold, rough surface of the symbol. Instantly, a wave of energy surged through him, filling him with a sense of purpose and determination.

"Let's keep moving," he said, his voice steady and strong. "We've got a mystery to solve."

And together, they ventured deeper into the darkness, ready to face whatever lay waiting for them in the hidden depths of Gravewood.

The sun dipped below the horizon, casting eerie shadows across the forest floor as Cameron and his friends emerged

STEPHANIE TYO

from the hidden tunnel. Their hearts raced with a mix of
excitement and trepidation, their minds buzzing with questions about the ancient symbol they discovered.

"Did you feel that?" Ollie asked, rubbing his arm where
the strange energy prickled his skin. "It's like something...
otherworldly."

"Definitely," Cameron agreed, his breath visible in the cool
evening air. "We need to figure out what that symbol means.
I have a feeling it's the key to unlocking another mystery here
in Gravewood."

"Let's head to the library tomorrow after school," Natalie
suggested, tucking a strand of hair behind her ear. "Maybe we
can find something in the history books about the symbol or
the place it led us to."

"Good idea," Ellie nodded, his face illuminated by the glow
of his flashlight. "But for now, we should call it a night. We
don't want to be wandering around in the dark with who
knows what lurks in the shadows."

As they made their way back to their homes, Cameron
couldn't shake the feeling they were being watched. The hairs
on the back of his neck stood on end, and he glanced over his
shoulder every few steps, convinced he would see something
sinister lurking out of sight.

"Guys, do you get the feeling we're not alone?" Cameron whispered, his voice tight with unease.

"Come on, Cam," Ellie said, rolling her eyes. "You're letting your imagination run wild."

But even as she dismissed his concerns, a chill swept through the group, and they picked up their pace, eager to put the darkness of the woods behind them.

As they reached the edge of the woods, ready to part ways for the night, a sudden gust of wind ripped through the trees, sending a shower of leaves swirling around them. And then, as quickly as it came, the wind died down, and an eerie silence settled over Gravewood.

"Did you guys hear that?" Ollie whispered, his eyes wide with fear.

"Probably the wind," Natalie replied, her voice unsteady despite her attempt to remain calm.

"Or maybe," Cameron hesitated, his heart pounding in his chest, "maybe it was something else."

"Cam, don't start," Ellie warned, his grip tightening on his flashlight. "We've gotten through enough supernatural stuff for one day."

"Right," Cameron agreed, swallowing hard. "See you all tomorrow at the library, then."

As they said their goodbyes and headed home, each more nervous than they would care to admit, Cameron couldn't shake the feeling they stumbled upon something far bigger and more dangerous than they could have ever imagined.

In the distance, hidden within the shadows of the woods, a pair of glowing eyes watched their every move. And as the last of the friends disappeared from sight, a low, menacing growl echoed through the night, leaving no doubt the mysteries of Gravewood far from over.

The following morning, Cameron awoke with a start, the chilling memory of glowing eyes and low growl still fresh in his mind. He sat up abruptly in bed, wiping beads of sweat from his brow as he tried to shake off his unease. The sun was already high in the sky, casting warm rays of light through his bedroom window. It should have been a typical, peaceful morning in Gravewood, but Cameron knew better.

"Get it together, Cam," he muttered to himself. "It was just your imagination."

"Cam? You alright?" Mrs. Hawthorne called from down-stairs, concern lacing her voice.

"Yep! Just had a weird dream, Mom!" Cameron replied, forcing cheerfulness into his words. He glanced at the clock on his nightstand; it was almost time to meet his friends at the library. Slipping out of bed, he got dressed quickly, his heart still pounding with anticipation.

"Are you sure you're okay?" his mother asked as he gulped down his breakfast. "You look a little pale."

"Really, Mom. I'm fine," Cameron insisted, waving away her concern. "Just excited to hang out with everyone today." Mrs. Hawthorne's worried gaze lingered on him for a moment longer before she nodded, giving him a small smile.

"Alright then. Have fun," she said, her voice hesitant but loving all the same.

"Thanks, Mom," Cameron replied, planting a quick kiss on her cheek before grabbing his backpack and rushing out the door.

As he made his way through the sun-dappled streets of Gravewood, Cameron couldn't help but feel a sense of foreboding gnawing at the edges of his mind. His thoughts drifted back to the previous night—the wind, the eerie silence, those glowing eyes... He shuddered involuntarily, chiding himself for letting his fears get the better of him.

"Cam! You made it!" Ellie called as he entered the library, snapping him out of his dark reverie. The others—Ollie, Natalie, and Ellie—gathered around a table piled high with books about Gravewood's history. Millie Finch stood nearby, her eyes scanning the shelves with practiced expertise.

"Hey, guys!" Cameron greeted them, trying to sound nonchalant. "What have we got here?"

"Millie's helping us dig deeper into the town's past," Ellie explained, her blue eyes gleaming with excitement. "We're looking for any information that could explain what happened last night."

"Or any other supernatural events that might be connected," Ollie added nervously, his fingers fidgeting with his glasses.

As they delved into the dusty pages of Gravewood's history, the friends found themselves drawn deeper into a web of unexplained phenomena, cryptic clues, and eerie encounters. With each new discovery, the atmosphere in the library grew more charged and tense—a palpable sense of anticipation and unease hanging heavy in the air.

"Guys, listen to this," Natalie whispered, her voice barely audible as she read from an old newspaper article. "It says here that there was a series of mysterious disappearances back in the 1800s—all on nights when the wind said to howl through the woods."

"Could it be connected to what we experienced last night?" Ellie asked, her green eyes wide with fear. Cameron looked around at his friends, their faces pale but determined, and felt a swell of pride mixed with apprehension.

"Whatever's going on," he said quietly, his voice steady despite the knot of dread tightening in his chest. "We'll figure it out. Together."

As they sat huddled together in the dim light of the library, surrounded by the secrets of Gravewood's past, they embarked on a journey that would test their courage and resolve like never before. And as he glanced over at Millie Finch, her eyes narrowed with concern. They're not alone in their quest to unravel the mysteries lurking in the shadows of their beloved town.

"Are you all prepared for what lies ahead?" Millie asked softly, her voice tinged with both caution and hope.

"Absolutely," Cameron replied firmly, his friends nodding in agreement. "Whatever it takes."

"Then let's continue," Millie said, her gaze steely and unwavering. "We have much to uncover."

As the friends delved deeper into the town's history, they couldn't shake the feeling they were being watched—somewhere out there, hidden within the darkness, those glowing eyes and menacing growls waited for them, hungry and relentless. But even in the face of this unknown threat, Cameron and his friends pressed on, determined to confront the supernatural forces that held Gravewood in their grip once and for all.

CHAPTER 19

The autumn wind howled through the streets of Gravewood, sending a shiver down the spines of the group of friends as they huddled together, seeking solace in each other's presence. Their quest for answers would lead them back to the one place where they always found comfort—the library. The ancient building loomed large before them, its heavy wooden doors creaking open to reveal the familiar maze of towering bookshelves and dusty tomes.

"Ah, there you all are," came the gentle voice of Millie from behind a mountain of books on a nearby table. She peered over her spectacles at the group, her eyes crinkling with warmth and kindness. "I've been expecting you."

Millie's short, gray hair framed her face like a halo, giving her an almost ethereal appearance. Her diminutive stature belied the vast reservoir of knowledge and wisdom she possessed. As she shuffled towards the group, her soft cardigan draped around her shoulders like a protective cloak, it was impossible not to be drawn to her kind demeanor.

"Come in, come in. I've put on a fresh pot of tea," Millie said, guiding the group further into the library. They followed her willingly, grateful for her steady presence amid the growing darkness that engulfed their once-peaceful town.

As they settled around the table, the friends couldn't help but exchange nervous glances. The weight of the curse and the secrets of Gravewood pressed down upon them, threatening to suffocate them under the burden of unanswered questions. Yet, even in their darkest moments, Millie remained a beacon of hope, guiding them through the fog of uncertainty with her unwavering belief in their ability to overcome the malevolent forces at play.

"Let's get started, shall we?" Millie said, opening an ancient tome with a soft sigh. The pages whispered faintly, as if they were eager to share the mysteries within. "I believe I've found something that might help us understand what's going on in Gravewood."

The group leaned in closer, each one of them keenly aware of every clue, every piece of information Millie unearthed for them, brought them one step closer to unraveling the tangled web of secrets ensnared their town.

As they delved deeper into the lore and history of Gravewood, guided by Millie's steady hand, the friends felt a renewed sense of purpose. Together, they could face whatever supernatural horrors lay ahead. And with Millie at their side, there was nothing they couldn't achieve.

"Millie, we can't thank you enough for all your help," said Ellie, her voice sincere and full of gratitude. The other group members nodded in agreement, their eyes reflecting a genuine appreciation for Millie's unwavering support.

"Really, we couldn't have come this far without you," added Cameron, running a hand through his hair. "You've been like a guardian angel to us throughout this entire journey."

Millie's cheeks flushed with warmth, her smile gentle yet proud. "My dear children, there is no need to thank me. It's been my pleasure to help guide you on this path. I've seen the determination and courage within each of you, and it filled my heart with hope for Gravewood's future."

As the group took a moment to absorb Millie's kind words, Natalie looked around at her friends, their faces etched with the resolve that had grown stronger with every obstacle they'd faced. She turned to Millie, her eyes shining with unshed tears. "Millie, I want to say... you've become like a grandmother to me. I lost mine when I was little, and having you in my life meant more to me than words can express."

"Natalie, my dear," Millie replied, her own eyes moistening, "you've shown me the strength and resilience that lie within the heart of our town's youth. You hold a special place in my heart, too, and I'm grateful to have had the chance to get to know you and be a part of your life."

"Your wisdom and kindness have inspired us all, Millie," said Ollie, his voice steady despite the emotion threatened to crack it. "You've taught us so much about Gravewood but also about ourselves. We're stronger because of you."

"Ah, Ollie," Millie said, reaching out to pat his hand. "You've always been a brave and resourceful young man, and it's been my honor to help you harness that strength for the greater good."

"Millie," began Ellie hesitantly, her eyes downcast. "You... you believed in me when no one else did. You saw something in me that I didn't even see in myself. I'll never forget what you've done for me and for all of us."

"Sweet Ellie," Millie said tenderly. "I've always known their greatness within you, waiting to be discovered. I'm so proud of how far you've come and the person you're becoming."

As the heartfelt conversations continued, the bond between Millie and the group of friends only grew stronger. They are united by a shared mission and by the love and trust they built together during their quest to save Gravewood from its supernatural curse. And though the road ahead was still uncertain, they knew, with Millie's guidance and the strength they drew from one another, they could face whatever horrors awaited them.

"Alright, my dear ones," Millie said softly, wiping away the last of her tears. "There's still much work to be done, and time waits for no one. Let's continue our journey and find the answers we seek, side by side."

With renewed determination, the group pressed on, the library's dusty volumes now imbued with the essence of their unbreakable bond—a testament to the power of friendship and the indomitable spirit of those who dare to stand against the darkness.

With their hearts swollen with gratitude, the group reluctantly left Millie's comforting presence at the library and ventured out into the fading twilight. As they approached Jazz Whittaker's abandoned house, a shiver ran down their spines. The eerie atmosphere was palpable; an unsettling silence filled the air, punctuated only by the creaking of the old house's timbers as they groaned under the weight of years.

"Guys, this place gives me the creeps," whispered Ellie, her voice over the rustling of leaves beneath their feet.

"Me too," agreed Cameron, his eyes darting to every shadowy corner, half-expecting some ghastly apparition to emerge. "But we need Jazz's help if we're going to solve this mystery and save Gravewood."

As they drew closer to the house, its unkempt appearance became more apparent. Broken windows stared blankly into the darkness, sharp shards of glass glinting menacingly in the moonlight. Weeds choked the once-manicured lawn, reaching up like twisted fingers toward the peeling paint of the weathered siding.

Taking a deep breath to steady herself, Ellie reached out a trembling hand and knocked on the heavy wooden door. It swung open with a low, mournful creak, revealing the disheveled figure of Jazz Whittaker.

"Ah! My young friends!" he exclaimed, his voice raspy yet warm. His long, unkempt gray hair hung in wild tangles around his face, framing a beard that had taken on a life of its own. With a flourish, he swept back into the dimly lit room behind him, gesturing for the group to follow.

"Welcome," he said, a twinkle in his eye betraying his delight at their visit. "I trust you've come seeking the wisdom of the ages."

"Actually, we're looking for your help, Jazz," Ellie replied, her voice steadying as she met his gaze. "We think you might be able to help us find the answers we need to save Gravewood from the curse."

"Ah, yes!" Jazz exclaimed, his eccentric behavior intensifying as he began to pace back and forth, his arms waving wildly. "The curse! A most fascinating tale, steeped in mystery and intrigue!"

Max couldn't help but roll his eyes at Jazz's theatrics. "Does he have to be so... weird?" he thought to himself. But Ellie determination reminded him they had no choice but to place their trust in this enigmatic figure.

"Jazz, please," she implored, her voice a mixture of desperation and resolve. "We need your knowledge. We need to understand the history of Gravewood and how to break the curse."

"Very well," Jazz acquiesced, his expression growing serious as he regarded each member of the group with a piercing gaze. "But I must warn you, the path ahead is fraught with danger and darkness."

"Whatever it takes," Ellie vowed, her eyes shining with determination. "We won't let Gravewood fall to this curse."

"Alright then, my brave young friends," Jazz said solemnly, his wild hair and beard now seeming less like the trappings of an eccentric recluse and more like the mark of a sage destined to guide them through the treacherous labyrinth of Gravewood's haunted past. "Let our journey into the unknown begin."

As Jazz led the group through the dimly lit corridors of his once-grand home, the air thickens with the weight of untold stories. The wallpaper began to peel away, baring the walls to the ravages of time like open wounds. Dust motes danced in the slivers of sunlight that pierced the gloom, their pirouettes accompanied by the creaking of ancient floorboards.

"Jazz," Ellie began, her voice tinged with a newfound respect, "we want to thank you for your insights into Gravewood's history and the curse. We know it's not easy to share this knowledge, but we're grateful for your guidance."

Jazz paused before an ornate wooden door and turned to face them, his eyes softening as he took in their earnest expressions. "It fills my heart to see young people so dedicated to saving their town," he replied, his voice strained by years of disuse. "But I must warn you, my friends, what lies behind this door could change your lives forever."

Without waiting for a response, Jazz pushed open the door, revealing a vast library filled to the brim with dusty tomes and weathered manuscripts. The room hummed with knowledge, each spine a window into the past, beckoning the group to step inside and lose themselves in its depths.

"Wow," breathed Ollie, his earlier skepticism momentarily forgotten as he gazed upon the literary treasure trove. "This is... incredible."

"Indeed." Jazz nodded, his eyes twinkling behind the veil of his unruly gray hair. "And I believe it is here we will find the answers you seek."

As they searched deeper into the labyrinthine library, the members of the group found themselves drawn to different corners of the room, each seeking a connection to the past that would help them unravel the mystery of the present. During this time, each member of the group had a poignant conversation with Jazz, showcasing the personal connections they formed with him.

"Jazz," whispered Ellie as she gingerly leafed through the brittle pages of a centuries-old diary. "I never thought I'd find someone who understands my fascination with Gravewood's history. Thank you."

"Ah, my dear," Jazz replied, the warmth in his voice chasing away the chill clung to the room's dark corners. "Your passion for your town's past is an inspiration. It reminds me of myself when I was young and full of dreams."

"Jazz, I..." Ollie hesitated, his usual bravado faltering as he met the historian's gaze. "I want to apologize for doubting you earlier. You've opened my eyes to the richness of our town's history. Thank you for trusting us."

"Ollie, fear not," Jazz said, placing a reassuring hand on the boy's shoulder. "It is natural to be skeptical of things we do not understand. Your courage will serve you well in the days ahead."

These intimate moments solidified the bond between Jazz and the group as they continued their search for answers within the walls of the musty library. The scent of aged parchment filled their nostrils, mingling with the faint aroma of candle wax, as the whispers of the past echoed through the shadows.

The atmosphere grew heavier with each passing moment, but the group remained undaunted, driven by their determination to save Gravewood from the curse that plagued it for so long. And as their connections with Jazz deepened, they found a true ally in their fight against the darkness.

The sun was setting as Millie and Jazz stood before the group, their faces illuminated by the fading rays of light. The friends spent countless hours in their company, uncovering long-hidden secrets and forging unbreakable bonds.

"Children," Millie said softly, her spectacles glinting in the twilight. "I cannot express how proud I am of each and every one of you. You have faced your fears head-on and come out stronger for it."

"Indeed," Jazz added, his beard swaying gently in the evening breeze. "Your courage and determination have brought hope to Gravewood once more. Remember, the future is yours to shape."

"Millie, Jazz," said Natalie, tears welling up in her eyes. "Thank you for everything. We won't let you down."

"Always remember," Millie's voice trembled with emotion, "that knowledge is a powerful weapon. Use it wisely, and never stop seeking the truth."

"Take care, my friends." Jazz smiled warmly. "May your journey be filled with light, even in the darkest of times."

As they walked away, the group watched them disappear into the encroaching shadows, their hearts filled with both sadness and gratitude.

Cameron gazed at the spot where Millie and Jazz stood, his thoughts racing. The knowledge they shared, the guidance they provided—he would carry these gifts with him for the rest of his days. "They believed in us," he thought, "and we'll make sure their faith wasn't misplaced."

Ellie's fingers traced the spine of a book Millie had given her. She could still feel the warmth of the librarian's embrace and the kindness in her eyes. "We were so lost before Millie and Jazz came into our lives," she reflected. "Now, we have a purpose, a reason to fight."

Natalie listened to the faint rustling of leaves and the gentle whispers of the wind echoing Jazz's words. "We're not alone," she realized. "No matter where we go, they'll always be with us in spirit."

"Come on, guys," Cameron said softly, breaking the silence. "We've got a lot of work to do."

As they turned to leave, a renewed sense of purpose surged through their veins. The road ahead would be fraught with dangers and uncertainties, but they're ready, armed with the wisdom and strength Millie and Jazz had so generously bestowed upon them.

And as the last glimmers of sunlight faded beneath the horizon, the heroes of Gravewood stepped into the night, their hearts alight with hope and determination.

The soft glow of the library's lamps bathed the group in a warm, amber light. Each member stood with their eyes fixed on the worn pages of the ancient books, savoring the last moments of calm before setting out on their perilous journey. Max's fingertips grazed the edge of a yellowed map, the ink bleeding through the parchment like veins under his skin.

"Are we all clear on the plan?" he asked, his voice a whisper.

Ellie nodded, her auburn hair tumbling over her shoulders. "We visit Jazz's house after this. He might have more information about the curse."

"Right," Cameron agreed, clenching his fists. "No time to waste."

As they exited the library, their footsteps echoed through the empty halls like ghosts of memories past. The heavy wooden doors creaked shut behind them, sealing away the comforting presence of Millie and her vast knowledge.

The walk to Jazz's house was shrouded in an eerie silence, broken only by the distant howling of wolves and the rustling of leaves beneath their feet. Moonlight filtered through the skeletal branches of the trees, casting elongated shadows on the ground like grasping hands.

"Jazz is... different," Natalie whispered, her blue eyes darting nervously from side to side. "But I trust him."

"Me too," Ellie murmured, rubbing her arms against the chilly air. "He's helped us so much already."

"Let's hope he can help us break this damn curse," Ollie muttered under his breath, his jaw clenched in determination.

Before long, they arrived at Jazz's decrepit house. The once-grand structure loomed before them, its crumbling walls draped in ivy and moss as if mourning the passage of time. A sense of foreboding weighed heavily on their hearts, but they steeled themselves and ventured inside.

"Jazz?" Ollie called out, his voice cracking slightly.

"Ah, my young friends!" Jazz appeared from behind a towering stack of books, his long, gray hair and beard giving him the look of an ancient wizard. "Welcome, welcome."

"Thank you for helping us," Ellie said sincerely, her eyes glistening with unshed tears. "We couldn't have made it this far without you."

"Your insights are invaluable," Natalie added, smiling faintly through her fears.

"Think nothing of it," Jazz replied, waving a dismissive hand. "Now, let's see if we can find some answers, shall we?"

As they delved into the mysteries surrounding Gravewood's curse, each member of the group found themselves drawing strength from their bond with Jazz. His eccentric wisdom and unwavering belief in them fueled their resolve.

"Time is running short," Ollie announced, his voice heavy with the weight of their task. "Let's regroup outside and discuss our next steps."

Gathered beneath the moonlit sky, they shared their thoughts and fears, each one bolstered by the support of their companions. And as they parted ways with Jazz, their hearts swelled with gratitude for the guidance he and Millie provided.

"Whatever happens next," Natalie whispered, her voice trembling with emotion, "we'll face it together."

"Because of them," Ellie agreed, her eyes shining with fierce conviction. "They believed in us."

Ollie nodded, the fire of determination burning brightly within him. "Let's make them proud."

With renewed vigor, the heroes of Gravewood stepped forward into the darkness, ready to challenge the unknown and restore peace to their haunted town.

CHAPTER 20

The air was heavy with a tense silence as the group of friends sat together in the dimly lit library, each lost in their own thoughts. The flickering light from the fireplace cast eerie shadows on the walls, amplifying the sense of mystery and horror that now surrounded them. The scent of old books and aged wood filled their nostrils as they contemplated their recent supernatural experiences.

Cameron absentmindedly traced patterns on the dusty wooden table before him, his brown eyes clouded as he reflected on the events that led to this point. He had always been known for his insatiable curiosity, often finding himself in trouble due to his impulsive nature. But never before his actions resulted in such dire consequences.

"Guys, I... I think I messed up," Cameron admitted, his voice a whisper. His fingers gripped the edge of the table, his knuckles turning white as he fought to control the emotions welling up inside him.

"Cam, don't blame yourself," Natalie reassured him, laying a comforting hand on his shoulder. "We all played a part in unraveling this curse."

"Still, it was my impulsiveness that started everything," Cameron sighed, feeling the weight of responsibility and guilt pressing down on him. "If I thought things through, maybe we wouldn't be in this mess."

As he uttered these words, the memory of finding the cursed artifact flashed in his mind—the cold metal tingling against his skin, the rush of excitement coursing through his veins, and the foreboding sense of danger lingered at the back of his mind. He realized the importance of thinking before acting and how his need for adventure drove them all into the depths of the supernatural world.

"Look, we can't change the past," Ellie chimed in, her determined gaze meeting Cameron's. "What's important now is that we stick together and figure out how to fix this."

"Besides, your curiosity isn't all bad," Natalie added with a small smile. "It's what brought us all together in the first place."

Cameron looked around at his friends, their faces illuminated by the flickering firelight, and a sliver of hope pierced through the overwhelming darkness surrounding them. They're right—it wasn't his impulsiveness that led them here; it was his unwavering sense of wonder and his courage to dive headfirst into the unknown.

"Alright," Cameron said, taking a deep breath as he pushed away the feelings of guilt and regret. "Let's work together and put an end to this curse. We've come this far, and I'm not backing down now."

His friends nodded in agreement, each wearing a determined expression on their faces. The air in the library lightens slightly as if acknowledging the newfound resolve within the group. As they delved deeper into the supernatural mystery entwined itself around their lives, Cameron couldn't help but feel a surge of gratitude for the friendships been forged in the face of terror and uncertainty.

Ellie stared into the fire, her piercing blue eyes reflecting its dancing flames. Its warmth on her face, reminding her of the countless hours she spent poring over dusty old books in the library, searching for clues that would help them unravel the curse. It was a journey of self-discovery that took her through the annals of history, from darkened tombs to ancient scrolls filled with cryptic symbols.

"Remember when we first discovered the Blackwell journals?" Ellie mused, her voice soft yet resolute. "I was so scared that I wouldn't be able to decipher the code, but I also knew that I couldn't let myself fail. My love for history and my intuition helped me push through that fear."

Ollie looked at her with admiration, his glasses catching the firelight as he nodded. "That was amazing, Ellie. You've proven how valuable your skills are, time and time again."

A shiver ran down his spine as he thought back to the moments when they confronted Gideon Blackwell's spirit. Ollie had always been gentle and kind-hearted, but there was a fierceness within him he hadn't realized he possessed until he faced the supernatural head-on. "You know," he began hesitantly, "I've never been one for confrontation, but this whole experience made me realize that I can stand up for what's right and protect those I care about."

"Like when you stood up to Gideon Blackwell," Cameron interjected, his voice laced with pride. "None of us will ever forget how brave you were in that moment."

A small smile tugged at the corner of Ollie's lips. "Thanks, Cameron. But I couldn't have done it without all of you by my side." He glanced at each of his friends in turn, feeling a warmth in his chest that had nothing to do with the fire before them. "Your support has given me the strength I needed to overcome my insecurities and face my fear of abandonment."

Ellie reached across the circle to squeeze Ollie's hand. "We're all in this together, Ollie. We've each grown so much since we first started investigating this curse, and we've become stronger as a result."

As they sat there in the dimly lit library, the air thick with tension and anticipation, the teens couldn't help but feel a sense of camaraderie and unity. They faced unimaginable horrors and uncovered long-hidden secrets, but through it all, their friendship only grew stronger. The uncertainty lay ahead, still frightening, but together, they would continue to unravel the mysteries surrounding them and, ultimately, put an end to Gideon Blackwell's curse once and for all.

The flickering flames from the fireplace cast eerie shadows across the library walls as Natalie stared at her once-pristine sketchbook, now filled with charcoal renderings of the supernatural encounters they faced. Her artistic eye allowed her to capture the ethereal beauty hidden within the terrifying moments they experienced together.

"Hey, Nat," Ellie said quietly, drawing Natalie's attention from her sketches. "I noticed you've been drawing a lot lately. It's really fascinating how you can find beauty in even the most frightening situations."

Natalie looked up at her friend and smiled softly. "Thanks, Ellie. I guess we all have our coping mechanisms. For me, it's art. When I draw, I can confront my fear of the unknown and see things from a different perspective." She traced her fingers along the edges of her latest sketch, depicting the chilling moment when Gideon Blackwell's spirit materialized before them.

"Your drawings are so powerful," Ellie remarked, her green eyes wide with admiration. "They remind me that we're not powerless against these supernatural forces. Just like you, I've learned to channel my own strengths to face my fears and fight for justice."

Natalie nodded, thinking back to the many times Ellie displayed unwavering determination and courage in the face of danger. "You've always had such a strong sense of justice, Ellie. It's inspiring."

Ellie shrugged modestly, but her cheeks flushed with pride. "I guess I've always been afraid of losing control over my own life. Seeing injustice and not being able to do anything about it was paralyzing. But now, after everything we've been through, I've found strength in my convictions."

"Isn't it amazing how much we've changed since this all began?" Natalie mused, her gaze drifting back to the dancing flames. "We've become stronger and more resilient, and we've learned to rely on each other."

"Exactly," Ellie agreed, her eyes shining with determination. "Together, we're unstoppable. No matter what lies ahead, I know that we'll face it head-on and put an end to this curse once and for all."

As the embers crackled and popped in the fireplace, Natalie felt a renewed sense of purpose and hope. With her friends by her side, she was ready to embrace the unknown and continue their journey towards justice and truth. For they were bound by something more powerful than fear—they were bound by friendship, and a shared strength that could conquer the darkest of forces.

The air in the room was thick with tension and anticipation, punctuated by the rhythmic ticking of the grandfather clock in the corner. As Cameron stared into the flickering flames in the fireplace, he couldn't help but feel a sense of pride swelling within him. The friends he made during this harrowing journey are like family to him now, each one having faced their own personal demons and grown stronger as a result.

"Remember when we first discovered Gideon Blackwell's photograph?" Cameron asked, his voice no more than a whisper, as if speaking of the ominous figure might summon him from the shadows. His friends nodded, each lost in their own memories of the events that led them to this point.

"Feels like a lifetime ago," Ollie murmured, his eyes wide and filled with wonder as he considered how much they all changed since that fateful day.

"Indeed," Ellie agreed, her fingers tracing the intricate patterns on the antique locket she wore around her neck. "We've each faced our fears and emerged stronger for it."

Cameron's thoughts turned to the moment he confronted Gideon Blackwell's spirit in the basement of the old house on Elm Street. It had been a dark, moonless night, and the damp air clung to his skin like a shroud. He could still hear the faint drip-drip-drip of water echoing through the dank chamber as he slowly descended the creaky stairs.

"Hey, Cam," Natalie said softly, her hand resting gently on his arm, pulling him back to the present. "You got really quiet there for a moment. What were you thinking about?"

"I... I was remembering the night I faced Gideon in the basement," Cameron admitted, his voice trembling slightly despite his best efforts to keep it steady. "I felt so alone down there, surrounded by darkness and fear. But you guys were there for me, and I realized that together, we're stronger than any evil force we might face."

"Exactly," Ellie chimed in, her brow furrowed with determination. "We've come so far, and we'll continue to stand together as we confront whatever lies ahead."

"United, we can overcome anything," Ellie added, her voice laced with conviction.

Cameron looked around at his friends, their faces illuminated by the warm glow of the fire. A renewed sense of courage and purpose coursing through him, fueled by the knowledge they're all in this fight together. And no matter what supernatural forces they faced, the strength of their bond was unbreakable.

As the clock struck midnight, the group exchanged steely glances, each silently reaffirming their commitment to one another. With a deep breath, they prepared to embark on the next leg of their journey, bound by friendship, courage, and an unwavering determination to end the curse that haunted Gravewood for centuries.

As the flames from the fire licked at the darkness, casting eerie shadows on the walls of the old library, Ellie found herself lost in thought. The flickering light danced across her face, accentuating the deep furrow formed between her brows.

"Hey," Ellie said gently, breaking the silence. "You look like you're a million miles away."

Ellie blinked, her piercing blue eyes refocusing on the present. "Sorry," she replied softly. "I was thinking about the time I deciphered those cryptic clues leading us to Gideon Blackwell's lair. I felt so much pressure to get it right. I'm terrified of letting everyone down."

Ollie looked up from his book, adjusting his glasses. "It's not easy to solve a riddle left behind by the supernatural. But you did it, Ellie. You used your intelligence and intuition to lead us to the truth."

A smile played at the corners of her lips as she recalled moments of triumph. Her fingers trembled as she traced the ancient symbols etched into the parchment, feeling a strange connection to the past. As the words revealed themselves, she'd experienced a surge of clarity, fueled by her love for history and determination to uncover the truth.

"Thanks, Ollie," she said, her voice filled with gratitude. "Your support means the world to me."

"Speaking of support," Ollie began, swallowing hard. "I remember when I stood up to Gideon Blackwell's spirit." He shuddered at the memory, recalling the chilling sensation that enveloped him in the presence of the malevolent being. "I was so scared of being abandoned and of losing you all. But that was the moment I realized how important loyalty is."

"Ollie, you've always been there for us," Natalie affirmed, her dark eyes shining with admiration. "Even when you were scared, you never once let us down."

"Exactly," Cameron chimed in. "You've got the heart of a lion, Ollie. We're lucky to have you by our side."

As the wind howled outside, rattling the windows and casting an ominous shadow across the library, the friends huddled closer together, each drawing strength from the others. Their connection carried them through the darkest moments and would continue to do so as they faced the unknown.

"United, we can defeat Gideon Blackwell and any other supernatural force that threatens Gravewood," Ellie declared, her voice resolute.

"Absolutely," Ollie agreed, his eyes filled with determination. "Together, we're stronger than anything that comes our way."

With every word spoken, the bond between them grew stronger, and their resolve unshakable. The fire crackled loudly, casting flickering patterns on the walls that danced in celebration of their unwavering loyalty. As the embers glowed, the friends looked at one another, knowing whatever horrors lay ahead, they'd face them head-on, united by friendship, courage, and a shared sense of purpose.

Natalie stood near the window, her dark brown hair blowing gently as the chill wind seeped through the cracks. The cold glass vibrated under her fingertips, and she could feel the goosebumps rising on her skin. Turning away from the haunting view outside, she glanced at a photograph she'd taken earlier. The image captured one of their numerous supernatural encounters—a scene both terrifying and beautiful in its own right.

"Hey, Natalie," Ellie approached, her curly red hair bouncing with each step. "Is that another one of your photos?"

"Y-yeah," Natalie stammered, startled by the abrupt question. She clutched the picture tightly but managed to hold it up for Ellie to see.

"Wow," Ellie breathed, her eyes wide with admiration. "You have such a gift, Natalie. Even when we're faced with something so frightening, you can still find beauty in it."

"Thanks, Ellie." Natalie smiled timidly, feeling a warmth spread within her chest. "I think... I think it's my way of coping with the fear of the unknown, you know? By capturing these moments, it makes them feel more real and less... terrifying."

"Your artistic perspective helped us tremendously, Natalie," Ellie agreed, her voice filled with gratitude. "I don't know how we would've made it this far without you."

"Speaking of Ellie," Natalie said, hesitating slightly before continuing. "You've been incredible, Ellie. You've always fought for justice, even when it meant confronting some really scary stuff."

Ellie shifted uncomfortably, her face turning a light shade of pink. "Well, I do what I think is right. And sometimes means facing my fear of losing control."

"Like when you stood up to Gideon Blackwell's spirit," Natalie recalled, her eyes flickering with awe. "You showed no fear, even when we were all terrified."

"Your tenacity is inspiring," Ollie chimed in, joining the conversation. "We've all learned so much from you, Ellie."

"Thank you," Ellie murmured, her cheeks flushed with pride. The wind outside picked up once more, its howl a reminder of the darkness still lingered beyond their sanctuary.

"Facing our fears and standing together is the only way we'll be able to defeat Gideon Blackwell and whatever other supernatural forces come our way," Natalie declared, her voice unwavering as she clung to the photo in her hands.

"Absolutely." Ellie nodded resolutely, her eyes gleaming with determination. "And we'll do it together. We've come too far not to."

The room filled with a sense of hope and resolve as their shared experiences bound them together. Each of them faced their own demons, but their friendship and collective strength would see them through the darkness, conquering their fears one moment at a time.

The wind outside howled like a wounded animal, its mournful cry penetrating the walls of their makeshift refuge. Cameron Hawthorne stood at the window, staring with furrowed brows into the storm-torn night. His heart pounded in his chest, and he couldn't help but shiver at the thought of what lay hidden in the darkness beyond.

"Hey, Cam." Ollie's voice broke through his thoughts as he approached, a warm mug of cocoa in hand. "You alright?"

Cameron turned to face his friend, his usual mischievous grin replaced by a somber expression. "Yeah, I guess," he replied, accepting the mug with a nod of gratitude. "It's just... everything we've been through. It's hard to wrap my head around it all."

Ollie nodded, understanding the weight of their shared experiences. "We've faced some pretty terrifying things, but we're still standing," he said, raising his mug slightly before taking a sip. "And we couldn't have done it without each other."

Cameron stared into the swirling liquid in his mug, memories of their harrowing journey flooding his mind. He recalled the supernatural horrors they encountered, and the terror gripped him during those moments. But each time, his friends had been there, supporting and encouraging him when he needed it most.

"Remember that night in the graveyard?" Cameron asked, a hint of a smile creeping across his face. "When we first encounter Gideon Blackwell's spirit? I don't think I would have made it out of there if you guys hadn't been with me."

"None of us would have," Ellie chimed in, joining the conversation. "That's the thing about friendship; it gives you the strength to face your fears and keep going, no matter how dark the road ahead may seem."

"True," Natalie agreed, her eyes shimmering with unshed tears. "We've all grown so much over the course of this adventure, and it's because we've had each other to lean on."

"Like that time in the basement," Cameron mused aloud, his voice over the wind's wail. "Facing Gideon Blackwell's spirit again, I felt so alone... but then I remembered that you guys were right there with me, even if I couldn't see you. That gave me the courage to confront him and not give in to my fear of isolation."

"Exactly," Ellie affirmed, her face set with determination. "We're stronger together than we ever could be apart."

As the storm raged outside, the words of friendship and support hung in the air like a warm embrace. Each friend understood they had changed, transformed by their harrowing experiences into something more resilient and tenacious than before. And as they stood together in the dimly lit room, their hearts filled with hope and resolve for the challenges yet to come, no matter what darkness awaited them, their bond would carry them through.

"Whatever happens next," he said, meeting the eyes of each of his friends in turn, "we'll face it together. And we'll win."

The wind outside howled like a wolf, branches scraping against the windowpane as Ellie stood beside Ollie. The flickering candlelight cast eerie shadows on the walls of the old room, making the ancient wallpaper appear to come alive with sinister intent. Her blue eyes glinted in the dim light, reflecting her thoughts back at her.

"Guys," Ellie spoke up, her voice steady despite the storm outside. "I want to say I'm so grateful for all of you. Your trust and camaraderie gave me the strength I needed to face this curse head-on." She smiled, brushing a strand of wavy blonde hair behind her ear.

"Remember when we found the cryptic clues? At first, I was terrified of failing and not being able to decipher them. But knowing that you all believed in me made it possible for me to embrace my intelligence and intuition. We've come so far because we've faced our fears together."

Ollie blushed, adjusting his glasses as he looked around at their friends. "Yeah," he agreed, his voice soft but full of conviction. "You guys have been amazing, really. I never thought I'd find people who'd be there for me no matter what, who'd never abandon me. You've helped me overcome so many insecurities, and I can't thank you enough for that."

As Ollie spoke, the scent of damp earth and musty wood filled the air, mingling with the faint aroma of the candle's wax. He recalled the moment he stood up to Gideon Blackwell's spirit, his heart pounding in his chest like a trapped bird as he faced his fear of abandonment. Through the unwavering loyalty of his friends, Ollie realized the importance of loyalty itself, as well as the courage that resided within him.

Ellie squeezed Ollie's hand gently, her fingers intertwining with his for a brief moment. "We're a team," she told him, the conviction in her voice unwavering. "We've grown stronger together because we've shared our strengths and weaknesses. And I know, without a doubt, that we can face anything as long as we have each other."

The air in the room hummed with energy as their words of friendship and support echoed through the space. The storm outside raged on, but within the walls of the old house, they found solace in one another's presence. Standing together, anchored by their unbreakable bond, they could conquer any darkness that lay ahead.

"Whatever comes next," Ellie said, her eyes locked onto Ollie's, "we'll be ready for it. And we'll face it together."

Natalie stood near the window, raindrops pelting the glass like a thousand tiny hammers, her heart swelling with gratitude. She gently traced the outline of an old tree outside with her finger, its branches swaying violently in the storm. The haunting beauty of the scene before her served as a reminder of how her artistic perspective guided her through the darkness, giving her the courage to face the unknown.

"Thank you," she murmured to her friends, her voice above the torrential downpour. "For understanding and accepting me, even when I couldn't make sense of my own thoughts."

"Always, Natalie," Ellie replied, her red curls bouncing as she nodded firmly. "We're in this together, no matter what."

A flash of lightning illuminated the room, casting eerie shadows on the walls. Ellie's eyes darted around, her petite frame tense but determined. Her unwavering sense of justice, fueled by her fear of losing control, pushed her to fight for their survival against all odds.

"Guys," Ellie began, her voice shaking slightly but full of conviction. "I want you to know I'm here, not because of what we've been through, but because I believe in our unity. Our determination made us strong, and it's given me the power to stand up for what's right, even when it terrifies me."

"Ellie, we're so proud of you," Cameron chimed in, his eyes shining with admiration. "Your courage inspires all of us."

"Thanks, Cam," Ellie said, a small smile tugging at the corners of her mouth. "Together, we can face any challenge, no matter how dark or frightening it may seem."

The wind howled outside, rattling the windowpanes, but within the confines of the ancient house, they found strength in each other's company. Natalie closed her eyes, taking a deep breath to steady herself. She could feel the love and loyalty bound them together like an unbreakable chain, giving her courage she possessed.

"Let's promise each other," Natalie said, her voice clear and resolute. "No matter what we face, we'll stick together, drawing on our strengths and supporting one another through thick and thin."

"Deal," Ellie agreed, her fiery determination mirrored in the eyes of her friends.

"Deal," Cameron, Ellie, and Ollie echoed in unison.

As the storm raged on outside, they stood together as one, their friendship a beacon of light amidst the encroaching darkness. With newfound hope and determination, they prepared themselves for whatever challenges lay ahead, knowing the strength they gained would see them through the darkest of times.

As the sun set behind the horizon, casting eerie shadows across the room, Cameron gazed out the window at the darkening sky. The crimson hues of dusk bleed into the inky blackness, painting a hauntingly beautiful scene that sent shivers down his spine.

"Guys," he began hesitantly, turning to face his friends. "Don't you ever feel like...like we've changed? Like, we're not who we used to be?"

Ellie leaned back against the wall, her blonde hair illuminated by the flickering candlelight. "I think... we've all grown," she mused thoughtfully. "We've faced things we never could have imagined, and together, we found a way through."

"Sometimes, I can still feel the chill of Gideon Blackwell's gaze on me," Ollie admitted, adjusting his glasses nervously. "But now, instead of running away, I stand my ground. It's. ..empowering, in a way."

"Facing the unknown was terrifying," Natalie confessed, her fingers tracing the outline of the camera hanging around her neck. "But it taught me how to find beauty even in the darkest places. And that's something I'll never forget."

"Everything we went through tested us and pushed us to our limits," Ellie added fiercely. "But in the end, we emerged stronger, braver, and more determined than ever."

The air pulsed with silent tension as the weight of their shared experiences hung heavy between them. Cameron's heart raced with the thrill of realization: they're no longer mere children stumbling through life's labyrinthine corridors. They became warriors, forged in the fires of adversity and tempered by the bonds of friendship.

"Let's make a pact," Cameron suggested, his eyes gleaming with determination. "No matter what happens, we'll always remember the lessons we've learned and the strength we've found in each other."

"Sounds like a promise worth making," Ellie said, her voice filled with conviction. She reached out her hand, palm open and inviting.

"Agreed," Ollie chimed in, placing his hand on top of Ellie's, his eyes shining with newfound confidence.

"Always," Natalie whispered, adding her hand to the growing pile, her fingers brushing against the smooth metal of her camera.

"Forever," Ellie declared, her small, steady hand completing the circle of unity.

With their hands joined together, they stood as one, their hearts swelling with a sense of hope and determination surged like a powerful undercurrent through their veins. In the fading light of day, the darkness could no longer hold any power over them. Together, they would forge their own path forward, eternally bound by the lessons they learned and the unwavering strength of their friendship.

THANK YOU

If you found this story enjoyable, I would greatly appreciate it if you could share your thoughts by leaving a review on Amazon or Goodreads. I value feedback from each and every one of my readers and look forward to hearing from you.

Website: www.stephanietyo.com

Facebook: https://www.facebook.com/StephanieTyoAuthor

Also By Stephanie Tyo

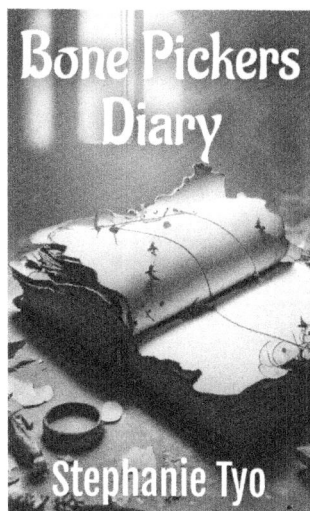

Bone Pickers Diary

Stephanie Tyo

About the Author

Stephanie Tyo, a resident of Cornwall, Ontario, seamlessly integrates empathy and intellect into her writing. Trained initially as a medical assistant and personal support worker, she currently pursues a Bachelor of Arts degree in Psychology and Women and Gender Studies, harbouring the ambition of growing into a therapist and eventually a psychologist.

Diversifying her exploration across various genres, Stephanie's passion for storytelling intertwines deeply with her unwavering commitment to lifelong learning—a value she aspires to instil in her readers. Central to Stephanie's life are her two teenage daughters, whose experiences serve as a wellspring of inspiration for her narratives.

Stephanie's stories, rich with authentic emotions and experiences, vividly mirror her fascination with the diverse spectrum of human life. Her work is a promise to resonate profoundly with readers who, like her, share a profound love for interesting narratives and an enduring dedication to continuous learning.

Website: www.stephanietyo.com

Facebook: https://www.facebook.com/StephanieTyoAuthor

Printed in Great Britain
by Amazon